Midnight in a Perfect Life

Midnight in a Perfect Life

MICHAEL COLLINS

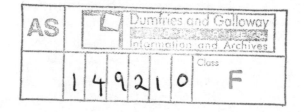
Weidenfeld & Nicolson

LONDON

First published in Great Britain in 2010 by Weidenfeld & Nicolson
An imprint of the Orion Publishing Group Ltd
Orion House, 5 Upper Saint Martin's Lane
London WC2H 9EA

An Hachette UK Company

1 3 5 7 9 10 8 6 4 2

A CIP catalogue record for this book
is available from the British Library.

ISBN 978 0 297 85988 8 (cased)
ISBN 978 0 297 85989 5 (trade paperback)

Typeset by Input Data Services Ltd,
Bridgwater, Somerset

Printed and bound in the UK by
Clays Ltd, St Ive's plc

The Orion Publishing Group's policy is to use papers
that are natural, renewable and recyclable products and
made from wood grown in sustainable forests. The logging
and manufacturing processes are expected to conform
to the environmental regulations of the country of origin.

www.orionbooks.co.uk

Dedicated to my parents, wife and children –
Nora, Eoin, Tess and Mairead!

Sincere thanks to:
Carol Kennedy
Kirsty Dunseath
Maggie McKernan
Dominique Bourgois
Emily Henry
Rich and Teri Frantz
William O'Rourke

One

This all began at the precipice of forty, in a childless marriage, when I was left confronting the statistical fact that I had fewer years ahead of me than behind me. My wife, Lori, was facing the same dilemma – impending mortality – though, three years older than I, at the stark age of forty-three, her crisis was more ominous. With her biological clock running down, and having been unable to get pregnant the old-fashioned way, she felt compelled to commend our bodies and souls to science, to have us sit in open-backed gowns, submitting to an inquisition of being probed and prodded in an attempt to spawn life.

Needless to say, it was the most vulnerable year of our marriage. In all likelihood conception would take place, not in the warmth of an embrace, but in a petri dish, sperm gingerly pushed through the outer membrane of an egg like some awkward adolescent tentatively entering a high school dance.

I was against the whole notion from the start.

I still remember the Sunday morning in fall when we tackled the clinic's screening paperwork. I implicitly understood what was at stake – *freedom*, not in a wholly selfish sense, yet I was conscious that on any other Sunday we would have stayed in bed, languidly undecided, responsible to and for no one, opting for a late breakfast or buffet-style brunch, perusing, in an offhand way, the impossible thickness of the weekend edition of *The New York Times*.

Already, in scanning the paperwork, aside from the volume of medical and financial worksheets, I had come across discount coupons for *Elmo* and *Barney* bedding at $199 plus shipping and handling, along with a red wax sealed envelope, more given to a royal proclamation of yore. It contained an application for tickets to a taping of *Bozo the Clown* – estimated waitlist for ticket availability, circa five years. The entire process underscored the inanity of a journey into the gilded world of childhood want.

So, too, the moment of decision was temporarily halted as Lori, in opening a pre-qualifying form asking her to document her sexual history, went into meltdown, confronting an abortion from her high school days when she had seemingly been able to get pregnant at the drop of a hat. Apparently, she had been carrying that guilt inside her head all her adult life, irrationally attributing her current inability to get pregnant as a punishment from God.

In my mind the abortion held no real significance within our relationship. It was ancient history, something I had heard of in passing early on in our relationship, and yet the abortion melancholy got us talking about God, or, more exactly, it got Lori talking about penance, while I argued, if God could really see all, would he really *want to anyway*? I mentioned the Holocaust and starvation in Africa. I said, 'Do you really think God *cares* about premarital sex?'

We ended up getting into a minor fight.

Like I said, the abortion story wasn't new to me. A kid named Donny something-*kowski* had gotten Lori pregnant. I had heard about the abortion for the first time about a year after we got together, while we were driving through a no-man's landscape between Milwaukee and Chicago after visiting her parents. All evening Lori's mother had been eulogizing Lori's former steady, The Ukrainian Prince, who had been a member of the state championship curling team the year a famed winter storm hit Eau Claire. Lori had 'carried a torch for him' through high school, that was how her mother put it, speaking with the unsettling pull of old world nostalgia, and she hinted that, but for unforeseen events, he would still have been part of their lives. Instead the Prince died less than a year later in the waning days of the Vietnam conflict in '71. Such was the short and bittersweet life of The Ukrainian Prince as far as the story went, except for the fact it had been the Prince who got Lori pregnant before pulling out for Vietnam.

But the real question facing us, beyond the philosophical and the spiritual, was, should Lori admit on the pre-qualifying form to the abortion? Did it have any bearing on how the clinic would proceed? The fine print talked about full medical disclosure.

Lori looked at me. 'Does admitting to an abortion when it was illegal mean I could still be charged?'

I said, 'Admit to nothing. Lie!'

She quieted. 'Sometimes I think it was maybe just a dream.'

I said, 'Maybe.'

I left Lori alone with the forms and used the phone in the master bedroom to put in my usual Sunday morning call to my mother at Potawatomi Assisted Living Suites (PALS).

The facility's claim to fame was its location, less than a mile from where Buddy Holly, Ritchie Valens, and the Big Bopper died in a plane crash in 1959, on what Don McLean described in American Pie as 'the day the music died.'

Whatever about the music, this was where my mother was supposed to die, though, in the string of broken promises that has defined my life, I was now confronting the prospect of defaulting on payment and unshackling myself of filial

3

responsibility, leaving her to the dogs of welfare.

I think my advancing age, and general sense of indeterminacy as a struggling novelist, exacerbated the callousness of the decision, though I allowed myself a complicated process of rationalization that the relationship between a parent and child was the only type of love that naturally grew toward separation. Still, I was aware of what I was doing – forsaking the living for the unborn. I had seen enough so-called darling offspring, so many alleged little geniuses, to understand I was simply abandoning my mother for the medically-assisted prospect of furthering the species, producing assholes who would most probably, likewise, forsake me in the future.

It wasn't the most fatherly of sentiments. I felt about as suitable for fatherhood as King Herod.

Of course, I might have begged Lori's understanding of my mother's circumstances, or been more forthright all along about my professional crisis, but I saw no measure of dignity or hope in such an appeal. Early on in our relationship, I had overcompensated in a way that worked against any measure of honesty with her, cavalierly spawning a series of lies concerning my financial success as a novelist and Hollywood script doctor.

The reality was otherwise.

Despite having had two books published, and a New York Times Notable Book of the Year to my credit, I was making less money than the secretaries at the colleges where I adjunct taught on occasion. Though, what was more troublesome and ominous, was that by the time I met Lori, my third novel, a work I'd slaved on for four years, had been summarily rejected by every publishing house in New York.

Of course, as our relationship developed, I eventually had to backtrack on my alleged access to vast wads of cash, entering

4

into a protracted double-talk about art with a capital A, about not selling out, and pushing a resurrected version of my failed novel that I'd simply begun to call The Opus.

If I can find Lori guilty of anything early on, it was her gullibility, or maybe her wanton decision not to want to see through me that hurt the most. She never challenged me directly. Maybe I lied too well. It is hard reassembling the past.

I can still remember one of our first official dates, watching her scan a book shelf in my apartment that held the numerous translations of my two novels. She had been genuinely awed at the prospect of what she described as 'being in the presence of a living writer.' I distinctly remember a feeling of pride, at being thought of in those terms given the reality of where my life was. She set my career in contradistinction to what she described as 'the peanut butter and jelly reality of ordinary existence.' At one time, she did see something in me that I hadn't seen in myself.

In fact, she was the one who pursued me. We had met, not once, but twice, before I got to know her. The first encounter I hadn't remembered specifically, until she relayed the circumstance. I had been on assignment for a men's magazine, profiling an Adopt-a-Dog-for-a-Day Program run by the Humane Society, an alleged way of picking up guarded, professional women at dog parks, when Lori's Doberman, Brutus, on furlough from Hell, looked up from lasciviously licking his man-sized balls and had a go at the mutt wire terrier I had adopted for the day.

All I could remember was the dog's balls.

The second occasion was at a Cancer Survivor Benefit. One of the survivors, Denise Klein, had taken a memoir night class I'd taught. Denise had been a personal friend of Lori. On seeing me again, Lori bid an exorbitant $950 to assure a place in a six week writing course I had donated to the benefit's silent auction.

We were into the third week of the course before I really took any notice of her. In the interval between our weekly meetings she had cropped her hair short in a style made famous by Mia Farrow in *Rosemary's Baby*. A week later, after I had effusively over-praised the emotional depth of her work – a clichéd ode to a childhood cat named *Toby* – in a post-coital embrace at my apartment, she owned up to the self-deprecating details of our first meeting at the dog park.

In retrospect, I understand it was her attraction to me that attracted me to her. She validated me in that sad and pathetic way all artists eventually come to define themselves – audience reaction.

It was after one of our first amorous encounters at my apartment, while spooning against me, she revealed her age and essential vulnerability. At thirty-seven, she openly admitted to feeling a sense of personal and spiritual confusion, of being emotionally lost, intimating, too, some less than spectacular relationships and confessing to a selfishness that had seen her focus too intently on her career. She described herself as 'Damaged Goods.'

In many ways, I was looking for something just short of perfect.

Through these early encounters, in the quiet space two adults can create for themselves in which Truth should surely live, I got the sense of her wariness of men in general, wrought specifically because of what happened to 'a friend of a friend' of hers, a divorcee who'd been tied to her bedpost by a one-night stand who'd sodomized her before leaving her bound to the bed. The woman's kid found her the next morning.

Against that apparent darkness within the male psyche, with that understanding of what human beings can do to one another, she had more or less withdrawn from dating. As she admitted, the good prospects had paired off one by one, or, as she wryly put it after we had come to know one another, all that was left were 'fags, and now, seemingly, writers.'

On the strength of those cocooned moments of intimacy, after dating for just three months, and with an understanding that one cannot live in a state of emotional isolation, I, at thirty-five, and Lori, at thirty-eight, committed our lives for better or worse in a quiet weekend elopement that saw us stand before a justice of the peace at the famed locks in Sault Ste. Marie.

Lori took just the Monday off work. There was no honeymoon.

I thought what developed over the following years was self-sustaining; we lived as adults, our wants minimal, immune to the dictates of fashion and impulse buying.

There was a hiccup in Lori's work, a brief period of unemployment due to a hostile take-over at her company that led me to forge her name and take out a line of equity against her condo to cover ourselves and my mother's care, though, in the end, Lori was rehired and promoted within the new structure.

Meanwhile, in the intervening years, I was left alone to write, unmoored from so-called real life on the back of Lori's resources, venturing further into the morass of The Opus, edging inexorably toward a quiet professional failure Lori graciously did not talk about, or did not fully understand.

However, providence did intervene early in the second year of our marriage, when my agent, based on material I'd sent him years before, secured a job for me as a ghost writer for the venerable crime writer Perry Fennimore. It was a position that potentially breathed new life into my career, and my bank account.

I think our lives could have remained even-keeled, seeing us through to retirement, but then our mutual friend, Denise Klein – the cancer survivor – had a relapse. After being denied an experimental bone marrow treatment by her insurance, she embarked on a quest to have another child, an elusive son, via a surrogate. She already had three teenage daughters.

It was a plaintive story she chronicled in a moving daily journal for *The Chicago Tribune* on love and the meaning of life, a memoir that was eerily poignant, including letters to her unborn child. She invoked God and Family as the great eternal, her teen daughters equal in their faith. They were the kind of family that would have cheerfully swapped out organs with one another, such was their love.

In the end, of course, Denise could not forestall the inevitable. In October of 1996, she became a footnote in the annals of medical journals, as having been the first woman to have her own fertilized egg implanted into a surrogate after her death.

On the way back from the funeral, I quipped about having half-expected one of the daughters to have been the surrogate. It proved a tipping point. Lori put her hands to her face and began to cry in inconsolable sobs. At the time, I'd not known the extent of her desire to have a child.

There had been talk of getting a cat, but never any mention of children. I thought as rational, modern adults, we had come to some unspoken agreement we were never going to have children, especially given our advancing ages. Philosophically I'd also connected our decision to a larger socio-historical view of pregnancy as nothing short of biology's way of controlling women as well as men. Hadn't we conquered pregnancy?

Trying to get pregnant seemed to me about as absurd as trying to get Polio.

In short, I'd assumed Lori was on the pill. After all, I knew about the abortion saga, but over the next year, the talk of downsizing started, of abandoning the condo for the experience of stay-at-home parenting, the desire to push a stroller through suburban parks at noon, to host play dates, to slave away on home-cooked meals, until one day Lori put it bluntly, with a slight tinge of hysteria: 'If The Opus is your intellectual destiny, the thing that will outlive you, then children are my biological destiny.'

She had equity in her condo. That was her mantra – the ace up her sleeve. The eventual disclosure regarding my having forged her name on the line of equity nearly destroyed our marriage. I had '*deceived* her, *lied* to her', her words delivered in an emotional torrent of pain, hurt, and indecision.

It took all my efforts to atone, and it was my job with the crime novelist, Perry Fennimore, that saved me. Improbably, after his own waning success, the novel I'd helped ghost write a year earlier had shot him to the top of the bestseller list, due in no small part to my work on his book, or so I'd been contending. I'd fortuitously lodged a cheque just a week prior to Lori discovering the irregularity with the line of equity, and I had begun, prematurely, to talk up a foreseeable big payday.

Still, what the entire episode did was subtly tip the balance of power in her favor, making me vulnerable and provisionally willing to ejaculate into a Dixie cup at some outpatient clinic.

Such was the complicated history of my relationship with Lori that colored my conversation with my mother, though I use the word 'conversation' loosely.

The call lasted five minutes and twenty seconds: two of those minutes spent as my mother was wheeled to the phone, another minute with her asking who I was, and another minute as I waited, listening to a nurse showing my mother a photograph of me.

I took a solace in her dementia. She would never really understand my betrayal. It was an uneventful call. At the end I said simply, 'I love you, Mom,' and hung up.

When I came back, Lori was waiting. She said, 'You look upset.' She wanted to know if everything was OK.

I said it was.

Lori went back to looking out the window.

I could see she had completed the form. She was waiting for a real estate agent to arrive and appraise the condo. According to the pre-qualifying paperwork, a provisional cost breakdown seemed to suggest services rendered could top $70,000.

She turned and looked at me again. 'You've not gotten any work done in days. I'm sorry.'

I knew a question was being asked of me. 'It's the peril of being a writer, living where you work.'

Lori hesitated. 'When you were on your trip to New York, did that publisher say anything about money?'

She was referring to the book deal I had told her was supposedly under consideration, given my work for Fennimore. Lori had been counting on the alleged deal money as we moved toward the prospect of having a child. It became part of the economics of our new life, and yet, the more she talked the harder it was to tell her the truth.

I said cautiously, 'A writer never talks money with an editor. It's a major faux pas within the industry. It betrays desperation.'

I could see her tensing up.

'Look, it's under review. These things take time. It's a cat and mouse game, figuring the relative worth of an intangible, working out what may potentially succeed or fail.'

Lori mouthed the word, 'OK.'

But it wasn't OK at all. There was no deal. In a meeting I had fucked up royally, and against the advice of my agent, Sheldon Pinkerton, I'd ended up having lunch with Fennimore's editor, armed with an *L.A. Times* review mentioning the renewed vigor in Fennimore's work. The reviewer had cited a passage, describing it as 'exemplary of an inveterate craftsmanship hewn of years of life lived ... a writer who has rendered the starkness of his characters with a precision devoid of judgment, capturing the essential coldness that may describe the human condition in the late twentieth century.'

The passage the reviewer quoted was something I had taken verbatim from my Opus. These were *my* words. I had underlined the passage in the unpublished Opus, pointing to it with a sense of vindication as the editor leaned forward over a $150 bottle of Bordeaux.

I wanted to stick my genius to him.

The next day I got a letter from the publishing house's lawyer accusing me of plagiarism, of grossly exaggerating my assistance to the writer, the letter outlining in legalese that all work produced or written for the writer was the copyright of Fennimore.

There was serious doubt I would ever write for the guy again. My agent wasn't returning any of my phone calls.

I heard Lori say something in the background, and looking up met her gaze with a coldness that underscored my growing depression, lost in a deeper and darker lie that I could not bring myself to admit to her.

There would be no deal.

Lori said quietly, 'Maybe you should call them tomorrow, just to see?' then bit into the softness of her lower lip, an anxious trait that still, despite everything, endeared her to me.

I gently stroked the side of her face and whispered, 'OK ...'

Sometimes our escape is not away, but further into something.

I could see Lori was trying hard. She raised her voice slightly, her brow furrowing with a determined expression. 'You're going to make it. I can feel it!' She put the flat of her hand over her stomach as if she were touching something sacred.

I staved off saying anything, and taking a step toward her embraced her in the jaded way a boxer might in the latter rounds of a fight, for, if things had been different, if I'd had a greater sense of life-long security, maybe I could have been the husband she seemed to think I could be. Love wasn't something I categorically rejected, but rather something I thought should be earned and not simply bestowed. Her enduring faith in *me*, or *us*, cut two ways. At times it felt like love, at other times, entrapment.

I had a sense of being disembodied, within and outside everything, as Lori turned us both toward the lake, our attention drawn to a solitary runner. She put her face to the cold window, her breath fogging the pane as she whispered, 'This is the second biggest city in America, and I can't hear a sound. This isn't living, up here in the sky. This is a glass cage.'

Further out beyond the runner, I saw the waves break against the shoreline, and in that moment, understood this was more than just a yearning in her, it was something deeply biological, something hardwired millennia ago. It was the kind of yearning that drove migration, that sent salmon swimming against currents, the kind of bewildering mating spectacle you saw on cable TV, the ardor of a black widow drawing her mate to union then killing him post coitus.

I might as well have interviewed a wildebeest on its existential sense of why it procreated, why it did not spare its offspring the terror of the hunting prides on the savanna. Of course the answer lay in that nihilism is a male disease of the soul, because we are not the bearers of life. Men do not carry hope the way women do.

In retrospect, this level of introspection constituted a mental breakdown, a foreshadowing of things to come, for one cannot dive so deep for so long and remain sane, or connected to so-called normal life. I know that now. We all have a breaking point.

Two

Sunday afternoon crept toward evening in elongated shadows. I held Lori in the cradle of a nebulous urban stillness only condo life in the upper stratosphere of a high rise could bestow. Maybe more so than it should have; I deeply regretted the looming loss of the place we had made our home. It defined the pinnacle of unencumbered adult life and love in the modern world, suggesting how far we'd come as a species from our days of insensible rutting in caves. With the prospect of these waning days of aerial inhabitation, I wanted to stand naked, suspended in blue sky, and one last time, wave back across history to let them know all was good here, that I had made it, or had, for a time.

The thought was broken by the shrill ring of the phone. Lori startled awake, instinctively stretching across me to get it because nobody ever called me. She whispered it was Deb, her squat sister and confidante. I could hear Deb squawking in the earpiece. Lori immediately tried to placate me, rolling her eyes as she got up and disappeared into the bathroom with the cordless phone. Evidently, this was a private conversation.

The mere fact that Deb had called heightened my sense of vulnerability and general anxiety that things were going on behind my back, that the future was a *fait accompli;* this despite the supposed agreement between me and Lori to keep our provisional investigations between only us, and not tell anybody.

Deb was one of my least favorite people in the world. After

hearing what I'd done behind Lori's back with the line of equity, her advice had been to file for a divorce, glibly commenting that the only thing a man should do behind a woman's back was zip up her dress. Since that time, she had persistently and annoyingly addressed me as 'The Embezzler!'

As I lay on the bed, I thought again about the impending prospect of life as I knew it ending, thought of simply walking away from everything given the potential futile endgame with Fennimore and the crisis over my mother's care. I imagined leaving a laconic scribble, something short of a suicide note, stating something to the effect that 'I was never the man you thought I was . . . Please do not try to find me.'

Of course I didn't run. There was no place to run. As you get older, you come to understand that. What I might have done to survive a decade earlier was no longer viable.

We are not the same throughout our lives. We change.

In the ensuing moments, just waiting there I had a dark vision of a prospective future life without Lori, as a greeter at Wal-Mart, for what talents did a writer possess really, not to mention a writer at forty?

I think if I were to define my marriage as time went on, it was founded on an underlying economic need, and therefore maybe truer to the original institution of marriage as the expressed notion of aggregating wealth or land, in short, toward security.

I'm not discounting attraction or carnal longing, but I think *Love*, as a guiding principle for happiness, is, for the most part, a modern conceit.

I don't think putting it thus so diminishes what I had with Lori.

In the background, I heard Lori say, 'Oh my God, he didn't!', breaking my train of thought; Lori getting sucked into the vortex that was Deb.

15

Deb was a real piece of work, a man-hater in the worst possible way, following the hell of an early marriage to some lowlife greaseball Fonzie wannabe she ran off with at eighteen, who eventually abandoned her, leaving her penniless with three children. She'd hitched that personal tragedy to a larger socio-historical context, to an indictment of what she called 'the patriarchal domination of Christianity,' something she'd obviously lifted from some self-help book. She referred to the twelve apostles as the first society of dead-beat dads in their abandonment of family and fishing net by the Sea of Galilee when they left to follow Jesus.

Her life was one long run-on sentence, and of such supposed import that she'd gotten herself on national TV, on *The Oprah Winfrey Show*, when Oprah was still fat and pretty inconsequential to anybody working a day job, touting her discovery of self, how she'd found meaning in life again as a female entrepreneur selling handicapped artists' Greeting Cards through a mail order business. The artists she represented were mostly victims of thalidomide who painted joyous scenes of optimism with their feet or mouths. Deb's catch phrase was, 'God has given me verses, not chapters,' which allowed her to take credit for what she was in life, for the day to day actions – the verses. I tuned out the backdrop of Lori's voice and stood by the window. A low bank of clouds was moving landward across the lake, drifting amidst the peaks of skyscrapers. Up here sometimes I could see everything, at other times nothing at all.

With a clawing sense of remorse, and to spur myself toward some decision, I called PALS a second time on the other line. It took ages for the staff to retrieve my mother. I felt my throat tighten just listening to my mother as she struggled to speak, slurring my name as if I were a stranger. She had given birth to me.

My mother's nurse got on the phone, abrupt and defensive, despite the cost of my mother's care. 'She had a pill a little after lunch and ... She has a routine ... We can't ...'

I raised my voice slightly. 'Thank you kindly ... for your invaluable service and compassion.' I knew the landmine of what I'd stumbled into, the late afternoon zombie haze of patient management, and I experienced a brief sense of the horror of what I was really paying to sustain. I heard my mother's voice again and said her name softly.

One of the indelible memories I still have of her was the way she used to say that everybody was the best in the world at something – it was just a matter of discovering what it was. She bestowed early on in my life an immeasurable sense of hope, of wanting to find that one thing, though, for a long time, I lived with the fear that maybe I might be best in the world at something like laying carpets.

My mother always smiled back when I said things like that. I remember asking her once what she was best in the world at. She answered, 'Raising you.'

I looked toward the bathroom door, wanting so badly for Lori to emerge, to catch me in this state, to come clean about the potential lawsuit with Fennimore's publisher and the precariousness of my mother's position. After all, Lori had revealed the details of her abortion.

I had my story, too, something that had changed me as much as Lori's abortion had changed her.

For years my mother and I had traveled with my father in his transient existence as a salesman, since it had been cheaper to have us travel with him than rent a long-term apartment. On a winter's night at the beginning of the Watergate hearings, while we were holed up at a roadside motel outside Muskegon, my father murdered a love interest of his, a middle-aged music teacher, before turning the gun to his own head.

Days later, in the wake of his suicide, a rumor surfaced concerning a box of correspondence from my father the music teacher had kept, in which he'd allegedly spoken of wanting to dispose of my mother and me.

I was fifteen at the time, and in the intervening years it was a rumor that came to haunt me more than his suicide.

I have carried a sense of oppressive servitude toward my mother since that time, especially through the initial years as we passed from one relative to another. I can attest she was never with another man after my father and was devoted to me with a love reserved for fairy tales. It was the simple act of dwelling upon her charity and love, setting it against my father's coldness, which won me a partial scholarship to Northwestern University and set me on the track to becoming a writer. With my application, I submitted an essay on Miller's *Death of a Salesman*, entitled, 'An Indictment of Capitalism – An Analysis of Willie Loman', adding to Loman's lament, 'After all the highways, and the trains, and the years, you end up worth more dead than alive,' my father's sardonic lament, 'We start out with such high expectations!'

I remember him staring at my mother and me, repeating that mantra. It was something that always augured the onset of his drinking and the eventual loosening and removal of his belt. I was punished for chores done with what he called 'an inattentive regard for authority,' and 'willful thoughtlessness towards all his sacrifices on my behalf.' He demanded a spit shine on his shoes to match the crispness of his starched shirts. A salesman survived on such things, on outward appearances, on the cold call of a handshake and a smile. I understand now there was valiance in having so little to rely on, to facing so many closed doors, so many rejections, dwelling on the successes, not the failures.

I know deep within my writing life skulks a sublimation of my father's untold story. I've been a ghost writer all my life.

In the end, I did not speak with my mother. She was too distressed and disoriented for there to be any appreciable conversation. I had intruded when I should not have. I politely thanked the nurse, set down the phone, cutting the connection across miles and years, and turned on the TV.

The Bears had lost again. We were midway through another losing season. My interest in sports had never been about the game as much as the tragedy of its fallen heroes; their strain against the inevitable march of time. The commentator was the great Iron Mike Ditka. Sidelined in his waning years to this useless job, it struck me how much of our life is lived in fading glory. I thought back to one of the last years Ditka had coached, how he'd gone crazy and attacked a fan in the stands; a bone-crushing former linebacker with probably the most glorious Eighties Super Bowl win to his credit reduced to such madness, his world unraveling around him.

As I kept staring at the TV, I thought, where does greatness go? I was conscious of watching a man who still wanted to hit something, hard. He just needed to know what to hit.

There was still that look in Ditka's eyes, a look I first saw in my father. On those drives north all those years ago, I remembered the way my father had made eye contact with women in other cars, and then how his eyes would connect with mine in the rear-view mirror. He would smile, and I would simply have to close my eyes.

It went that way between us. In retrospect, I've often wondered if he was not trying to tell me something about life, about how you have to make do with quiet indiscretions, that we all need a measure of freedom. In those years, he'd come to calling me Captain Obvious.

I remember an incident at a roadside urinal far north into Michigan. We had slept overnight in the car. My father had the hangman's noose of his tie dangling from his pocket as he washed against the coming dawn, readying to visit this and that country middle school. He looked up and placed the noose around my neck.

He began talking about responsibility, about the weight of life, about what it takes to survive in this world. I don't remember his exact words, only the intensity of his voice, the hot warmth of his Old Spice aftershave. He talked in a measured way, looking directly into my eyes, tightening the noose around my throat. He said something akin to the fact he saw a younger version of himself in me. I felt the noose press against my windpipe. He wanted me to stop looking at things with such intensity. He wanted me to laugh. All I felt was the clouding, euphoric sensation of light headedness, of slowly being choked to death. I think this was his idea of wisdom, trying to turn me from my basic instincts, to lead me elsewhere.

An hour later we stopped for pie and coffee at a diner. My father talked in that familiar and charming way he used with women. He had a wad of bills, all singles wrapped around a twenty dollar note. He set his hand on my head. He said to the woman that I was in training. I was going to make up for the mistakes he'd made over the years. I was his 'reclaimed innocence.'

It was a poetic sensibility that women liked, tapping a deeper sense within us all that we could have been better if only we had tried harder, if only we had known better, if somebody had shown us the path. He spoke in his roundabout way of the unbridled sense of good faith that lies within us all, asserting our complicity in wanting to be deceived, for, 'otherwise we become too modern, too cynical.' That was how he put it in the early light of a throwaway morning so many years ago.

He understood need in the way only a salesman can.

There are times when I think I drove my father to want to kill us. I shouldn't have defied him. I had no business looking at him. It was something I overheard my mother say just once, in a hushed call to her aunt, making me feel that possibly the greatest gift we possess is to remain quiet in the face of the obvious; that Truth is not always worth facing.

I stared again at the post-game coverage, inhabiting the misery of someone else. I could have watched Ditka climbing the stands after that fan for the rest of my life, Ditka as noble as Sisyphus, his plight no less heroic than that of the ancients.

But the intercom buzzed. The real estate agent was in the lobby.

I shouted to Lori. She didn't respond. I put my head to the bathroom door. She was crying and talking about the abortion.

Three

In the weeks before our first fertility clinic appointment, it happened my agent was talking to me again. We were trying to shore up relations with Fennimore and his editor. I agreed to admit to being rash and drunk in New York, sticking in the caveat I had taken medication. I was willing to put something in writing to avoid any legal ramifications, not wanting to embarrass all parties concerned or make public exactly how much I had contributed to Fennimore's latest novel.

It was during one of those protracted conversations I got a call-waiting beep. It was Lori. She was in a state of euphoria. The date of our fertility appointment had been confirmed.

When I got back to my agent, I related the news. He nearly jumped down the phone. Infertility was *hot*. There was a book in it, or at least a series of articles in a major magazine, a seed toward securing a non-fiction deal. I don't think I'd ever heard that much enthusiasm in his voice, although there are no small ideas, no small books, when you're dealing with an agent.

'This could be your ticket to the big time!' he shouted. 'This is right up your alley! Let me make a few calls and get back to you!'

And suddenly he was gone, leaving me holding the phone.

And, yet, as I set the phone down and the more I thought about it, a non-fiction deal was 'up my alley.' I had a sense of the commercial non-fiction industry given that through the lean years in New York, I had scavenged a living doing freelance work for a vast array of men's magazines. I had contributed to columns such as *The Sexual Aptitude Test (SAT)*, Larry the Bartender's advice column: *On Babes, Jobs, and Other Stuff that Screws up Guys' Lives*, Health Club Dating Tips with pithy sub-headings like, *It's easy to find panting, half-naked women at the gym. The hard part is getting anywhere with them*, and frivolous pieces concerning, among other things, women's opinions on penis size and type.

Of course, in the end, I despaired of such articles, of being one of several non-credited contributors. My literary career had stalled, and I was hard at work on the morass of The Opus. A new editor at my publishing house had declined the eight hundred page tome I'd given her, blaming her decision on a shift in the house's editorial focus, but lauding The Opus' genius. She had just been looking for a different kind of genius.

We parted on the best of terms as she picked up the lunch tab and kissed me like Judas at The Last Supper, leaving me to the yawning chasm of professional failure.

I was just shy of my thirty-fourth birthday.

I still had an abiding sense back then that what I was writing *was* genius. I'd made an appeal to my agent to submit the draft to numerous other publishers, but was stymied by his insistence that the industry was in flux, and that I should work outside the pressures of ordinary existence. He spoke to me like an aesthete when really he wanted me to leave him the hell alone.

In the end, a survival instinct kicked in and I abandoned New York for something closer to home – Chicago. I came back broke, or nearly broke, racking up credit card debts until I could no longer transfer the balance to a no-interest grace-period card.

At first, Chicago proved no panacea. In fact, I deteriorated further. At my wits end, the only writing job I secured in a six month trawl of agencies was a part-time day job writing safety manuals for the Department of Motor Vehicles that lasted all of a month. It set me again on a path of aimless wanderings toward despair. It was while on one of these walks, holed up at a café scribbling notes in an attempt at inspiration, that I happened upon a job posting in an underground weekly called *The Stranger*: they were looking for 'a self-starter, a self-motivated writer interested in exploring the new media of emerging on-line technologies!'

It was the technical aspect of the job that immediately lured me, affording me a potential chance to leave behind the dead world of print, to escape the cave of publishing despair, though, when I went for interview, I learned the true nature of the work was writing for a pornographic start-up called *The Portal of Venus*.

The Portal was in the process of digitizing a library of porn into a detailed database of fetishes to be sold over something called the Internet, using a Hyper Text Markup Language (HTML), terms that were geek speak to the average person.

I got the job based on the material I'd written for the men's magazines.

In retrospect, I feel that in many ways it was the newness of the technology which had initially inured me to what was actually being peddled, an incongruous mix of high technology and base immorality.

In the course of a day I moved between rooms filled with banks of IBM servers and 486-based systems and photo shoot assignments a floor below featuring a jaded assortment of runaways and drug users in a shrink wrap type pornography that didn't demand beauty, just desperation.

A sacrilegious series called 'The Good News' featured plain-faced nuns going door-to-door in what always turned out to be bizarre, improbable sexual encounters. Supposedly, *The Portal* had ordered the most nuns' habits in the Midwest the previous year. I guess I believed it. Old-style Catholicism had tanked. *The Portal* had also ordered the most Intel 486 processors in the greater Chicagoland area and had early adopter status in using beta releases of Microsoft Windows 3.1, working with telecommunication giants in setting up switch boxes and routers for pushing data down phone lines.

The Portal ended up introducing me to a subculture of pornography I'd hitherto known nothing about, though in some ways it was strangely democratic and authentic, serving a baser need than the so-called legitimacy of the airbrushed ex-cheerleader All-American Pets of the Month; the women were ordinary in a way that established the underlying reality of sex as well . . . sex.

The job proved a professional stay of execution, and allowed me to return from absolute darkness, connecting me once more with human life. I told myself I was biding my time. Actors washed dishes between jobs; this was no different. In their day, even the greats like Hemingway and Fitzgerald had plied their craft in Hollywood with no great success. This was no different, though one day, against a tide of mounting personal pressure after an all-nighter of heroic struggle on The Opus, I ended up stinking drunk at work, quoting it, when my boss, Max Chapman, overheard me lamenting the death of Art and high culture, slamming the debased shit we were all engaged in at *The Portal*.

I'd never had direct dealings with Chapman, just knew of him as incongruously authoritative given what he was actually selling.

Chapman cut me right off, critiquing me in a way I'd not been challenged since college. There was something immediately charismatic about him. As a self-described 'humanist', he was versed in an existentialist understanding of what he called 'the true human condition' – a phrase that sobered me right up.

He talked my language, or to be more exact he deconstructed everything I held sacred with a daunting sense of academic conviction and, dare I say it, unmitigated truth. According to him we were in search of personal perfection where nobody would ever grow old, all cocks would be huge, all tits surgically enhanced and pussies wet and trimmed. This was 'the nature of human yearning stripped of all moral anxieties', the direction he felt all of science and technology should be heading toward – 'the immutability of the flesh,' the only logical course for history in the absence of a hereafter, or as he put it, 'The endgame of Western Art will see us worshipping the cock similar to the giant phalluses of primitive African art.'

It had been hard following his exact logic that first time. He'd caught me off guard. Like I said, that day I had been drunk and self-absorbed, though in a strange way I was still philosophically aligned with him. The underlying nature of *The Portal*'s pornography was tied to a complicated voyeuristic angst. It was ordinary and debased – viewers on the outside looking in, sex organs, gaping asshole cream pies, of cocks shoved through gloryholes, all anonymous carnal sex acts. According to Chapman, and he stressed this with the unnerving conviction of one who knew what he was talking about, 'the French kiss was the only act you couldn't get away with in pornography.'

On other occasions, as I got to know him, he was more centered, less philosophical, describing *The Portal* as an economic experiment, 'a first iteration of what we were all promised with globalization – a post-modern service sector where once people got tired of jerking off, they were going to want to buy something on-line.'

It was like he was two people within one person. I came to learn that.

He had an MBA from a real college back east, nascent blue chip smarts you didn't find just anywhere. He was forthright and focused in the way all true visionaries are, and he'd sunk a shitload of money into this new technology.

I had a sense he could have been anything he wanted to be. He defined everything I ever wanted to be – iconoclastic and rich. I still remember his catch phrase, 'Vice is always at the vanguard of progress!'

One day as I was working he stopped and gave me a challenge to write something depraved and real, or as he worded it, 'You have to kill someone for anybody to give a damn anymore!' He delivered the advice after having actually taken the time to read my on-going Opus which he felt was 'a work of *minor genius*, but unduly influenced by nineteenth century literature, which was too ponderous and philosophically remote for the modern age, given our general access to pussy.'

I knew in my heart he was right.

For the remainder of my tenure at *The Portal* I came under his scrutiny, or guidance, I could never really figure which.

He took my literary smarts and re-assigned me to write testimonials and forum pieces, fictional letters that pushed the bounds of incredulity, letters from supposed girlfriends confessing to having cheated on their ill-equipped boyfriends, revealing size mattered, all insipidly transparent, and yet deeply wounding, written so penis pumps, cock rings, pocket pussies, and blowup Annie dolls could be discreetly shipped to P.O. boxes.

My only solace, it was all written under a pseudonym, in a bifurcation of self, or more plainly, a splitting of personalities. I have written under so many names, lived so many lives.

In the most forthright and professional manner, he took to

stopping me in the hallway, wanting to know how things were proceeding for me in general, setting out questions such as, 'Are you happy with who you are?', 'Have you decided yet what you want from life?', 'Where do you see yourself in five years?' – declarative, human resource type questions. His was a secular sort of mantra, in which he asserted self-doubt was the only true sin a man could commit against himself. He told me he had disconnected what he did from who he was – finding the two mutually exclusive. On his desk, he had a picture prominently displayed of his wife, three kids and a dog all standing by a log cabin.

I personally diagnosed him early on as a schizophrenic. He referred to women exclusively as 'tail!'

If I'd been less broke, I might have challenged his notion of free will in general, especially given the psychological fallout of where pornography inevitably ended up, in the hands of junior-high kids, corrupting and skewing the formative years of fading innocence and emerging sexual awareness.

Through that summer, I often stopped between assignments to listen on the radio to an aged Harry Carey singing, 'Take Me Out to the Ballpark,' reviving memories casting back to childhood. I remembered drives north with my father, the car tuned to WGN broadcasts, kids cheering on a perennial losing team. Dreams of a pennant run were dead by The All-Star Break, where all one could hope for was to catch a fly ball or an autograph.

My father called each Cubs losing season the last grand act of American working class heroism. He was a life-long fan.

And yet in the end, I think it was Chapman's subtle influence that did change my fortunes, for while working through one of my daily tasks, sorting the mail, I came across a dubious snuff tape the authenticity of which I immediately doubted, given its overt philosophical nature.

The silent, grainy tape turned out to be a gruesome recasting of Søren Kierkegaard's *Fear and Trembling*, a moral tale about religious faith in the face of absolute absurdity.

The original account centered on a medieval fable concerning a knight's unrequited love for a princess, charting the stages of the knight's spiritual loss and reconciliation.

The disturbing text of *Fear and Trembling* was displayed throughout the tape as a backdrop scrolling script, detailing the various stages of spiritual crisis the perpetrator, dressed as Kierkegaard's *Knight of Infinite Resignation*, experienced as he slowly strangled his hooded victim.

> *'I believe nevertheless that I shall get her, in virtue, that is, of the absurd, in virtue of the fact that with God all things are possible.'*

It was a direct quote from Kierkegaard, and yet it read like the ultimate stalker note.

The tape was so *apropos* everything Chapman had referenced over the summer, the mire of sexual dystopia and religious loss. I knew, too, Chapman had the technical resources at his disposal to arrange for such a taping. We had connected philosophically.

Prompted by what I felt was his personal validation of me as an artist I took the tape as a source of inspiration and left *The Portal*. In the ensuing months, I used Kierkegaard's parable to infuse The Opus with dramatic immediacy and tension, incorporating the sequences on the tape into an existential crisis bound up in a murder mystery, which I forwarded to my agent, requesting he reposition me as a crime writer.

Though nothing came of my efforts immediately, it was the reconstituted Opus that did find its way into the hands of Fennimore, who ended up hiring me to ghostwrite for him.

*

It was against such thoughts, and a fundamental belief that one should never wholly abandon hope or opportunity, I went into survival mode, and committed to that sense of *self* Chapman had talked about so fervently.

I decided I wouldn't tell Lori about the plan to document the fertility process, and simply take whatever offer my agent secured. I knew recording our journey would be anathema to her. She was deeply superstitious, in atonement mode about the abortion. Any perceived notion of cashing in on this last gasp procedure, what she was calling 'her second chance', she would have seen as a jinx.

And yet here lay a chance to redeem not only myself, but her as well!

Four

Investing in the non-fiction book idea seemed the path of least resistance, for fiction, in its truest and maybe most elite sense – as intellectual searching and questioning – had died in the last throes of nineteenth-century humanist inquiry. I was with Chapman on that point.

I decided I had suffered enough.

The editor who eventually bit on the concept was Marv Schwartz – Schwartzy – a reptilian wattle-necked man on his fifth marriage, which somehow uniquely qualified him on the subject of sex and relationships. Ironically, it was Schwartzy who'd given me the dog park assignment that had led to my initial encounter with Lori. I'd met him at a party while he was visiting Chicago. I'd been telling someone how in Japan when a person achieved an orgasm, they said, 'I just went' instead of 'I just came.' That sort of information passed as high culture with Schwartzy.

Schwartzy's latest incarnation was as an editor for *Modern Male*, a news-stand glossy that always had tanned guys with six-packs staring out at you. It was basically a beer commercial trying to be a magazine. I'd no pretensions about its literary merit – it was point-of-sales stuff, the sort of thing the masses thumbed through – but, more importantly, it was also the kind of thing editors at publishing houses trawled for *hot* subjects, for potential books, or so said my agent.

As a potential foreword on the subject, I drew first upon my personal association with Denise Klein, since she had been the catalyst prompting Lori's desire to have a child.

After so many years of being sequestered, writing in my underwear, within the shadowy, autobiographical world of The Opus, there was something redemptive in having a project that took me outside the house each day. I understood more so than most the psychological vigilance of a generation of house-bound June Cleavers resorting to pearls and heels while vacuuming, intuitively aware of what it takes to define oneself when alone for the greater part of a day.

I left most mornings with Lori, sharing for the first time the intimacy of the early commute amidst the throng and bustle of the El ride downtown. I told her in an offhand manner that I was researching a *'period'* piece in a double-entendre that satisfied the writer in me, all part of the ongoing negotiations with the New York editor, who was leaning toward signing me in a two-book deal. I told Lori it augured a long-term faith in my work.

Regretfully, I could not stop myself from pushing good fortune, or to put it another way, lying to her. But then it was hard denying the intensity of the change that had come over her.

She had taken to buying a copy of *Parenting* magazine at the news-stand by the El, a slick glossy fetish she clutched like some sacred text, a talisman to her commitment to a new lifestyle. I couldn't help wondering how they filled it each month, but of course they did, with a gamut of sections that covered subjects from pregnancy planners and fertility calculators, to baby naming, breast feeding and pumps, teething and tantrums, postpartum blues, and inane articles on hosting the perfect birthday party for a one-year-old.

It was an advertiser's wet dream, emotional blackmail pitched through the glossy spreads, with cherub-faced six-month-olds in terrycloth towels holding rubber ducks, and four-year-olds squeezing puppies amid fields of lavender. Who could possibly deny them anything?

In many ways, in its streamlined content, its laundry list of ad hoc advice and snippet articles, the magazine was really no different from the day-to-day operations at *The Portal of Venus*. I could imagine both magazines being owned by the same shadowy holding concern, by my Blue Chip Boss, Max Chapman. Everything was about money in the end.

I remember us being stranded on an El train for an hour, during one morning's commute, Lori reading an alarmist article, entitled: 'College Financial Planning – *The Bottom Line!*', the excruciating pun visually reinforced in a masthead featuring an array of bare-assed nine-month-olds clutching scrolled diplomas, when an old black musician pushed into our compartment. He opened a worn velvet-lined case, took out a battered saxophone and began to play a soulful blues that captured the grief of Southern slavery in a way I had never fully understood before.

It caught me unaware, the suggestive power of creativity. I saw the potential of human life in that moment, the dexterity of fingers on the keys, the exalted state of human expression given breath in a scale of notes, in a music played by some ragtag figure of slum upbringing and undoubted, untutored genius. I was about to say something, but kept quiet. I stared at Lori. She was unmoved, intently filling out some ungodly complicated financial worksheet associated with the financial planning article.

For all his effort, when the El lurched forward again, I saw the musician got about a three dollar take of dimes and nickels.

I spent my days in the cloistered hush of the reading room at *The Harold Washington Library*, hidden for the most part amidst a flotsam of homeless come in out of the cold, who simply stared at the periodicals and newspapers.

As a stalling tactic over the initial days before I tackled the Klein material, I checked out microfiche from various newspapers concerning my father's murder of his lover and his subsequent suicide, staring again at the black and white shot of the squat ranch house where he had died, his Ford Fairmont parked out back.

It had been well over a decade since I'd pulled out the Associated Press story. From the mere reportage of these scant details, I had somehow reconstituted the last hours of my father's life, the culmination of a stark story that flitted between his imagined early days before my mother and me, to where he found himself in his later years, blowing his brains out in a ranch house on a lonely stretch of county road.

I had written both of my novels under a pseudonym. The removal of my own name gave me a sense of artistic distance. In another shot, taken by a local photographer, I saw a distant image of my mother stranded at a motel the morning after my father's suicide. I thought it defined the mood of my first novel and, if not for my mother still being alive, might have demanded, as much as you can demand anything from a publisher, having them use the shot for the cover. For me, the image was a conduit into a life that went beyond my own, a touchstone that let me inhabit the history of both my parents.

Through the process of observation, in watching the way my mother stood by the window at so many motels, I had come to understand the silent gaze of a country girl who had lost everything, her brother killed in the defense of the 38th parallel. In one lifetime, she had passed from the agrarian domesticity of an Iowa farm, a *Petticoat Junction* existence, straight through to the darkness of *A Long Day's Journey into Night*.

In the end, I did tell my mother about my novel, secure to

a point that she would never read it. She had cataracts. Yet, the novel was picked up by Books on Tape. She ordered it, and in the early days of her failing memory, she came to listen to the dark confessional analysis of my father's relationship with her.

I see it as the pivotal event that changed us both and hastened her retreat toward senility. At times, I've wondered if she was not a prisoner to me in the end. I suspect so, for in visiting her in the weeks after I discovered the cassette beside her bed, her revisionist history of her relationship with my father morphed into a story she would tell umpteen times, of how my father had courted her with a pickup line of old-world charm. He had allegedly gone around confessing to everybody who'd listen – 'I saw her from behind and had to run up to see if she was as good looking from the front.'

It is a hopeless romantic vignette, but seemed to bring her solace. And despite my understanding of their later relationship, I believe it must have started just so. Who we are at the beginning of a relationship is not necessarily the person we end up being.

After stalling over the historical record of my father's death, I finally got to the Denise Klein material. I checked out the microfiche archives of *The Chicago Tribune*, chronicling her open forum series of letters to the paper, and had the pages run off by a librarian.

Immediately I was struck by the starkness of the banner title, 'Midnight in a Perfect Life,' suggestive of how quickly and deeply her life had changed. I had not read her series while she was dying, too caught up in my own work, but now in scrolling through the words of a woman no longer alive, it affected me more intensely than it might otherwise have done.

There was something straightforward and honest in her writing, or at least, in the published material.

Truth be told, when she took my class, I had never fully come to terms with her struggle and her cloying reliance on faith and the hereafter. We had a rocky relationship artistically. She accepted Jesus in a way I couldn't understand. Of course, intellectually, I understood the concept of a 'leap of faith,' but my criticism was that I didn't see how Jesus had earned her faith in him. I hadn't put it that way. Instead, I expressed it with the characteristic murk of erudite urbanity that defined my underlying sense of inferiority: I said that she had not fully inhabited the concept of the INEFFABLE.

I might as well have written something in Chinese. I had laid all this on a dying woman who had taken the class merely as a catharsis, to explore self-expression and an inward journey. Her audience was herself, a simple reconciliation with life's end, a final expression of who and what she was.

Looking up from the microfiche, I paused, remembering how her reaction to my initial criticism had been a radical shift of tone, her second piece an ill-conceived medical take on her first chemotherapy session. It focused heavily on procedure and was overly reliant on the credibility of scientific terminology. That, she felt, had been my chief complaint about her first piece – *credibility*. I'd cut this second submission to ribbons as *un-emotive* and it soured our working relationship still further.

Yet, in now looking back at her letters to the paper, I saw how her work had evolved. She had taken to heart my criticism of her religious internalization of her personal crisis and illness, and transformed her experience into something more outwardly engaging and ultimately readable. She had done what I had failed to do, adapt, recreate her own voice, and find an audience.

In its revised and published form, her first chemotherapy session began with her throwing up alone in the parking lot after the procedure. Then the scene cut to her arriving home, greeted by her three beautiful daughters. The girls had shaved their heads at a Chemo Solidarity Party. She described them as looking like Auschwitz prisoners. Suddenly struck by the horror of what would eventually befall her, she began screaming at them, before breaking down and falling to her knees. The last image saw her gathering up the silky mound of her daughters' hair with what she described as *The Grief of Rapunzel*, the title of the piece.

That a life could continue to be expressed on a thin strip of microfiche renewed within me that deeper sense of what the written word represented. It bridged a divide between life and death, ennobled the art of writing, set it apart from so-called normality.

I saw a clarity and honesty that cut through the conceit of fiction, seeing for the first time the rationale for the proliferation of non-fiction, the declarative openness of the *I* voice, eclipsing the age of metaphor, when people may have been unwilling, or disallowed, to speak so openly.

Five

It snowed throughout the morning as I finally finished my work at the library. I felt a sense of accomplishment I had not experienced in a long time as I gathered up the entire sequence of Denise's letters in a manila envelope, along with the printed copy of all the work she had submitted through-out the course.

At a bank of public phones in the vestibule of the library, I called Lori. I wanted to come clean with her, felt honesty should prevail as we moved forward. I was ready to lay out who and what I was, what I feared and hoped for in life; also where I *really* stood with the New York editor.

Regrettably, I got her voice mail. I didn't leave a message.

It was just going on 1 p.m., and I felt at odds as to what to do next. Already, a lambent light was tending toward a lengthening of shadows and there were lights on in the building across the street. I didn't feel like heading home and having my sense of purpose truncated. I wanted to be out, amidst life.

As I stood in the colossus of the Harold Washington Library foyer, I stared up into the ceiling, ruminating on the fact that, despite an uncaring public, money and a place like this had been set aside to create a storehouse of who and what we are as a people. I thought of the three dollar take of the saxophone player, of the relative obscurity of one life destined to play the blues. The reality was, you could only do what you could to the best of your ability, and the rest be damned.

I picked up a phone book, intent on mining the Denise Klein story now that I had gathered the information on her, setting it at least as a preface to my own non-fiction. All I needed was Frank Klein's approval as executor of what Denise had produced, along with maybe a brief interview giving Frank's perspective on what had transpired during the flux of her sickness, her quest for a child, and eventual death. Almost a year and a half had passed.

I tried the number listed at the top of Denise's assignments but it was disconnected. The phone book wasn't much help so I called directory assistance. It took three calls to different Frank Kleins, before I got through to the right Frank Klein. I half-expected him not to be there, given the time of day. He struggled to remember me at first. He was in the midst of changing a diaper, or so he told me. I could hear the child, Frank Junior, crying in the background. Frank agreed to meet me that same afternoon, asking me to bring along a gallon of milk and a carton of Marlboro.

An hour later, I took the train out to Skokie, and then a taxi to an address I had hurriedly scribbled on the back of the manila envelope containing Denise's work.

I arrived at a run-down apartment complex that made me wonder if I'd mistakenly written the wrong street number. But then, in a first floor window I saw the figure of Frank Klein, dressed in Bermuda shorts and a faded golf shirt. He was watching me. There was a stroller and a snow shovel in the miniature strip of graveled garden.

He extended his arms behind the closed window, suggestive of a self-deprecating irony that would define my visit with him.

In a small living room with an over-sized TV set at an ungodly volume, I watched a mouse drop an anvil on a cat's head as Frank took the milk then peeled the gold strip off the cigarette casing in a slow, deliberate motion. He relayed to me the desperate circumstances of what he called 'living in the shadow of post-traumatic publicity hype, the reality when the cameras stop rolling.'

He qualified the remark later with a more culturally significant quote, asking, 'What do you think it's like to be baby Jessica, to be pulled from the well under the scrutiny of a nation? Where do you go from there?'

It was hard hearing him over the noise of the TV. I had a tape-recorder in my pocket, attempting to capture the exchange. I watched him tap the cigarette against the palm of his hand in a way that betrayed how old he truly was. He lit up in a cloud of smoke. He was fifty-two years of age living in bachelor squalor. Denise had been a decade his junior. The anomaly in his life was the kid in the playpen, big-headed and naked, save for a sagging diaper.

Frank saw me looking and said pre-emptively, 'From a medical standpoint, I think the only thing that would have been worse would be a clone. I'd have had to look at myself all day long.'

I looked at the kid and then at Frank. 'He's a good looking kid, Frank. He's got your eyes.'

Frank nodded. 'Let's just hope he doesn't see what I see.'

That was the general tenor of how our conversation developed. Frank smelt of the sickly sweetness of metabolized hard liquor. It was a Thursday afternoon, and he didn't even comment on the fact he was not working. A bottle of Scotch was set out on the kitchen table.

He told me that he had lost his house to bankruptcy even before Frank Junior was born, a measure he conceded partly undertaken to offset having to pay for his daughters' college fees, but also to escape the medical bills that had followed

Denise to the grave. 'They didn't fix her,' he said loudly. 'You saw what they did to her! All they did was prolong her agony, and then those goddamn sharks lined up and demanded their money. For what, tell me?'

There was, of course, no answer to the question. I said softly, 'It bought her time, Frank. It allowed her to make plans.'

I watched Frank nod obligingly and then go toward the refrigerator to fill his glass with ice. He said with his back turned to me, 'Everybody wants to be with Jesus, just not right now! Isn't that the irony of religion?'

I took the opportunity to stand and look around. The kid cooed and Frank attended to him, making baby-talk. He was a good father.

All that remained of his life now was the fallout of a distant existence. I stared at a series of photographs he had tacked up on the wall. One was of his wedding day; the others of his daughters. All three were beauties in their own right, the shots of them mostly taken through high school in the heady days of their mother's illness. In one they were posing in shorts and tee shirts with the words LOVE, FAMILY and GOD embossed in a stylized script, holding aloft signs outside a car dealership during a charity car wash.

Frank raised his voice, and I turned. 'In the end I felt like I was sending them out there like the three little pigs . . . I don't think we can hope for brick houses anymore. Reality lies somewhere between the straw and stick ones!' He said pointedly, 'You can quote me on that. It's all part of the public record, the bankruptcy papers, and I got my "get out of jail free card." I think the financial system has that sort of *out* built into it . . . they statistically account for failure . . .'

I pretended to write down what he said. He seemed to want to say something meaningful, continuing to speak in a halting series of disconnects between pulls on his cigarette.

In a strange way, it was refreshing to find someone more jaded than I.

Our conversation was cut short as a smell of shit invaded the dank claustrophobia of the room. Frank changed Frank Junior on a pullout sofa with an overhanging naked bulb. The place looked like an operating theater.

Later I sat in the grim confines of the kitchen drinking neat Scotch and listening to Frank talk between sips. He turned his glass in a slow meditative swirl, as the kid gnawed on fish sticks in a highchair, then cleaned the kid up and sat him on his knee.

In a former time, I thought, they could have been some sideshow attraction, a medical wonder – though not a clone, Frank Junior did look like a miniature Frank. In fact, that was the confounding thing about it, how un-special the kid was in light of everything that had gone into creating him. I looked at Frank and thought, how could anyone survive this vacuum of social isolation and remain sane?

Frank said, 'We still have a free stay at Disneyland. But there's a catch, you got to get there first. I might as well have a free stay on the Moon for all it's worth.'

I smiled obligingly in the way men might pass certain truths between them.

In the end, I didn't mention why I had come, nor did Frank ask. As I was getting ready to leave, I said, 'Do you miss her, Frank?' It was a question delivered with the cheap sentiment of a daytime talk show host.

Frank looked at me, considering his response. 'I think in a marriage when two people come together they create a third … entity …' He seemed to struggle with his analogy for a moment. 'You know, maybe like a band coming together.

What would Keith Richards be without a Jagger, without *The Stones*?' He said dryly, 'Is that *literary* enough for you?'

It smacked of the suggestion he knew why I was there, but I think the quote passed as a genuine testament to his enduring sense of what had befallen him, of how his life had turned out.

As I headed for the door, Frank rose and put his hand on my shoulder. The kid was balanced on his hip. I think he was trying to regain a measure of familiarity, like he had put me out with his 'Is that *literary* enough for you' comment. He looked right at me. 'If it means anything, you pushed Denise to find something deeper within her.'

I nodded in acknowledgement, but Frank kept talking. 'I remember her coming back home and screaming and cursing, reading your comments aloud to the girls and being so damned mad at you, then afterward being mad at herself...'

I said quietly, with a move toward ending our conversation, 'That's part of the process of self-discovery.'

Frank cut in. 'What she wanted was to be *remembered* more than anything else!'

I looked toward the kid and then at Frank, 'We all seek that, every last one of us. We've just got to find that one thing we're good at.'

I suddenly felt overwhelmed with the memory of my mother and wanted to leave. I looked at my watch, but Frank wasn't done.

I could tell he was more drunk now than when I had arrived and could see he was struggling to finish what he really wanted to communicate. I had breached a dam of emotion deep within him for my own end.

'Let me ask you something ...' he said eventually. 'You think you can give yourself cancer?'

This, I knew, was Frank talking to Frank.

'For almost two years before Denise got sick we hadn't slept together. She'd pretty much died inside.' He touched his heart with his drink. 'We were just going through the motions, waiting for the girls to get out of high school. Denise slept on the couch. It was out in the open with the girls. They sided with her for the most part.' He stopped for a moment, his concentration broken. 'By the way, don't have all girls ...' His eyes got big when he said it.

I nodded, 'I'll remember that, Frank.'

He was quiet for a moment. Then he started again. 'You know, if Denise was alive right now we'd be divorced. That's what Jessie ... my eldest daughter told me right after Denise died. She said it in the hallway before Denise was even cold. It was like she'd been waiting to say it all along.'

I watched Frank lower his head, suddenly caught in the memory.

I said softly, 'That was grief talking is all that was, Frank ...'

He shrugged and took a deep breath. 'So why don't any of them call me?' There was a rush of emotion in his voice.

The exchange darkened the general perspective I had of him. He was more complicated, the situation darker, than I had ever imagined. This was a side of Denise Klein's family life I knew nothing about.

Disconcertingly, Frank still had his hand on my shoulder. I could feel the pressure of his fingers as he adjusted his balance, trying to remain upright.

I said with the forced optimism of a hostage negotiator, 'People come around in their own time ... and as for divorce or anything like that ... I don't think we can ever be sure of what might have been. That's the mystery of life. You can't beat yourself up over what is done. She didn't leave between relapses, did she?'

Frank took a step back and, raising his glass, agreed in the most amenable way, shaking off his depression for my sake, and the kid's. 'Maybe you're right! Maybe I'm just remembering it wrong.' He saluted and drank his Scotch in one long gulp. As the kid reached for the glass, he abruptly pulled it away and said, 'I think if I wait long enough I got a drinking buddy here in Frank Junior, someone I can win over to my side!'

I smiled. 'There's always a silver lining to life.'

Frank laughed off the sentiment, then he said sardonically, 'Now I know you're full of it. I was looking for some honesty here. I thought that's what you were peddling, but now I know you're full of crap!' He stopped abruptly, pulled a mock serious face, and leaned toward the kid like they were sharing something between them. 'Here's the way it is. The kid's not happy. He wants me to ask you to leave.'

It was a jaded ventriloquist act. I thought, was this how Frank acted when he was alone with the kid, asking and answering his own questions?

I had taken Frank someplace he had not wanted to go. I regretted it immediately. I had pointed to a futility he already understood. Where was the genius, or the compassion, in that?

It was a charge my father had leveled at me in his own way in the years leading up to his suicide. I had made us all uncomfortable, pushing us, my mother included, toward what each of us knew, but none of us wanted to acknowledge – the fact that my father had other women, that his heart lay elsewhere.

In the end, I left the apartment in almost the same manner I had arrived, watching Frank watch me from the sliding patio window. It was as if I could have been coming or going – a moment out of time, an eternal re-run playing at Frank's Place.

I wrote that down on the manila envelope as the taxi pulled away, trying to crawl away from a personal sense of my own guilt, to keep myself from thinking of my father or mother.

Six

In the lead-up to our first visit to the fertility clinic I occupied myself with description, trying to capture the desperation of all our lives with the detached eye of an outsider. I wrote up the piece on Frank and faxed it to one of Schwartzy's editorial minions, who ended up calling it 'too existential and dark.'

'These are direct quotes from a real conversation,' I shouted. 'You can't censor reality. Life is existential! Life *is* dark!'

In the midst of the spat, I demanded to speak with Schwartzy again to underscore what I was going to deliver. He was indisposed. He never took my calls, all of which set me ill-at-ease, doubting the veracity of our deal. No contract had appeared. It was more a horse dealer's handshake of good faith, all part of the indeterminacy of the publishing world that had driven me over the edge in New York.

I had begun to suffer that same sickening feeling and fitful sleep. It was like prodding an old wound. I also started to have vivid dreams about my father, taken back to the circumstances surrounding his suicide, the intensity of that time always at the back of my waking consciousness.

It was against those unsettling feelings that Lori and I entered the black monolithic landmark of the *Hancock* building, and took the lift forty floors to the clinic of Dr Jay Goldfarb. I noted the ankle-length of her fur-lined coat, knowing I would write something about the atavism of animal skin, the primal nature of what we were embarking upon.

Lori saw me looking at her and took it as concern. She

smiled. She was uncomplicated in a way I marveled at. It was one of her most endearing qualities, what I called the survival instinct of ordinariness.

Already I had dubbed her, for my article-in-progress, *Miss Conception* – she, a case study in the ingestion of birth control and weight loss pills, in the havoc science has played on the female body. As for male fertility issues, I'd decided on a catchy banner, *Sperms of Endearment*. A run-through of various insemination interventions was going to go under the heading *Semenar*; my initial idea, a support group of sperm sitting round a table playing cards, talking frankly about feeling tired. It was all there, or there about, in my head.

I knew Goldfarb was renowned in the field of infertility treatment, and as we reached his clinic, I was set to wryly capture our initial encounter. Nothing, however, prepared me for what materialized when the elevator doors opened, the vastly lucrative world of the elective medical procedure. The foyer was a vault of emerald-veined marble with columns inlaid with a pantheon of naked faux granite and marble statues. It was like a day spa of the Gods, or an art gallery, not a medical clinic.

I turned in a sort of vertigo at what modern success could afford those who'd made it. It was nothing short of a total commitment to excess, a calculated full-on visual assault designed to arrest the rational mind, and by logical extension, to bear testament to its founder's genius. In those initial moments, I thought maybe this was how a slave in Egyptian times rationalized dying in the creation of the pyramids. At some point we become inculcated in the dreams of others.

Just one look at Lori confirmed my suspicion. She was standing beside a life-size statue of *Venus*, a woman of such fabled beauty men would slaughter for the right to impregnate her. Another statue, *Shy Lover*, featured a virginal bridesmaid in a sheer vestment, gracefully holding up her arms, her face hidden, her shyness making her all the more seductive. Another statue was looking into a fountain – Narcissus who fell in love with his own reflection, spurning sex, fated to watch his own image until he died.

What was Goldfarb insinuating with the sexual foibles of these mythical figures? Two Trojan warriors with phallic helmets guarding the reception desk made me understand I was being had by a guy with money to burn.

I was about to say as much to Lori, but she had crossed the foyer.

Goldfarb had miraculously materialized.

He was and was not what I expected. Maybe I didn't know what I expected really. He ended up being one of those pasty types of below-average physique who had succeeded neither in sport nor with girls in high school, not freakish enough to be into comic book clubs or chess club, yet sagacious enough not to waste their time on such pursuits; one of those cerebral beings who pass unnoticed through school, biding their time, accomplished in the As they pull in calculus and biology. That he, of all people, *Dr No Prom*, now spent half his life between the parted legs of women must have been a dream come true.

This was just the sort of observation Schwartzy demanded of his writers.

The message of my yet-to-be-written article was simple, supporting the idea that sexual conquest for the male was not so much about appeal as tenacity, averages, play-books and odds. In each ejaculation the male shot forth an average of 384.2 million sperm; this, compared to the monthly ovulation of a single egg in the female. Nature had sided with probability.

We all ended up standing by a wall of pictures attesting to the clinic's success – in fact, disquieting shots not just of single births, but bassinets of twins, triplets, quadruplets and even sextuplets. Childless couples were having litters, not families. Such was the moral, ethical, and financial conundrum of this science: the more implanted eggs, the greater the chance of conception, yet with multiple-embryo pregnancies, so, too, would come the dilemma of multi-fetal reduction – abortion.

At some stage in this process we'd take the life of innocents through selective reduction. We'd cull Angels.

I said, as we entered Goldfarb's office, 'Wasn't it Mailer who said any act of sex without the prospect of conception is invalid and soul-endangering?'

Lori squeezed my arm nervously as Goldfarb replied, without missing a heartbeat, 'I think a more interesting question is, who do you think Mailer was talking about, men or women?' Tacitly reassuming control, he added, 'We're going to need a sperm sample from you, if you're up for it.'

Then he fixed his attention on Lori.

Under the garish light of his office the mood turned decidedly clinical. Plastic models of female and male anatomy were set off to one side of the desk, and in the centre stood an open theater of a medical table with a set of stainless steel stirrups that looked like motorcycle handlebars.

The official terminology of what we were embarking on went under the name of Assisted Reproductive Technologies (ART). Given Lori's age, Goldfarb began by talking about changes in egg number and quality in relation to a subject's age. All the eggs a woman ever produced were already present in the ovaries of the developing fetus as early as the tenth week of intrauterine life. From then on there was a reduction in number over time and a precipitous deterioration of egg quality between thirty-eight to forty years, causing chromosomal abnormalities and increased risk of Down's Syndrome.

The reality of modern existence was that it took almost

until middle age to attain economic stability. Evolution lagged behind. This was the frailty of forty. Thousands of years ago, we'd undoubtedly have been dead by now.

For a time Goldfarb spoke of the risk of uterine cancer just before menopause, and the marked increase in the number of radical hysterectomies involving the removal of the entire reproductive apparatus of women, the uterus, ovaries, and fallopian tubes, especially in women who had not carried. This led eventually to his asking Lori about her sexual history, Goldfarb tacitly challenging where she had check-marked *No* under previous pregnancies. I suppose he knew there must have been in most instances. Few escaped high school unscathed.

Goldfarb changed her answer on the form to *Yes*. 'I understand the sense of reservation here, the reluctance to divulge information in this age of lawsuits.' He looked up from the form. 'But before assessing medical interventions, we need to establish your true sexual history, from frequency of sex to menstrual cycles, pregnancies and miscarriages.'

He directed his gaze at me for a moment. 'Both your sexual histories.'

I simply nodded and observed, as he turned his attention back to Lori, a faint scar running just behind his hairline, suggestive of a recent face tuck. He said to Lori, 'How many weeks did you carry?'

'Five ... five months,' she replied quietly.

My throat tightened, not at the betrayal, since I already knew about the abortion. It was just I had assumed it had occurred relatively early in the pregnancy.

Lori reached for my hand, which I gave her.

Goldfarb's face betrayed no emotion. 'Second trimester ...' His pen was poised over the form. 'What about complications ... sepsis, or excessive bleeding?'

'Sepsis ...' Lori whispered.

51

I felt the pressure of her fingers.

'And it was treated where, and with what?'

Lori struggled for a moment. 'The place … the place I had gone to … Penicillin, I think that's what I got … I can't remember. We had to go back that day. I was bleeding badly.'

The *we* struck me.

Goldfarb said, 'This was pre-Roe v. Wade?'

Lori nodded. 'In high-school …'

'You're lucky to be alive,' Goldfarb said candidly. 'I don't want to make you live through this again, but was this a partial birth abortion?'

Lori's eyes glossed. 'I don't know what …'

'The fetus was delivered alive?'

Lori hesitated, before meeting his eyes. 'Yes.'

I could feel the intensity of the exchange heighten, Goldfarb's volley of questions delivered with medical detachment.

It did nothing to assuage Lori's sense of guilt.

I felt my presence was adding to her growing consternation. Ostensibly, this was a rundown of her sexual past and under normal medical circumstances my being there would have been at her discretion.

These were her secrets, not mine.

Still Goldfarb pushed. 'Looking back, did you have a feeling that something was different, a sensation of scar tissue building up, a feeling of …'

He let Lori put a name to the feeling. 'Blockage,' she said quietly.

Goldfarb repeated the word. 'Maybe we'll check for obstruction of the cervix. In certain cases there can be damage to the cervix or uterus in late stage procedures.'

Lori raised her voice slightly. She was shivering. 'I was pregnant again after that … after the first one.'

I felt myself swallow, but tried to betray nothing. I touched my thumb against the soft fat of her palm.

Her body was trembling with emotion. She began to cry softly, closing and opening her eyes, before wiping her left cheek with the back of my hand.

In that momentary hesitation, in simply trying to regain her composure, I saw Goldfarb subtly checked his watch. We were on a schedule. He said coldly, 'How long after the first pregnancy?'

Lori looked up, and cleared her throat and said with a sudden determination, 'Not long ... I carried for only six weeks. He was killed in Vietnam ... the father I mean.'

Goldfarb kept writing notes then began moving through a questionnaire in a rapid-fire succession.

'Are your menstrual cycles regular?'

'No.'

'Do you pass clots?'

'Yes.'

'Do you experience severe menstrual cramping?'

'Yes.'

'Any sense of discomfort during intercourse?'

'Yes.'

'Are you able to achieve orgasm?'

She didn't answer.

Goldfarb asked the question again.

Lori brought my hand to her heart. 'I *feel* love.'

Despite my best intentions, all I heard in my head were the theatrics of faked orgasm, what the readers of the men's magazines feared, the most intimate of betrayals.

Lori disengaged her hand.

I was above all this. I kept telling myself that. In the context of this setting, what Lori said meant nothing. I wanted to stop her from continuing.

This was where such journeys led, to intimate disclosures and heartache.

I glared at Goldfarb. He tacitly kept writing. I wanted to know how many interviews had he conducted like this, confidant to the protracted psychological and sociological crisis of so many abortion stories, to so many past histories and regrets.

Under different circumstances, I might have pointedly asked him. This is where I wanted to delve now, escape the personal drama, probe the greater societal issue of reproduction and sex in general. So much of adolescent American female sexuality was seemingly defined, first by a reckless impressionability of peer pressure, then by an about face moral one-eighty in later life, a rejection of past sins, a retreat toward a reactionary PTA sexuality of Reformed-Cock-Suckers!

I tried to capture the phrase just so, to commit it to memory, to find a measure of objective journalistic distance, as Goldfarb, holding a plastic model of a pear-shaped uterus aloft like a chalice, began outlining his determination and course of action, speaking into a small tape recorder, as we officially became part of a medical record.

At one point, he stopped the recording momentarily, and looking at me pointedly, said, 'We'll need a blood and sperm sample to initiate tests on you,' his eyes indicating I should leave.

I looked between him and Lori. She didn't meet my gaze, her fur coat wrapped around her, one of the pockets centered over her stomach.

She looked like some sad marsupial.

Seven

For the better part of a month, Lori's confession about her faked orgasms arrested all discussion regarding where we wanted to go as a couple, and what *we* truly desired.

I watched as a level of desperation took hold of her. One only had to check the cabinet to see she wasn't thinking straight, the over-the-counter naturopath vitamins, herbs and pills she was taking, Vitamin C, Vitamin E, Zinc, Centrum Silver Anti-oxidants, Siberian Ginseng, Carnitine, Arginine, Selenium, Garlic extract, and Bee Pollen, along with prescription fertility drugs – Clomid and injectables that came with hypodermic needles.

Goldfarb had given her a biometric chart related to her cycle. It looked like some vast constellation, hinting at the great mystery that was Life.

I remained guarded, wary of prematurely broaching where we stood, especially when Lori abruptly attempted reconciliation, leaving a cheap photocopied coupon on my side of the bed that read, 'Redeem for Hugs Anytime.' The coupon had come from a *Friendship Kit* Deb hawked with her Greeting Card business. It was the sort of sentiment that kept the confectionery business afloat.

I felt the decided coolness that had prevailed between us in the intervening weeks since the visit to Goldfarb's clinic had played to my advantage. The longer we didn't talk the better. I had even disappeared for an alleged business trip to New York, staying really at a shit motel along the Indiana Dunes.

I came back with a defiant air of independent confidence that things were on the upswing for me professionally, throwing in the vague threat I was considering renting a studio to get down to writing.

It was a complicated dance between alienating her and pushing us toward what people were calling these days 'a reality check!'

The truth was, with no definitive price tag on fertility treatments, there wasn't enough money to pretend about moving to the suburbs. We would have gone into debt beyond our means. The associated costs kept rising in a flood of literature, but especially as Lori's case seemed like it wasn't that straight forward. I think even Lori had come round to that fact despite the pills and herbs she was downing. In going through her purse another day I found a past due bill for the condo mortgage. We were already sinking.

In retrospect, I felt Goldfarb had done us a favor, and cut to the heart of something that went beyond the mere pursuit of a child. *He* had created this vacuum of indecision, inadvertently giving us time to think.

This was a midlife crisis. That's all it was. I had come round to that conclusion early on. I was just waiting for Lori to get it. There was nothing wrong with us as we were. I wanted that to be the prevailing sentiment when we made up. We had been duped by the mania of the popular media pushing pregnancy, pushed toward something neither of us really wanted.

I had my speech ready, the pitch at a childless marital redemption, pushing the relative ease empty-nesters shared, indeed looked forward to, what were now dubbed *The Golden Years*. It wasn't an entirely melancholy prospect at all really. I thought I could sell her on the idea of an early sun-kissed retirement to Arizona.

Now a month on, the first overture toward reconciliation was at hand, but I still knew it wasn't time yet. I still had this scenario in my head of us prematurely coupling after a slobbering litany of supposed misinterpretations of one another's words, where I would be obliged to say I wanted a child through the sheer force of her will.

To that end, with our collective futures in the balance, I knew the best defense was a good offense, so I changed the word *Hugs* to *Shrugs* and went to brush my teeth.

When I came back into the bedroom, Lori was apparently asleep, her back turned to my side of the bed.

The coupon was gone.

If the problem had been kept solely between us, I think that Lori and I would have prevailed, arriving at the counsel of our mutual benefit, but I knew I was fighting an invisible enemy in Deb. She had infiltrated our silence with calls to Lori at work.

Regrettably, Deb had got to me too, sidelining my work with Schwartzy, for just days after our meeting with Goldfarb, she pitched videotaping Lori's fertility treatment as a potential *Health Channel* exclusive. Without a business plan, she even managed to rope in Goldfarb behind my back. Seeing the marketing angle, he signed a legal waiver and Deb became amateur producer, director and camerawoman to the intimacy of Lori's journey.

On top of everything, she had the audacity to call me for my agent's name with a view to a potential book deal, the book a secondary concern, since she was focused 'on the new media.'

I wanted to slit her throat.

On the occasions I suffered her presence, she was always dressed in elastic banded polyester pants that rode high over the oval egg of her gut, a flounce of ruffled lace collar hinting at something approximating femininity, along with a dribble of fake pearls dangling over her trademark pink heart sweat-shirts. At times I wondered what she would have been like if she had been born beautiful, if the entirety of her existence hadn't been given to an over-wrought defense mechanism against the judgment of men.

I was at least willing to talk of such things, to drag forth the philosophical and moral implications of where we stood as the opposite sex. Of course we never arrived at such a talk.

In the end, Deb's involvement was one of the most demean-ing, soul-wearying experiences of my life. As things pro-gressed in the following weeks, as she and Lori hung out, as they began to visit Goldfarb without me, I came to view her as a case study in excruciating ordinariness, the epitome of an abject democracy of self-starters in which the only prerequisite for success was an unflappable sense of self. She was a work-in-progress, pumped up by accreditation certificates in *person-centered growth*, *potential fulfillment* and *self-actualization*, along with astrology and cosmetology con-centrations; she, the patron saint of Ordinary, *Ordinariness* her most prized asset.

Behind her back, I exclusively referred to her as *Humpty Dumpty's Ex*, the reason *Humpty Dumpty* fell or, more prob-ably, *jumped*. For all my ridiculing and despising of her, in the end my own desperation prevailed, and I tried to piggyback on her enterprise.

I called her up, positioning myself as potential wordsmith who could craft a broad and sweeping narrative of what was at stake for Lori, a proposition Deb uncharacteristically agreed to, initially without objection. What made Deb's selective editing cut however were two inane biological quips I made under the sway of over-familiarity, namely that human intelligence was presumed to be tied to the cranial dimensions of what could pass through a woman's pelvis, along with a factoid from the animal kingdom that, in times of drought, a kangaroo could regulate the growth rate of an embryo. This latter quote was colored by a god-awful socio-economic remark I made about poverty and the unemployed, taken totally out of context.

Deb made me look like a racist, misogynist ass.

I had misjudged her, realizing all too late her underlying, willful nastiness. She was anything but ordinary.

The fruits of her efforts culminated in a home-made tape of Lori's visits to Goldfarb, something Lori came to rely on as postmortem to each insemination failure, viewing the jittery footage over and over, as if she might be able to detect something she had done wrong.

It was disconcerting as hell and pathetic from my point of view, footage that saw Lori initially waving at a camera like someone about to leave on vacation. The tape, a compendium of her visits, eventually took the format of a series of director's takes, grey static beginning each take, then the starkness of a date-time stamp, then a slow fade-in of sound and raw video that always began with Lori's arrival at the check-in desk, the breathiness of expectation caught in her speech and the muffled thump of her heart as she passed the statues of the Gods.

Then it was on to a series of takes spliced together in uneven cuts, adding to the documentary feel of the tape; scenes of Lori undressing, folding her clothing over a chair, delivering a stock-take of what she was feeling, a monologue that modulated over the months between hope and desperation, the irrational resilient faith of someone inculcated in a cult, a zealot's earnestness punctuated by tears and fitful nodding as she put on a backless gown and waited, alone.

She had taken to wearing a small cross, which she kissed, setting it between her breasts. The next scenes were always the same, under the garish light of the office theater, Lori on her back, the imperfection of her pear-shaped thighs in the air, the waxy paper crinkling beneath her buttocks, the clinical snap of synthetic gloves and ooze of KY jelly, an overture toward the serious business of creating life.

Then it was either stock footage of a laboratory procedure with a wiggling sperm breaking the membrane of an egg in a petri dish, or dramatic tunneling footage of a lens worming its way up through the cervix into the uterus, the dubbed voice of Goldfarb reciting his hocus pocus incantation of esoteric medical terminology.

What was missing each time was the final, triumphant breakthrough, the successful implantation of a fertilized egg, the pulse of a heartbeat – Life.

For now, that was to be denied Lori, leaving her lost in the emotional isolation of guilt, underscored by the fact that she had in the past been pregnant, not once, but *twice*.

In the interim, I tried again to connect with Schwartzy, to gain a measure of assurance that things were still good between us. It didn't matter if I never went through the fertility process. He would be none the wiser. I had planned on writing under a pseudonym for the mileage of mystery. I would be the consummate insider. If I could attach the wry sensibility of a male voice, I felt I could undermine the essential mania of the process.

In wading through the medical literature on fertility at the library, after what had been, otherwise, a day of aimless wandering, I came across a factoid I felt would appeal to his general predilection for cultural smarts, and to his sensibility as a Jew in particular. One of Lori's key fertility treatments was a series of injections of human menopausal gonadotropin (HMG).

HMG was comprised of extracts from postmenopausal women's urine, though the kicker was that the breakthrough fertility procedure had been pioneered in Italy by a relative of Pope Pius XII, who'd coordinated massive urine collections from the retirement homes of nuns. HMG remained culturally relevant, since today retirement homes were still a primary source of urine for fertility treatment drugs.

I called Schwartzy from a payphone in the library foyer and left an enigmatic message on his voice mail suggesting I had information on a vast Papal conspiracy surrounding the issue of fertility.

For the better part of a week I waited for a message from Schwartzy. There was no response. I called a few more times, jacked up by a heightened anxiety, insinuating I was considering shopping the information around if I didn't hear from him soon.

I think reality hit in that week as to where I really stood as a writer. I called my agent. There had been no further word from Fennimore's people. There wouldn't be. The call to my agent lasted a matter of a minute. He didn't even try to do what any good agent would have done, lie to me.

I took the opportunity to immediately make amends with Lori.

Without referencing the looming mortgage crisis with the condo, I discussed again the idea of the sublet, speaking of how I felt the neighborhood was conducive to the writing life, not just because of the progress my agent was making with negotiations on the 'fat contract.' If things worked out with Goldfarb, I would need a legitimate office, a quiet space away from the baby.

I knew merely mentioning the prospective baby would allow me to reclaim a measure of compassion and decency in her eyes.

I was desperate.

In a come-to-Jesus talk Lori revealed, among other things, her own vulnerability, admitting to being behind in payments on the condo. She showed me the bank statements. She pushed to know where things stood in New York with the deal.

I told her I was in the process of making suggested edits, but I was close. I could see the finish line. I made the animated motion of a runner breaking the tape. The editor just wanted to pitch the best possible book to the editorial committee. She was discussing a multi-book deal, the house viewing me as a potential long-term prospect, a young writer they could nurture.

The sublet was the ideal space for me to focus. It seemed plausible in the mere telling of it. Here was our escape plan, our out from absolute financial ruination.

I couldn't tell if she could see through me or not, but she acquiesced. I could see her struggling to come to terms with everything that was happening to *us*, and to her. It wasn't fair!

I held her for a time, until she even magnanimously offered to hold off on further treatments until *we* heard something from New York.

I didn't answer her. It wasn't really what she wanted to hear.

A half hour later, I knelt in the bathroom as Lori sat on the toilet, and under her guidance, swabbed her thigh with rubbing alcohol, then slowly injected a two inch needle into her sub-cutaneous fat as she winced and set her head against my shoulder.

Eight

On the morning I set off to try to secure an apartment in the gay district, all I could do was make light of the potential move, smiling and saying jokingly, despite everything, 'Remember what you said when we first started dating, that all you were left with were "fags and writers"?'

At one time that wry sensibility might have passed as romantic honesty as to where we really stood. Now, the comment was met with a stony silence, though Lori tried as best she could and said finally, 'Call me if it looks like it might work.'

It was hard recovering what we'd had between us. It changed from minute to minute.

In the hallway while leaving, I was confronted by Deb, who stopped me and said, 'Here's something for your office, Karl!'

Obviously, she'd been kept abreast of economic developments. She unraveled a poster of a kitten on a pile of books. The caption beneath read – 'Help, I'm ten stories up!'

I said, 'Kittens and literature. Doesn't it say something about that in the Bible as foreshadowing The End of Times?'

'Well, here's something you might find more fulfilling. I got it for Lori.' She handed me a book.

It was a signed *Oprah* edition of Mitch Albom's *Tuesdays with Morrie: An Old Man, a Young Man, and Life's Greatest Lesson* – a dime-store take on the meaning of life and death that had sent the entire nation running for a box of Kleenex.

Not bothering to do me the courtesy of looking at me

directly, Deb casually called out Lori's name, before inquiring if I'd read 'Mitch's masterpiece.'

I said, 'I'm awaiting the Jack Kevorkian foreword edition of the book!'

She glared at me. 'You're such an asshole, Karl.'

She tried to go by me, but I blocked her passage. 'You know, a more interesting story is how Mitch had so many Tuesdays on his hands for Morrie, and how he just happened to get a book out of it. I figure he had one hand on the typewriter as Morrie was drawing his last breath. His death was a fuckin' circus, Deb! Who talks like that? Who dies like that? You want the reality of dying in the modern age, go see my mother! I'm more of an expert on the act of dying than goddamn Mitch Tuesday and his goddamn life affirming aphorisms!'

'So why haven't you written about it? That's what you are, allegedly, a writer – right? You've got Mondays through Fridays. At least Mitch did something with his Tuesdays.'

'OK, Deb, how about this for reality! A take on the carnal side of life's desires, a rumination on the age-old struggle between faith and faithlessness, something catchy like – *Fridays with Trixie: An Old Man, a Young Woman, and Something Worth Going to Hell For?*'

'Do it Karl, do anything but what you're currently doing, which is *nothing*!'

On the trip up North, I tried to blank out Deb's indictment. Staring out from the train I was conscious of the shamble of life in the flotsam of so many screaming children in the caged recess yards of public schools, and I thought, how was it that Lori and I could not produce just one more soul to add to this multitude? Life didn't seem that precious or hard to conceive.

For the remainder of the trip, I simply shut my eyes.

I was early for my appointment, so resorted to a specialty

coffee shop, *Caribou Coffee*, a Madison Avenue marketing conceit featuring a rustic Alaskan theme, with a central fireplace and flannel-backed chairs. Incongruously, it was the central meeting place in the gay neighborhood during daylight hours.

In the main, I avoided such coffee shops, saw them for what they were, modern offices of the dispossessed.

I tried to free my mind of everything that had gone on with Deb, and simply looked around me, my attention eventually drawn to an unframed photograph of vast tundra with a frozen lake at the base of a jagged rise of snow-capped mountains. On closer inspection, I saw a lone Caribou almost lost within the composition, its earthen hide blending against the sparse rocky tundra. The antlered head was raised in alertness, its breath a small cloud of mist – the overall effect starkly majestic, naturalistic, transcendent.

It put me in mind of what must have undoubtedly drawn a disturbed Chris McCandless into the wild, our peculiar American phenomenon of seeking guidance or redemption within nature.

The sublet was around the corner and it proved a story unto itself. As I had suspected, things were not altogether above board.

For over forty-five minutes I endured an ungodly complicated affair brokered by the apartment's Russian janitor, Ivan, along with his nephew, Vladimir, both in for a take on whatever was agreed on as rent.

Ivan had a habit of not understanding things when it suited him that made negotiation hard. The upshot was that the regular tenant was gone *indefinitely*. Ivan didn't know where to, or for how long, and seemed indignant at being asked, then pretended not to understand further questions. Annoyingly, throughout the entire viewing, he had his hand out, a peasant's rough paw with blackened nails, the other buried deep in his anorak pocket.

Inside the apartment I observed a pubescent girl in an oversized smock cleaning out the refrigerator. On her haunches, she nodded deferentially, before lowering her eyes as Ivan said something abruptly in Russian, cajoled a moment later by Vladimir who winked at her.

I watched them out of the corner of my eye as Ivan edged me toward a bedroom with a small bathroom. 'Utilities *free* for you as part of my deal, Mr Karl,' the *Mr Karl* a title of supposed respect he had annoyingly adopted.

Returning to the kitchenette, I saw a stash of plastic garbage bags containing personal items ready to be thrown out, suggesting the move was less than voluntary, and recent. More ominous still were the small brown vials and syringes sticking out of one of the bags. A smell of bleach failed to cover up the unmistakable smell of infirmity.

It all gave me the creeps, more so when I saw the sole personal effect that had survived the departure of the phantom tenant – a well worn La-Z-Boy chair, its backing missing. The exposed structure revealed a matrix of metal frame. In a macabre way, set alone in the barren room, it looked like some crude instrument of torture.

Ivan caught me eying it and offered it to me for first eighty, then sixty, finally settling on fifty bucks in a deal I never agreed to, vigorously shaking my hand, which he seemed to take as a bargaining strategy. He called me 'the thinking American!' when I told him what I did for a living. He nudged Vladimir. 'We will have to watch this *Mr Karl*.'

There was no getting around him. The chair was mine. In fact, he also had a roll top desk for my writing and was insistent about my having it.

We didn't ever discuss a price.

Nor was there any formal contract. He didn't believe in the written word.

I said, 'You and the rest of the known world!' but he didn't get the joke.

Already we had moved on. This was Ivan's deal, his sublet.

In the end, we shook hands as I took on an *unofficial* month-to-month lease at a bar across from the apartment, but not before being forced to down three vodka shots despite my protests that it was only 10 a.m. This was how it was done in Russia. I was obliged to pay for the bottle of vodka which Ivan kept within reach.

As I was getting up to leave, Ivan grabbed my arm. He had become visibly drunk, or ruminative, in a matter of minutes. I felt the pressure of his hand on my arm as he produced from the depths of his anorak pocket three ivory-colored chess pieces – a pawn, a King, and a bishop. He set them before the shot glasses and started talking in gibberish Russian and English about each piece.

Seemingly, he had something to say. Everybody did in the end. He touched the side of my head with his index finger.

What I gathered was that the pieces defined a political or religious cosmology for him. It was hard to follow exactly. He positioned the King and bishop in a series of complicated chess moves, hither and thither over an unseen board, invariably coming back to the pawn, moving it in a series of simple forward steps, something I think he wanted to impress upon me as noble and democratic, or maybe it was the opposite. Like I said, my head was already spinning.

When I left him, he had a throat hold on the King, and things were turning decidedly ugly for royalty.

*

It was still morning as I retreated to *Caribou*, feeling the effects of the vodka. I called Lori with the good news we had the apartment on a month-to-month basis.

I got no reply and suddenly remembered she was off again with Goldfarb, in the midst of another check-up. That's why Deb had been at the house, to accompany her. From the vantage point of the coffee shop, I could just about see the tip of the Hancock building down in the city.

I called Schwartzy's machine as well and said in a conspiratorial tone, 'You know the Pope sanctions all nunneries to collect the urine of nuns for fertility treatments? I've got a title for the article – "Holy Water!" Give me a call, Schwartzy. I know you respect tenacity. I'm not going away!'

I returned to my seat, regretting almost immediately having given him information I knew he'd use. I felt lost to that familiar weightlessness of a day with no foreseeable end or purpose. I think it was the combination of the drink and Schwartzy that got to me.

I looked across to the bar. Ivan was still visible. He embodied an old-world scavenging survival instinct that connected with my father. In simply looking across the street to the bar, I was suddenly aware something had fundamentally changed within us. It had happened figuratively between the bar and *Caribou* – where a drink of coffee cost more than a beer, and everybody was drinking coffee.

I could never have imagined my father, or any of his generation, making such a choice and not getting drunk.

I wrote the line down on a napkin, felt a rush of inspiration. I was thinking again like a writer, or so I wanted to believe. I had become stagnant, too removed from life. It put me in mind of something Chapman had said regarding The Opus, calling it 'curiously arresting and yet soulless,' candidly wanting to know if I felt in any real sense that the world was inhabited by living, breathing people.

As I looked up, I saw the young girl in the smock from the apartment cross the street toward the apartment complex. She was obviously skipping school. She was followed shortly afterward by Vladimir, a dead ringer for Dolph Lundgren with a hard body reminiscent of designer underwear ads or the centerfold of a gay magazine. He was attached to Ivan in some sort of indentured servitude.

I wondered what the hell someone like him really thought of America.

I got up and tried Lori's number one more time. There was still no reply.

I was onto my second cup of coffee, sobering up, when a group of men entered the shop, engaged in an animated conversation. They ended up taking a seat near me so I got the gist of their conversation.

Apparently, in an attempt to offset paying out huge life insurance claims, the industry was luring HIV positive persons with enticing 'life settlements', one-time cash payouts, or buyouts, depending on how you viewed it, granting instant economic security. The conversation swung between the mercenary nature of the insurance industry, to a *what if* scenario about what you could do with such a windfall.

It raised the issue of mortality in a way I had never really considered before. There are few times when such questions move beyond the realm of the abstract, when the finiteness of our existence is laid so bare.

One of the men was seriously considering the option.

I turned slightly, looked at the guy who was considering the buyout.

In his early forties, he didn't look sick. I didn't really know if people were still dying of AIDS outside of Africa. This guy looked healthy in a lean Ken doll way. He had a fake tan and was wearing a salmon shirt and penny loafers, in what amounted to a sort of unofficial uniform of unencumbered gay life.

I thought, why *wouldn't* he take the offer? When do we ever get such wagers?

The only other person I knew who had confronted such a question had been Denise Klein, her battle more dramatic in the radical surgical mastectomy she had undergone. Her instinctive reaction after her relapse had been a push for transcendence, a desire to create new life.

It begged the question, where did male transcendence lie?

I was suddenly conscious of just how exclusively male this coffee shop was. How would each, outside the traditional union of marriage and children, reconcile with mortality in their failing years, each destined to hospices of male companionship, reliant on the solace of friendship, on a bond of a different order.

What came to mind as I sat sobering up were those societies through the ages, loyalty sealed with blood, in which, for the most part, from the crusades to the trenches of the great wars, men took leave of this world, not in the arms of women, but among their fellow men.

In Greek society, homosexual love was revered – as much an intellectual union as sexual, wrought of a different aspiration, the surrogacy of passing on wisdom and tradition. And, lest we forget, the founding tenets of philosophy and the rational life took place in the bathhouses amidst a sect of men.

Nine

The détente I had reached with Lori faded once more in her growing anxiety regarding treatments that yielded no pregnancies. The procedure had taken primacy in her life in a way I could not understand. She knew the reality of our finances. This was not like her. I saw a credit card application on the table.

Our relationship waxed and waned. In many ways I felt I had become obsolete to the procedure. On that first and only meeting with Goldfarb, I had banked a sperm deposit that had run into the hundreds of millions. At times, I felt like the deposed king of some as yet uncreated line of descendants, conscious of potential and nothing else.

Lori's efforts were more complicated. She was still *harvesting* her eggs. I think the disparity of the terms killed something within and between us.

My day-to-day existence played itself out in a series of Beckett-like wanderings up around the apartment where I was supposed to be writing.

I rarely went there at all, just carted some of my books there simply for effect. Ivan was always around, along with Vladimir and the girl in the smock. There were move-ins and outs. I could see it from the road as I passed by, the transience of our lives, all too apparent. This was a place of silent death, of plague.

Whenever I saw Ivan, he stopped amidst a move and

shouted, 'The Thinking American!' like he thought ideas were a joke.

I felt, too, the burn of the girl's stare following me.

All I did was roam the bleakness of the lake shore, awaiting inspiration with a pen and paper in my pocket, feeling an emotional sickness, utter worthlessness at how things had turned out with Schwartzy, which was underscored one morning as a man veered into my path and whispered, 'You want to suck my cock?'

I kept walking, my eyes momentarily closed as I swallowed with the visceral sensation of someone sticking their cock down my throat.

In the mere act of being out at this hour, in this neighborhood, when people of honest character were in their allotted place of employment, did I pass for the sort of guy who might suck somebody's cock? A creature already culled from the herd of normal existence?

I wondered, how long would it take before the shock of such an affront would wear off, before I would come to see myself as this guy had seen me, a potential cock-sucker, consenting to gag on some penis in a rundown apartment at 10:30 in the morning, or hanging around some public restroom in a midday ejaculatory hopelessness, wanting simply to experience a momentary sense of release?

There were individuals who lived such lives. I had just encountered one of them.

Given this chilling scenario, I rallied a sense of purpose and turned once more to the Frank Klein material, dwelling on the existential underpinning of the dialogue transcribed from the tape of our encounter.

The meeting with him still haunted me. There was something infinitely sad about his existence. Collating the transcript

73

and the portfolio of material on Denise, I attempted to create a narrative of their distinct and separate lives.

I gathered, too, the newspaper articles relating to my father's suicide, reading through them again and again, material I had framed into not one but two novels so many years ago. The question I was left facing was, where had that talent gone, the sleight-of-hand to create something substantive from the mere fragments of a life – had this gift been eclipsed in bad conscience, in the underlying guilt of what I had done to my mother?

I knew the answer, the locus of my psychological blockage, a moral twinge short-circuiting my gut instinct.

On previous visits to see my mother, I had sometimes considered the feasibility of placing a pillow over her face, of bringing to an end what in so many ways had already ended. It would have solved a lot of problems.

I felt I would long for that release when my time came.

I began taking the El further out toward the suburbs after leaving Lori, transferring to the CTA which stopped a block from Frank's apartment, dogging him in the way you might investigate a suspect. It reminded me of how I had followed my father years before.

I don't know exactly what I hoped to accomplish in watching over Frank. I thought that maybe I was trying to attach myself to a certain narrative, to find the clarity of a voice, see the distinct honor in his ruinous life, to find the heroic.

At other times I wondered if I wasn't appealing to Denise, calling across some cosmic void, atoning for the way I had treated her. Characteristic of some archaic Catholic desperation, I hoped that in heaven she might intercede on our behalf so that Lori might end up pregnant.

It was a disquieting revelation that such a sentiment still

lurked within me, that notion of being forced to do something for the sake of someone else's welfare. Or maybe what I truly thought was the bawling of a child might strike some nerve, some instinct for survival, for choice to be eclipsed by necessity.

Whatever the underlying fixation with Frank, there was something honest about him that drew me to him. I wanted to absorb that state of fatalism he occupied. He lived as a caricature of himself, somehow surviving in the 'afterglow of publicity' as he had so candidly put it. I thought I could learn something from him about the act of modern survival.

Despite the enduring poverty he lived through, I came to observe how he took Frank Junior out most days in a stroller to a convenience store. The staple items he gathered were milk, bread, cereal, beer and cigarettes, the basic food groups of resignation.

Like I said, I don't know why I fixated on him, but as time passed, I mailed him, on occasion, a few bottles of Scotch and cartons of cigarettes, waiting to see him retrieve them.

He unwrapped the presents right at the doorway with a deliberateness that seemed to suggest he considered these were cosmic gifts, that he could be bought and sold, or appeased with such offerings. I never once saw him look up to see if anyone was watching.

At one stage, I considered sending him a gun, just to see how far he might go. I could push the narrative strand of his life toward some glum conclusion, some endgame involving a single gunshot, mirroring the arc of my father's life. After all, that is where all stories ultimately lead – to an end.

I was still debating the integrity of such a move when, getting off the bus one morning, I noticed a woman park outside Frank's apartment. In her late thirties, she looked average in an average sort of way.

It turned out the woman was the clerk at the convenience store Frank frequented. I suppose that's why they call them convenience stores. It was a twist I would never have come up with, but the vagaries of life have a way of tabulating their own meaning.

Anyway, I investigated this woman.

Her name was Cheryl, or at least that's what her nametag said. In the convenience store I overhead her talking to Frank, aimless chatter about absolutely nothing of importance.

Frank wanted cigarettes. That was typical Frank. His needs were basic.

I loved it, this element of intrigue, what life can serve up. I got up close to Cheryl, smelt the cheapness of her perfume. She wore an inordinate amount of jewelry on her fingers and her nails were painted. She had eyelashes like Tammie Faye Baker. There was a sense of improvement about her. She genuinely thought she was pretty.

I thought to myself, people like this never commit suicide.

Anyway, I began to think of this Cheryl amidst the grander scheme of things, awaiting the appointed arrival of Frank into her life, or maybe it was the other way around. In my preferred version she was ancillary to Frank. It was Frank who needed saving.

There was something truly engaging in watching their relationship develop, being privy to these trysts, to this penny opera, observing the small graces gained against apparent anonymity.

It is how I had ultimately come to reconcile my father's ways. We are nothing as humans if we cannot maintain a secret life, if we cannot live beyond the ordinary. Somehow Chapman, too, had arrived at this idea, risking everything, for what, but to feel alive?

In many ways, I envied, and was glad for Frank at the same

time. We were compatriots as males, and yet, despite Frank Junior, Frank was getting laid. In fact, on close inspection, this Cheryl was not bad. She had a chorus-line figure women had once aspired to in an age before dieting. She was *literally* a handful.

In peering in at the tableau of life's goings on, in imagining Frank and Cheryl together, I felt I was learning something deeply significant.

Again, the two reminded me of my father and his lovers, that illicit sense of togetherness. Of course Denise was dead. It was not entirely the same circumstance, yet it drew me back to a very vulnerable time in my life, to the crushing childhood misunderstanding of what love really meant, facing the apparent contradiction of my father loving more than one person.

I began to imagine what Frank was doing in there to Cheryl, imagined also a ghostly Denise hovering, watching over Frank and Frank Junior, grieved at the choice Frank had made in Cheryl, or possibly blessing this union.

Of course, at times I wanted Frank to be the moral standard bearer, a paragon of ascetic abstinence, or at least to reflect upon such things in the aftermath of sex. I think his position and life's experience warranted such thoughts.

One afternoon, after watching the curtains close on the street-level living room, I got antsy. Frank was with Cheryl. She had arrived in a Cutlass Supreme that had a piece of two by four as a bumper.

Across the way, Frank Klein had found a solace I could not achieve. Disguising my voice, I called him from a pay phone.

When he answered, I said, 'This is your conscience, Frank. Now listen carefully. I want you to fuck the shit out of that cunt Cheryl and then throw her out! This is all wrong, Frank! We both know it!'

I hadn't planned on using an expletive but I think the name Cheryl lent itself to a certain sleaze. I watched the window as I spoke. The curtains eventually parted.

Frank was still in his Bermuda shorts and Hawaiian shirt, the phone in his hand and the receiver to his ear. He seemed to regard the world with the same look he had when opening the presents I sent him. In the background, I could hear Frank Junior cooing, the television turned up loud, just as it always was at Frank's place.

Then Frank saw me. His eyes met my eyes.

I looked away, but I didn't put down the phone. My heart skipped a beat. 'What the hell do you want from me?' Frank's voice asked.

I hesitated, looked up again and stared across the distance separating us. 'I want you to be happy, Frank, that's all.'

He seemed to consider the statement, before turning toward the interior of the room so he was out of sight for a moment. I heard the muffled sound of a hand over the phone. Then he re-appeared along with Cheryl who was wearing only a bra and panties. She was holding Frank Junior in her arms.

Frank said, 'Do you think it's that easy for us here?' He opened his arm in an expansive gesture encompassing what his life now was.

My heart was still racing. I said, 'It should be, Frank. You did nothing wrong. I'm sorry if I spoke out of turn just now. I was just thinking you could do better is all.'

'Karl?'

'Yes, Frank.'

'I've seen you around. I've got all this on tape.' He held up a small recorder.

I felt myself struggling for words, for some magnanimous tone that might counter his anger. 'I appreciate your right to privacy, Frank. I'm pulling for you is all. Just give yourself permission to live again, Frank. And for the record, I don't think Denise had your interests at heart.'

Frank raised his voice. 'I don't want you to mention *Denise's* name ever again! I see you around here and I'm calling the cops, you got me?'

'You got my word on it, Frank.'

I set down the phone, feeling his eyes burn a hole in my back as I walked away.

It was the closest I came to actually losing everything. For a week I dreaded a call from the police. Thankfully, Frank had the decency to not get anybody else involved. Maybe he was ashamed of Cheryl, or he knew I was right.

Still, it had been a close call.

For sanity's sake I began a trawl of the free weeklies, a different type of humiliation that saw me submit my résumé to interrogation by a series of Goth and Vamp secretaries at various papers, all *Nine Inch Nails* and *Smashing Pumpkin* devotees attired in the perfunctory black teeshirts and Doc Marten lace ups, all this before I finally got to speak to an actual grown-up at *The Stranger*.

The lead story the previous week had been an interview with Marilyn Manson who had allegedly undergone surgery to remove two ribs so he could suck his own cock.

The story described self-love few have ever fully attained.

In a bio section was a picture of Manson, a.k.a. Brian Hugh Warner, from his boyhood in Canton, Ohio, with his dog. The piece described his father as a furniture salesman and Vietnam vet. The father looked not unlike my own.

I read the interview in the waiting room at *The Stranger*'s industrial redbrick loft, before meeting with the Editor-in-Chief and owner of the weekly, Nathanial (Nate) Hoffman, a trust fund heir to an old world fortune. In his mid-thirties,

Nate had the beginnings of a double-chin, and looked particularly ordinary, especially given the general tenor of the magazine. His only touch of rebellion was his Doc Marten shoes and a small diamond earring.

I couldn't tell whether he was gay or not.

It turned out Nate had been part owner of *The Portal*, something I hadn't known until he made mention of having seen me there as he perused my résumé. Not mentioning *The Portal* was a glaring omission, suggestive of my relative failure and a need to cover my tracks.

I said by way of explanation, 'I was researching a book at the time.'

Nate looked directly at me. 'Is that what you're doing here?'

I hesitated in answering, but Nate didn't press me. Instead he said, 'You know, Max was jailed on sex-related charges. He ended up getting off lightly, given the fact he was a person of interest in the disappearance of a runaway they were never able to pin on him.'

I shifted in my seat. 'I didn't know that. I wouldn't have figured him for that type. What I remember most about him was he had a saying, "Vice is always at the vanguard of progress." He seemed above it all.'

Nate set aside my résumé. 'Max always felt he was above everybody else. If you stare into the abyss, the abyss eventually stares into you!'

I said, 'I got out of the abyss in time then.'

Nate said flatly, 'Me too . . .'

There was a sudden stalemate between us, then he said, 'You were interviewed in the case, right?'

I said, 'I think we all were.'

Nate seemed to concede it as fact. 'You know I said to Max when he was out on bond on the lesser charges, "You don't even have to confess anything, but think about the parents not ever knowing what happened." Max had two girls of his own. I asked him, "What if it was you waiting a lifetime, never knowing?" I asked him where the body was.'

I asked quietly, 'Did he ever admit anything?'

Nate shook his head, then he picked up my résumé with a professional flourish, scanning it for a matter of a minute or so.

His tone changed. 'I see here you haven't published for the better part of a decade.' He set the résumé aside. 'I'm sorry, I just can't put Max out of my head. I don't know how to proceed with a real interview.'

I readied myself to leave, but Nate preempted me saying, 'Let me ask you a purely academic question, if you could have earthly fame at the expense of a hereafter, would you take it?'

'No.'

He raised his eyebrows. 'With all due respect, you're a liar, then, or you've lost your sense of ambition. Which is it?'

I rose and extended my hand, 'I want to thank you for your time.'

Nate, likewise, rose, and extended his hand. 'I'm sorry. It's this Max stuff. For the longest time the police suspected me. I was his business partner. He'd conned me into the porn business. You could see how the police would suspect it wasn't just Max, how they thought I had to be in on it.'

I was almost to the door when I stopped and turned again. 'As a matter of clarification, Nate, regarding my writing life, I was the ghostwriter behind crime novelist Perry Fennimore's last bestseller. I hitched myself to fame and money, Nate, and then I walked away from it. I'm currently working on something outside the domain of commercial taste. I've set my sights on literary immortality. It's not all about money. I would have thought you would have learned that given how it turned out for Max.'

Nate said in a contrite way, 'You're right. Look, let me see what we might have coming through the pipeline. I'll be in touch.'

Ten

We talked little as Lori prepared for what she had decided would be her last checkup. I hadn't asked if it was her decision, or Goldfarb's. We forsook marking the occasion of her appointment, proceeding as normal, though we were set to move to the sublet in the gay neighborhood the next day.

A week previous the condo had sold above the asking price. I was thankful for such small mercies, that things were maybe on the upswing for us. This was a temporary move. I wanted to impress this upon Lori, but decided against saying anything.

Deb was on hand during the morning with a video camera in tow, adding her own undercurrent of passive aggressiveness as I skulked around getting ready to leave.

I heard her talking in a furtive manner behind my back, but I was preoccupied, for despite the awkwardness of the interview with Nate Hoffman, he had put some work my way. I was set to go on my first assignment, an interview with a touring troupe of former Soviet street performance artists.

The pay was one hundred and twenty-five bucks, not that I revealed the figure to Lori. Rather, I dwelt on the cosmopolitan chic of performance art, describing how it broke down the dynamics of the Cold War era in a free exchange of ideas, speaking with a socio-political gravitas to the video camera since Deb had it turned toward me.

'Our children are inheriting a safer world. We have emerged from the shadow of the nuclear age.'

Deb piped up behind the lens, '*The Stranger*, Karl, just for point of clarification, that's a free weekly for fags written by fags, right?'

'Bigotry is our next great challenge, Deb. And the term is, "Alternative Lifestyle"! What would you have me do, Deb? Write up yet another leftovers recipe for *Good Housekeeping* or test the latest advances in feather dusters for *Family Circle*? Is that your idea of journalistic integrity?'

'You're such a self-aggrandizing asshole, Karl.'

Two hours later, against the rumble of the El track, my pager vibrated, and Lori's number appeared on the LCD.

I didn't call my voice mail.

She called three more times in the space of fifteen minutes.

I figured the results had not been good.

I closed my eyes momentarily, caught between relief that things were finally over, and a genuine sense of compassion toward Lori. I understood deep down what it was to have something you wanted so desperately taken away from you, if one could dare compare the rejection of a novel with her circumstance.

I thought back to her initial optimism in the trips downtown, to the image of the black musician, when, for a brief instant, I felt I had come to understand the sense of possibility and wonder a child might bring.

Now the journey was over.

In the end, I knew there was nothing I could offer but the same fumbling words I had uttered on previous occasions. There are times when words do not suffice, when a person should be left alone.

That is how I rationalized not going home.

The boutique hotel seemed upscale for what was supposedly a vagabond performance troupe. Their dubious press release, done in a banal, anarchistic splash of red letters, had an unattributed quote calling the troupe's work 'a miasmal post-apocalyptic new order totalitarian nightmare, wholly Eastern in its prophetic vision.'

In fact, the troupe's presence in the lobby had already caused quite some consternation by the time I arrived.

There were two distinct groups. The first, a half-dozen or so figures wearing black military uniforms and blank featureless masks; the other, more numerous, as many as fifteen, dressed grub-like in black plastic pupae suits made out of garbage bags.

Almost on cue with my arrival, a few of the expressionless masked figures produced bullhorns, and began shouting unintelligible Russian, while the grubs assumed the position of . . . well, grubs. The remaining masked figures then drew forth billy-clubs and started attacking the grubs, who began writhing on the marbled floor.

It was bedlam, a maelstrom of shouting against a backdrop of hissing interference pouring from a boom box with a turntable built into it.

I had a professional fast action camera, loaned to me by *The Stranger*, which I immediately retrieved in order to capture the frenetic rise in action, focusing on some of the grubs curled inward in silent agony. Then, the ill-formed heads emerged, instinctively turning in my direction, the primitive mouths opening in warped screams reminiscent of William Hurt in his isolation tank in *Altered States*.

At that point a strobe light began to flash, while, incongruously, against the totalitarian brutality, a woman in her early twenties appeared, naked, save for her military boots. Like a ring girl at a fight, she carried a placard over her head that read – I Have Nothing to Sell You! —

She had the figure of a dancer, the delicate bones of her

ribcage showing as she held the placard aloft, her nipples a deep sanguine color in the strobe light, her pubic hair shaved to a perfect V. Her arrival only increased the intensity of the attack on the grubs, rising decibels of static morphing into the warbled sound of a vinyl record being turned backward.

In the midst of this mayhem, the performance was shut down by hotel management and the arrival of four cop cars.

The cops immediately moved in on the woman carrying the placard.

A heated argument ensued.

After things settled down, I met Aleksey Romanoff, the leader of the troupe. Dressed in existential black leather pants and a turtleneck, Aleksey dragged on an unfiltered cigarette, his eyes magnified by a pair of round wire-rimmed glasses in a style made famous by John Lennon. He took my arm in a characteristically Russian act of intensity, turning me away from the hotel staff.

I said, in what could have been considered too conciliatory a tone for a journalist, 'I think they should have let you finish.'

Aleksey's forehead wrinkled. He let go of my arm as he inhaled, then shook his head. 'No . . . the day the peoples will not stop is day it is too late, you will understand of course.'

I pretended to write down his comment in my small notepad, then turning the course of the conversation around, I said abruptly, 'Let me ask you, can you make a living doing this?'

Aleksey scoffed. 'The day we are making the moneys is day is too late for all of us, you will understand. We have bread for the soul. That is how we survive.'

This was the gist of his mantra. It didn't account for the fact the troupe had not only managed to travel from Russia, but were staying at a boutique hotel with tables strewn with top shelf vodka tonics at twelve bucks a pop.

I didn't see any bread.

Aleksey seemed to sense the contradiction, but instead of answering, he set his cigarette in his mouth and said, 'If you will please be so kind,' while putting his hands over my eyes, directing in his blunt English, 'What is it you remember just now of this performance? Please you will tell me if it is good for you.'

What I saw in the sudden sensory deprivation of blackness shocked me. It was the V between the woman's legs, but I lied and said, 'The faces of the grubs . . .'

A foreign voice, a woman's, interrupted, her English more exact. 'You see, Aleksey . . . I don't know why I have to trim my box. Nobody cares about my *box*!'

Aleksey's grip tightened over my eyes. 'Wait!' He put his mouth close to my ear, 'I think the subject is not so happy with you. Can you please describe her *box*?'

Again the woman protested. 'You cannot lead a subject like this! My *box* is nothing compared to the suffering of the grubs.'

Aleksey persisted. He said something in Russian, then, 'Please answer, if it will be possible . . . You are American critic. Your opinion matters greatly.'

He re-adjusted his hold over my eyes. 'Please, focus on the *box*.'

I smelt the tobacco and vodka on his breath as I said, with a half-laugh, 'Maybe if I could see the *box* again?'

The woman raised her voice. 'This is ridiculous! Give it up, Aleksey . . . Showing my *box* would be an act of pornography, not art . . . Would you not agree, kind sir?'

I felt the question directed at me.

Exasperated, Aleksey removed his hands. 'You are ruining the experiment as always, Marina! You are not *so* good a subject!' He turned, called for another drink and simply walked away. He was seemingly done with me.

I self-consciously averted my eyes immediately from Marina and stared at the grubs who had reconciled with the masked military figures. They were all drinking and smoking, the best of friends.

Marina seemed to wait. She was watching me.

I turned and smiled. I couldn't think of a sensible thing to say. She looked even more beautiful clothed, like some exotic Puss in Boots, svelte in an intoxicating European sort of way. Her short, spiked hairdo was dyed a vibrant shade of red. She wore no bra.

Someone gave her a Budweiser which she accepted.

I stiffly handed her my business card.

'A *business* card! Tell me, kind sir, you are a famous American journalist and I have made it to the big time!'

I held her gaze. 'I'm not a journalist. I'm a novelist.' I pointed toward the card, immediately regretting having done so.

I watched her stare at the card, then laugh. 'Forgive me, but I cannot imagine Tolstoy or Dostoevsky with such a card as this!' She waved the card like it was an exhibit. 'What has this world come to when novelists have business cards?'

I didn't get to answer. She turned her attention to the troupe. 'I suppose this all bores you, vagabond European intellectual dress-up art, right? Tell me, are you comfortable with your democracy and your business cards?'

At that moment, she epitomized the sort of languid woman with heartfelt political inclinations I had always longed to converse with in college. I was at a loss for words, but recovered with an aloof defensiveness. 'Let's just say I'm glad I was on the winning side of history, if that's what you are asking … that I was on the side of the wall everybody else wanted to be on.'

I watched her take a swig of her beer. 'So, Mr Democracy has brass balls after all! But, you presume too much. How do you know I'm not just visiting your side of the wall?'

I think everything else in my life dissolved in that moment, that if one can submit to the influence of another body and soul, it regrettably happened on Lori's saddest day on Earth.

I felt the vibration of my pager again against my heart. It was like the dull sting of Cupid's arrow.

Marina called to Aleksey, who was off with the grubs. They turned out to be an all female ensemble. Aleksey was laughing it up with a petite, demure pixie with a pageboy haircut. He came over and introduced the pixie to me as Natasha, which somehow induced her to burst her sides laughing. She extended her hand toward me.

I could tell Aleksey was on his way to getting drunk. He pointed at me, wagging his finger in my face while looking at Marina. 'Be most careful, these Americans with their money will do anything to buy you, Marina.' He broke off into his clandestine tongue, then turned and addressed me. 'This game, it will start in one hours! We must go. Goodbye!'

I looked at him.

'The Bulls! The *Jordan*!' he said with exaggerated emphasis, pointing to his watch. 'In one hours, please, goodbye?'

But Marina didn't leave. 'Listen Aleksey, our dear American friend here is a famous novelist. He has a card! He was telling to me about life on our side of the wall.'

Aleksey looked over the rim of his glasses at the card and Natasha burst out laughing again. They were hammered.

I interjected. 'Come now, Marina, I don't think that was my point exactly.' I experienced a sense of heightened euphoria using her name.

Marina winked, as if we were sharing a joke. 'Which was?'

'What I think is there's one kind of prison where man is behind bars, and everything he desires is outside; and there's another kind where these things are behind the bars, and man is outside. That's the essence of my politics.'

Marina feigned alarm. 'Let me guess, you are an FBI operative sent here to spy on us?' She extended her wrists toward me. 'I understand your policies on national defense. I suppose you will want to handcuff me for un-American activities?'

It was the most erotic non-erotic thing anybody had ever said to me. Again the events of the previous months were shed in a rapture of being near her, though I said stiffly, 'I go by a principle of presumed innocence.'

Marina lowered her wrists. 'This is a legal or personal statute, this presumed innocence?'

'Both . . .'

Marina shook her head gravely. 'You see what we are discovering now in America, Aleksey, this presumed innocence! Mother Russia should have dropped the bomb when she had the chance! We would have won. I think these Americans are chicken shits!'

I will freely admit, all I did was stare at the points of her nipples under her tee-shirt, but I felt this ache within me. Being around her, this kitsch free-spirit roaming continents, enlivened me. Her sense of possibility snared me, drew me to her, a feeling heightened by the subconscious awareness of Lori and what awaited me at home, the passing of unsustainable life within her, the interminable shadowy sin of adolescence defining her.

Aleksey cut in and said, 'One hours for the Jordan, if you will, please come!', wheeling a reluctant Marina toward the exit to the awaiting grubs and uniformed militia.

I shouted after her. 'When you get down to the ghetto, to

the United Center, tell me what the hell you think about the NBA, Jordan, and our so-called democracy! You have my card!'

Seeing her leave in such company was akin to watching something out of *A Clockwork Orange*.

Eleven

The moon showed over the lake like a Eucharist by the time I walked off the surreal effect of the troupe, or more honestly, trying to blank the image of Marina from my mind.

I couldn't help thinking about the fact she was occupying the same city as I was that night, and somehow it set my heart beating faster. All I could see when I closed my eyes was the V between her legs.

It was, I supposed, a measure of true Art.

I called the boutique hotel from a phone at a bar after downing three whiskey sours in quick succession. I left a rambling quasi-political message, saying, 'This is Mr Democracy calling. Listen, Miss Cold War, I was serious about you giving me a cultural perspective on what you saw tonight at the game. I think you had it easy, you and your Berlin Wall. The reality here is there's nothing to tear down, no apparent enemy. It's a different psychosis . . .'

I left my home phone number at the end of the message.

When I entered the condo it was devoid of furniture, boxes piled high, save for the TV and a camera and tripod in the middle of the floor beside an empty carton of ice cream and a spoon.

The VHS tape Deb had been making documenting Lori's journey was playing with the volume turned low.

It took a moment before I found Lori.

She was in the living room, staring at the moon, her face pressed against the glass.

I said her name.

She didn't turn. 'I paged you all afternoon. Where were you?'

'Working . . . I told you . . . remember?'

I moved toward her, then thought better of it and stopped dead.

I saw a hot pack on her abdomen, a sure sign, if I really needed one, that she had menstruated.

All told, the preceding months had cost a total of $57,000.

Lori put the palm of her hand to the underside of her nose and let out a long breath. 'I want to know what purpose feels like.' Her right hand became a closed fist over her heart.

I said, like some amateur off-Broadway actor, 'There's always the next time . . .'

She turned toward me, then back to the window, shaking her head. 'My uterine wall can't hold a pregnancy. There is no next time!'

I said quietly, 'You get older Lori, things change at a biological level . . . it's nothing more than that.'

She wiped her nose again. She didn't turn around.

I took a step towards her, but she raised her hand. 'Don't . . .'

Beyond the window, I could see it had begun to snow out over the lake, the sky dull in the settling evening.

Lori let out a long sigh. 'I called Donny tonight.'

I hesitated, not quite understanding. '*Donny?*'

'My high school sweetheart!'

I didn't fully understand. I thought this Donny character had been killed in Vietnam, or that's what the story had been all along.

Lori turned and looked at me defiantly. Her eyes had the swollen look of someone who had cried themselves out. 'See Karl, we're all liars in the end . . . We all have our secrets!'

93

I tensed at the accusation and most particularly the word 'liars!'

Her eyes were wide as saucers. 'I'm not a fool! I know what you *are* . . .' She was pointing at me.

I had never seen her like this. I started to say something pre-emptive, to stave off the worst, 'How am I a liar?', but Lori talked over me.

'*You* don't get to talk . . . you listen to me, goddamn you!'

She had been waiting all evening to say what she had to say.

Despite what she had said at Goldfarb's office, it turned out Donny hadn't died in Vietnam. It was something her father had made up on the way back home after her abortion. He had driven her to get the abortion. She described the day in infinitesimal detail, her father pulling off the side of the road, and without looking at her, saying defiantly, 'Donny is *dead*'. It put into perspective her relationship with him, how he never called. Even when we had visited, he treated her like she didn't exist. In the act of taking her to the clinic he had committed his soul to hell.

I had a vivid memory as she spoke of the no man's land between Chicago and Milwaukee we had traversed years before, when I had first heard the truncated abortion story.

I stayed quiet as she talked. It was, as she said, her turn. When she got started, she couldn't stop.

I learned Don worked construction. He was divorced and living in Green Bay. He had joint custody of his two boys. His ex had remarried. It was a sordid, low class soap opera of suburbia.

What I got from the way she talked was a conversation tinged with the melancholy of catch-up, of a man broadsided by his past in a call out of the blue.

I didn't ask how she had got his number, or why she had called him. It didn't matter. What I came to understand were

94

the terms of their relationship, the depth of where her heart lay, Donny pervading her waking consciousness in a way I had never known about.

She talked for what seemed like hours before she got round to telling me how Donny said Donny Junior had real scholarship potential, when the sudden realization brooked within her of what she had cast aside so many years ago.

I watched her whole body slacken, observed the jolt of uncontrollable sobs as she broke down under the weight of so many years of grief.

She wouldn't suffer me touching her. For what seemed a lifetime, I simply stood amidst a pile of boxes, and could think of absolutely nothing.

Eventually she recovered and passed by me without saying a word. She went into the kitchen, then arrived at the notion of getting blitzed.

I heard her rummaging through some boxes.

She retrieved a bottle of cooking sherry. She wasn't a drinker.

I started to say something to that effect, that it wasn't a good idea. Next thing I knew hand grenades were being thrown across the kitchen.

She was tanked in the first twenty minutes.

If there had been a bed, I would have set her in it, but it had been disassembled, so I left her cradled in the darkening space of what had been our living room, in a metaphor that didn't bear elaborating on.

She kept calling me a fraud over and over again, trying to hit me with her fists, until she threw up, and eventually passed out.

In a way it would have been a natural end to things. There are few times the occasion for departure presents itself so absolutely, and if this were anything other than what it was, real life, I might have ventured toward the door.

Instead, I simply retreated to the guest bedroom.

I was drifting toward sleep when the phone rang. I shuffled about, trying to get to it, and lost the call.

Minutes later it rang again.

It was Marina. She said in a rush of breath, 'You are a very busy *American*. I am sorry to call you at these hours.'

I felt a high school rush of butterflies. 'No ... no ... I'm here ...' I hesitated, looking furtively toward the living room. Lori was still marooned and alone.

Marina talked loudly, in the heightened voice of one who had evidently been drinking. 'May I confirm something with you of very much importance, *Mr Democracy?*'

Her former command of English had faltered. I tried to say something again, but she cut me off.

'Yes. To this question of much importance ... I was speaking with professor of this sociology you have in New York City who tells me that the Americans do not pick up the phone on first ring. He says Americans must wait three times before picking it up ... *three times*. He says to me it is so caller will not think his fellow American is without friends and just waiting beside the phone. Is this true of your society? Do you have such fear of this personal failings?'

I played it straight, though my heart was pounding. 'I don't like to generalize. I think that is the first rule for any good sociologist. We are *all* exceptions.'

In a sudden moment of silence, I heard the din of a crowd roaring, and realized Marina was still at the stadium.

She raised her voice. 'How am I to confirm things if you will not answer?'

I felt a thrill of excitement at the mere sound of her voice, that, and the fact she had decided to call me. Betraying nothing, I said directly, 'Why are you in America?'

'This again, please? Why are you *not* in Russia?'

'Maybe I'll go there . . .'

'*Maybe* . . . Don't lie to me, *Mr Democracy*. You are an obsessed people. You are all great assholes. Name one country that borders the Caspian Sea.'

'Is that why you called me twice, to prove my ignorance of geography?'

She said hotly, 'I am returning your call, *Mr Democracy*. You called to me at my hotel with your *ridiculous* message!' Then out of nowhere she said in a patronizing tone, 'You are married man. This is it. I am understanding completely, *Mr Democracy*. I have called you at home and this wife is now listening. I have got you into trouble? You are chicken shit husband!'

Instinctively looking toward the living room again, I suddenly threw aside the calm facade. 'That's not it. I'm sorry . . . I was sleeping.'

Marina cut me off. 'Do not lie, *Mr Democracy*. On this message you left you were talking such sweet words like a man who wanted to get into my pants.'

'You mean you're wearing them?'

'Fuck you . . . You think Marina is your whore? You are nothing, you hear, *nothing*! You are no different, I am seeing this now.' She stopped abruptly. 'I am going to tell a story to you . . .'

'Listen, Marina,' I pleaded, but she shouted, 'I, Marina, am telling to you my story! You will please listen! There was a married man who comes home to find a line of men waiting outside his house. He does not understand this, so he speaks with a man standing in the line, "Kind, sir, what is going on here?" and the man answers, "Oh, you do not know, I am so sorry, but we are lining up to fuck your wife. Maybe, you should think about divorcing her." The married man, he

97

answered, "No, I cannot divorce her. If I do this, I would have to go to the back of the line."'

She hung up, leaving me to sit alone, mystified at how things had changed in the course of a single phone call.

I turned on the small portable TV, tuning in the grainy image of ungainly seven foot players traversing the court like giraffe, trying to catch a glimpse of Marina in the stands.

It was the first time I had felt Love in the way it was described in romance novels – wholly irrational, where another human being could occupy your heart and soul for the entirety of your natural life. Marina connected me to the legitimacy of an emotion I had never fully experienced in my forty years on Earth.

I ended up dialing the boutique hotel just after midnight. I got through to her room's answering machine and left a short, professional message.

I said, 'I would like to continue our discussion at a further point at your convenience, if it would so please you,' affecting the grammatical stiffness of her speech, influenced by the intoxication of want.

Twelve

Through the early hours of approaching dawn I lay awake, listening as a loose rain hit the window. It turned to sleet and finally snow.

It was one of those days in which we were lost to the clouds. The world beneath had ceased to be, or that it is how I imagined it. I felt cold, remote and alone.

I didn't really know where things stood as I began tip-toeing around, trying to uncover various pots and utensils to prepare breakfast while Lori slept off the effects of alcohol. In opening one of the taped boxes in the kitchen, I stupidly slashed my palm with a box cutter. It took a long time for the blood to stop.

At one point, I heard coughing, thought Lori was awake, and braced myself for what was to come. From the doorway I saw that she was still asleep, naked on her stomach, her head cocked at an awkward angle. She had thrown up during the night. When she breathed it was in sinusy gasps.

In the kitchen, I set two pop tarts in the toaster, suddenly aware my thoughts were elsewhere. I was thinking of Marina, or more exactly I was processing the absolute disdain she would have expressed at the thought of eating such garish child food, describing us in her characteristic ridicule as crass and ordinary.

It was disconcerting to find her lurking at the edge of conscious thought, given what the day held. I felt a sudden self-consciousness, imagined arguing with her right there in the kitchen, defending, among other things, the odor of percolating coffee and the spring-loaded Pavlovian release of pop tarts as truer to the hopes and aspirations of vast tracts of humanity. Nobody had ever revolted against the influence of pop tarts, except hard-line communists, and look where it had gotten them.

I felt the words of a rebuttal taking shape for the article I had yet to write about the troupe, provisionally titled *Socialism and Twelve Dollar Top Shelf Vodka.*

The sting of her story about the witless husband still hurt. I didn't want to admit it, maybe all the more because of the stilted way she had told it, in her drunken English, but she had spoken from the heart.

And yet, despite her insult, I had this strange thought of what it might have been like to be with her now, if through some sleight of circumstances I could interchange her with Lori, if we could pass through relationships without regret or breakups, one minute occupying one life, another the next.

Is this what Lori wanted with Donny? I felt the tincture of jealousy or some emotion I could not readily define.

Lori emerged and went toward the bathroom. She said in a faltering way, 'Last night ... what I said. I was drunk. I'm sorry.'

Of course, most of what she had said was before she got drunk. Still, it was a measure of leverage I hadn't expected.

She contritely met my eyes again as she sat on the toilet in full view.

I had weathered a storm. In fact, in Lori's obvious contrition, in her willingness to move forward, I understood she was under the delusion that she had injured me with the disclosure of having called Donny. It was she who had been unfaithful.

In a strange way the slight from Marina only served to highlight what I had with Lori, the flash point of Marina's anger betraying that, whatever my initial infatuation, it would never have amounted to anything between us. I had made an ass of myself, overreached in a way that would have brought only humiliation. I wanted to believe that. We were as Lori had pronounced early in our relationship, 'Damaged Goods.'

Lori came out of the bathroom, and creeping up behind me put her arms around my waist.

She pressed up against me.

I shifted and turned.

She immediately froze. 'My God ...' She reached for my face. A series of scratches ran from the corner of my left eye along the side of my face. She tried to say something else, but I pulled her close, set my chin on the crown of her head, as she whispered, 'I don't remember any of it ...'

'You got drunk too quickly was all.'

We said nothing for a time. I turned and felt her weight, sensed her heart race then settle.

She began to talk softly. 'This was never about not loving you. I want you to know that ... A person can get lost in wanting something so badly they don't see what they already have.'

We had subtly moved on. When she finished, I said, 'Can I ask you something? At Goldfarb's ... What you said about that second time with Donny. If he wasn't dead, why didn't you have the baby?'

She squeezed my hand. 'Donny wasn't the father.' She raised her voice slightly. 'I could have lied, right? Does that make me less of a person in your eyes?'

I shook my head, interlaced my hands with hers.

She whispered, 'I sometimes wonder why you stay with me.'

Before we left the condo I watched Lori lean over the sink, and put in her contacts, tipping her head back like she was putting in new eyes.

I could see, too, the swollen track marks along the pale of her thigh where she had injected herself with HMG.

It was hard to believe it was all over.

Deb arrived before noon, accompanied by two movers in gray shirts, muscling her way through the towering boxes, rolling her eyes, exasperated, shouting she was double-parked below.

In a way, her overbearing nature made it easier to leave the apartment. I merely caught Lori's eyes as we shut the door.

The sky had cleared in patches of pale blue and the fresh snow made my eyes hurt as we exited the foyer for the last time.

Deb's business associate, 'handicapable' Ray, was waiting for us, frantically sketching with a brush in his mouth in a series of agitated jerks. He had tiny ill-formed hands. He looked up at me for the briefest of moments, then stopped sketching and began fumbling with the complicated apparatus of his modified car.

I liked Ray. Seeing him always made me feel slightly better about myself. I think we could have been actual friends if it hadn't been for Deb.

Despite being raised a ward of the state in Louisiana, he exuded a Capote-like Southern quality of mannered gentility. I had this idea of him as the bastard of one of a breed of Southern gentlemen given to a slightly effeminate affectation for seersucker suits, pocket watches and a drawling twang best suited to the practice of law. I imagined a jilted mistress concealing her pregnancy for too long in the bindings of a corset, twisting poor Ray into knots inside her.

A cigar smoldering in an ashtray filled the car with the aroma of a tobacco plantation.

Ray licked his lips, parched, as Deb reached into the console and gave him a drink from a 7-Eleven Slurpee. It was the only act of genuine kindness I'd ever seen her exhibit.

We were beginning again, though, as Ray pulled out, Deb killed the mood by saying, 'So how's that Opus of yours coming along?' but then stopped abruptly. It was the first time she had looked directly at me, seeing the scratches on my face.

Her eyes flitted between me and Lori

I saw Lori disengage and stare out the window.

For a time we were all silent.

It began to snow in a swirl of light lake-effect flakes. Ray took Halsted as opposed to Lake Shore Drive.

Set back from the lakeshore sky-rises lay an older Chicago, a patchwork of neighborhoods that had once served the bustling stockyards and holding pens, a place of meat markets and abattoirs. I leaned forward to try to relieve the tension and tapped Ray on the shoulder. 'You ever read Upton Sinclair's *The Jungle*, Ray?'

Deb said sharply, 'He doesn't like to talk when he's driving, Karl.'

I leaned back, but Lori said defiantly, 'What about it?' She looked directly at me.

I said with a strident sense of academic authority, '*The Jungle* was set right here in Chicago, in what was formerly the meatpacking district. Sinclair single-handedly reformed the slaughter standards. He called the industry "an incarnation of a monster devouring with a thousand mouths, trampling with a thousand hoofs; a Great Butcher – the spirit of Capitalism made flesh."'

Deb stared hard at Lori. She didn't like Lori siding with me. She turned toward Ray and said, 'That sound like commie talk to you, Ray?' She put the straw of the giant Slurpee to Ray's lips again.

When he sucked, it sounded like someone on life support.

As we passed the Biograph Theater I piped up, 'That's where public enemy number one, John Dillinger, was shot down by the Feds.'

Lori had her face to the window. Her head moved ever so slightly in acknowledgement. I tried to hold her hand but she moved it away. I could tell she didn't want to get caught in a show of overt affection around Deb. It defined what I had always considered to be one of our problems, Deb's persistent interference.

Another few blocks and Ray turned at an old-fashioned English phone booth painted candy apple red.

Deb clapped her hands. 'Welcome to Queersville!' with an edge of scorn that couldn't be interpreted otherwise.

I ignored her baiting. She was turned sideways now, looking between Ray, me and Lori. 'You want some history, Karl, a history of the voracious meat-eating industry? That bar there was frequented by the gay cannibal eater Jeffrey Dahmer – you know, the guy who kept the heads and genitals of his victims in his freezer.'

'I think *eater* after cannibal is redundant, Deb, just as a point of fact, you being so literate and all.'

Deb snapped, 'Tell that to the guys he ate!'

Ray piped up with his usual droll humor. 'Isn't that a sushi bar over there, Deb?' I don't think it was a remark against me, as much as he had to side with Deb in all matters.

Deb let out a squeal of laughter. 'Jesus, you make me piss myself, Ray!' Just saying it got her roaring again. She explained the joke to Lori. 'Raw meat, get it?'

Seeing Ray's eyes in the rear-view mirror I experienced a shuddering sense of déjà vu, taken back across a lifetime, my father staring at me on so many highways.

I broke eye contact with Ray and reaching for Lori's hand again, I said, 'Here linger the ghosts of a rough-hewn, hard-working class of Catholic-sized families ...'

Lori buried her face in her hands and started sobbing.

Deb erupted, 'Jesus Christ! What the hell are you bringing her here for, Karl? If nobody's going to talk about the eight-hundred pound Gorilla in the room, then I will. This is a place you move out of, not in to! He's not worth it, Lori. We all know there's no contract, tell him. You're washed up, Karl!'

Suddenly I was hitting Ray's seat hard, shouting, 'Let me the fuck out!'

Lori started screaming with a shrill hysteria, everything escalating in a matter of seconds.

I shouted, 'Pull the fuck over, Ray!'

Ray swerved before the car jerked to a stop.

'Tell him it's *over*, Lori!' Deb started punching me. 'You don't touch him, goddamn you!'

I caught the door handle as the car pulled away, and running alongside, shouted, 'Don't let her do this to us, Lori, *DON'T!*'

Deb's window was rolled down partway. She stuck her head out. 'You're a loser! You always were! One call to a sperm bank and you're obsolete! You got that, Karl? She doesn't need your shit!'

I kicked the side of the car. 'I'm not the fucking problem.

She is! That abortionist fuck! Tell Deb about Donny, Lori! Tell her about the second guy too!'

I'd overstepped the line. Seeing the pain in Lori's face, I felt nothing but remorse, but it was too late.

Thirteen

Lori didn't call through Friday or Saturday. I knew the undue influence Deb could exert over her. I felt if she didn't call on Sunday, then it was truly over between us.

All Saturday night and into Sunday morning, it snowed heavily as I stayed holed up at the sublet, intent on focusing on the article about the troupe and trying not to dwell on my personal circumstances. It was the first legitimate assignment I had been given in years. Monday was the deadline.

I got up from the roll top desk and listened to the sound of a scraping shovel as Ivan cleared the courtyard.

The article had been going slowly, in a figurative but also literal sense, due to the box cutter wound. I was not prone to hypochondria, but the entire area had become swollen in an angry pocket of infection.

Flushing the wound under a faucet, I teased apart the sides of the cut, the pearly color of tendons showing. I thought, was this how I might die, an accidental cut from opening a box? It brought to mind Tolstoy's *The Death of Ivan Ilyich*, Ilyich dying slowly after an injury sustained while showing an upholsterer how he wanted his curtains hung. It was an irony I thought someone like Marina would have appreciated. I was still smarting from the phone call. She had not called me back either.

Wanting to include a line from Tolstoy, if only to impress her, I instinctively turned to where I'd kept my college texts at the condo, to the left of my writing desk, only to realize that they, along with most everything else, were still with the movers.

I left the apartment, in search of Tolstoy, walking against the buffeting wind toward the El and riding the train over to Wicker Park, past the notorious ghetto of Cabrini Green, the darkened façade of slum rises. In the distance, I could see something going on near a burned out basketball court. I tracked a series of local network TV vans and reporters on the scene until the El dog-legged West, the train heading alongside a blackish river and a labyrinth of old industrial buildings. It was a former wasteland, now an emerging Chicano area with tarred roofs and giant billboard signs. I could see solitary lives flitting past behind barred windows in the upper floors of the apartments abutting the tracks. It was the sort of ride I thought Marina should have taken. American history went beyond the domain of boutique hotels, to these innumerable enclaves from an older era, a time that preceded notions of lifestyle or leisure, to the work-a-day existence of immigrants who had abandoned the agrarian nightmare at the turn of the century.

I wanted to say such things to Marina. I was above the illusion of pink glazed pop tarts, closer to her than she realized.

I thought of calling from a pay phone, but didn't.

At a one-hour photo store I dropped off the roll of film I'd shot of the troupe. Then I made my way toward an old secondhand bookstore where I had sold text books years previous, finding a copy of *Tolstoy's Collected Writings* in the muskiness of the basement, among shelves of old books pawned by former students.

It was dispiriting that the *Collected Writings* had fared no different, the relative utility of the book lasting a semester. It had last been used by a Loyola student in '78. Scrawled all over the pages was 'Disco Sucks!' set against the iconic prism of Pink Floyd's *Dark Side of the Moon*.

Through the early afternoon, I stayed in the shabby enclave of the store's reading room, lost in a cocoon of transient, academic intimacy, alone with a repository of texts containing the collective genius of so many centuries.

In paging through *Tolstoy*'s work, I came upon his Ilyich story, scanning for the line I needed: *Tolstoy*'s indictment of Ilyich's life, rendered with characteristic Russian directness, 'Ivan Ilyich's life had been most simple and most ordinary and therefore most terrible'.

It was a line so simple and yet so absolutely honest and sad, it made me wonder if it was the English translation, or was this how Russians spoke in their own tongue, with the eerie candor of philosophers? It was the sort of line that hit hard in adolescence, a line disaffected English teachers were forever referring to, steering the impressionable into the troubled waters of seeking that which is other than ordinary.

The question they never answered was, how did a person survive outside the ordinary, and what was so terrible about ordinary anyway?

I arrived home to an empty apartment. I had, in a way, despite everything, been expecting Lori.

I tried not to think, opening my file on the troupe and adding the Tolstoy line.

I was as yet undecided on how I should portray Marina.

A futile hour later I put on a pot of coffee, heard my phone ring, and picking it up expected to hear either Lori or Marina's voice.

It was neither.

On the line was the administrative director at my mother's care facility, Jane Cantwell – a compassionless bitch who lived in a world of black ink solvency, and who I was firmly convinced drowned kittens for fun in her spare time.

Jane feigned a voice of concern. She referred to my having not called my mother over the last two weekends, along with the listing change for my number.

Then she got to the real reason for her call.

I listened to her clipped voice speaking down to me, informing me in no uncertain terms of PALS' strict policy regarding *arrears for a period of two consecutive months*, which was a violation of the contract and therefore subject to a termination of the resident's stay at the discretion of the board.

I cut her off at that point, invoking her name with affable informality, like it was just a dreadful oversight. 'I just moved, Jane. My life has been topsy-turvy.'

She tried to say something, but in my distressed state I talked over her, letting her have it. I spoke with a heightened intensity about my mother's abiding commitment to *American Liberty*, her sacrifice to God and country, the demise of a cherished family holding as her two older brothers had been shipped out and killed in Korea in defense of the 38th parallel.

I hit the high and low points of a life in the grandiose manner we expect from our presidents, but of course, Cantwell didn't bite. The truth is, if the likes of Martin Luther King, Jr. had made his 'I Have a Dream' speech in the service of something personal, and not in general terms, I don't think he could have secured a free Happy Meal at McDonald's, let alone the rights of a people. There exists a strain of language we speak among ourselves in our day-to-day life that is unromantic, that goes undocumented and cuts to the heartlessness underlying human existence – a language of economic survival.

When I finished, Cantwell said, 'You're aware of our three percent administrative late fee.'

I said, 'I am now, Jane, thank you *so* very much.' She hung up.

The call sent me further into a funk. We had a history, or at least I tied Cantwell to a certain vitriolic self-loathing that had defined my leaving New York. At the time, Cantwell had driven me to distraction with questionnaires, so-called *information gathering* and *introspective soul mining*, with the view to allegedly providing a holistic approach to care commensurate with advancing assisted-living retirees' goals for varying degrees of personal independence.

It was the sort of semantic hoodwink that drove me wild. I'd intuited from the start it was an endgame concerning vast sums of *money*, which was why I'd looked up her credentials. Her undergraduate degree was in English, with a concentration in Early American Literature, a disquieting fact that undoubtedly accounted for the shameless lifting of a line from Thoreau's *Walden* – 'To affect the quality of the day – is the highest of arts!' embossed in italics on PALS' revised Mission Statement.

I'd kept the entire juggernaut of pamphlets, looked on the whole charade with an artist's reserve, viewing it as part of the post-modern service sector *mind fuck* of Orwellian doublespeak that saw the introduction of a fee-for-service structure, in which such tasks as bathing, dressing, grooming, and toileting were all treated as discreet 'modalities of assistance.'

It was something I could maybe have stomached, but when I visited my mother, I found deterioration in *real* service. My mother's nurse explained that in re-defining 'non-medical services' as those that lay outside the domain of medication management, Cantwell had fired a hoard of qualified medical staff. Their replacements were non-paid interns and students from a nearby community college who worked in exchange for accreditation in things like 'Homecare Aid', 'Hospice

Assistance', 'Geriatric Nutrition Aid', and 'Ass-Wipe Management'.

The truth about geriatric care lay between *incredulity* and *reality* – incredulity at its exorbitant expense, versus the alternative reality of having your loved one stuck in a La-Z-Boy at your own house for the rest of your life.

At one point I had discussed the situation with Chapman, asking for an advance on my paycheck which had led him to a comparative analysis of Eskimo culture, where according to him, during the disruption of their ancient ways in the face of modernity the aged had to be forcibly taken to the edge of the ice and abandoned – whereas in earlier times, with a greater sense of an afterlife, the elderly had simply left the igloo to die alone.

It begged the question, why did we cling so to life? It was a question Chapman hinted was at the heart of an underlying crisis we all faced – our fear of death in a Godless universe.

I thought what the modern world needed was a fleet of buses to come in the night, to ease the process of decision making for the elderly, freeing us of the moral quandary of death and dying.

Turning to my computer, I opened up a new document and paraphrased something he had said, 'If modern life teaches us anything, it should be to consider with equal measure, not only how to live life, but also how to end it.'

I got no further. It read like the beginning of a suicide note. Of course, it put me also in mind of what Chapman had potentially done to the missing girl. My thoughts had drifted to the snuff tape on more than one occasion, not that I ever fully allowed myself to investigate the connection. I still had the tape. It was with me in the apartment, something I had taken with me as a precautionary measure when I'd initially moved boxes up here.

I felt weariness settle. I had fallen out of practice of really writing in the way I had in years past. I put the tape out of my mind.

Over a cup of coffee, I picked up a credit card application I'd partially filled out, offering a six month grace period on balance transfers. On the application cover, a good-looking, middle-aged woman was standing on the deck of an A-frame beach front property, wearing a loose knit sweater and cradling a latte, as she watched breakwater foam against the sunrise. Only the VISA logo discreetly placed in the upper right-hand corner betrayed what was really being advertised. At what other time in history could a society so blatantly deny the truth of both our individual and collective crises, simply hiding behind debt in the hope of better times?

There was no economic underpinning to anything, no real sense of absolute worth – not that it stopped me from completing what was my umpteenth application and lying about my salary.

It was as I was folding the glossy application form that I had a sudden compunction to contact Marina. I wanted to listen to her hard-line realism, hear her defend a totalitarian regime of fiscal literalists, with their planned economies, mountains of shoddily made shoes, their bread lines and grinding poverty. I wanted to have her argue against a currency disconnected from the gold standard, a nation living on the audaciousness of promissory notes backed with blind religious faith – 'In God We Trust'.

I wanted her to explain all this to me, or, truthfully, I just wanted to hear her voice. I dialed her hotel number, my heart racing as the operator answered, but hung up when he asked me to identify myself.

*

As seven o'clock Sunday dissolved into eight, and with still no sign of Lori, I ate a simple peanut butter and jelly sandwich and drank a tall glass of cold milk with a deliberate slowness, unencumbered by the presence of anybody else. It felt good to inhabit such solitude.

Essentially I was starting over again.

I set my plate and glass in the sink, rinsed them and left the items to dry. At my desk, I shuffled again through the photographs from the one-hour store, the shots of the grubs and totalitarian guards capturing a stylized, avant-garde politics few Americans could relate to in any real sense, suggesting we had all lost our way. I thought, what if we lost that ability along with other things, such as Love or Understanding or Compassion, or maybe we had already?

In sorting through the initial shots, admittedly, the protest seemed entirely too self-conscious, askew of a Western political sensibility, and it probably would have remained so, if not for the images of Marina's emergence, walking through the bedlam with a beauty you could not have imagined inhabiting the same frame. Even with an amateur eye, the eroticism of her presence was undeniable, as I'd caught her mid-stride with her sign held aloft. She offered something totally at odds with the abstract struggle between the grubs and masked guards.

In the article I likened her to a breed of women who had defined their revolutionary instinct through their femininity, Lady Godiva to Delacroix's bare-breasted matriarch leading the populist Parisian revolution against the crown; women who had displayed their nakedness as symbols of the motherland.

I felt enlivened merely typing her name – Marina, this Madonna of Stalingrad. She offered a vision of something that existed outside the marketplace, the political invective of the entire troupe eclipsed by the curved lines of her figure, suggesting that before there was politics or war, before there was ideology, there was simply Beauty.

In the final stages of reviewing the article, I stood for a time by the window. It was the good feeling of a day's work near completion.

I watched as the snow continued to fall in hypnotic floating flakes. This was how I had envisioned my life during my initial success with my first two novels, unmoored and left alone with my thoughts in a freedom few were truly equipped to experience.

It felt like home in the quiet of evening. Time had ceased to mean anything. It was as if I had lived here all my life.

A taxi's glow caught my attention as I continued to stand by the window.

Seconds later, I watched Lori materialize, dressed in moon boots and a long winter coat. She struggled with an overnight bag, leaning back into the cab to pay the driver.

For a moment, I thought about killing the lights, pretending I wasn't home as she entered the courtyard and buzzed down below. It was like an electric shock. Turning toward my bedroom, I looked at the computer screen glowing in the dark, searching for some revelatory inspiration or courage, then simply buzzed her in.

I had stood on the threshold of a new life for a mere three days.

Out in the hallway, I watched Lori rise up the corkscrew staircase, a spiraling double-helix of DNA, an abject metaphor for our troubles, though this wasn't the time for metaphors. To deflect the awkwardness of the last few steps, I said, 'Who needs a Stair Master, living on the fourth floor. This is a physical honesty few people know anymore.'

Lori's face was flushed from the climb, probably more so

from the long drawn-out struggle she had inevitably had with Deb.

I took her shoulder bag and newspaper without ceremony as if she had just come home from the office. She moved tentatively through the empty living room, surveying, too, the kitchenette. I realized she had never been to the apartment.

In the small bedroom the file I was working on was open, along with a scattering of pages, photographs and *Tolstoy's Collected Writings*.

Lori ran her finger along the spine and said with a tremulous effort, 'Who reads Tolstoy?' She turned and added, 'You seem settled ... I didn't mean to interrupt your work.'

'I was stopping for the night anyway.'

She hesitated. 'I could blame Deb ... That would be the easiest way out, right?'

I figured she had been rehearsing those lines all the way from the suburbs. I said, 'She's your sister. I figure that's what sisters do, look out for one another.'

She kept looking around. 'I can't even take credit for being here. It was Ray's doing. He kicked me out of Deb's.'

I said, 'Ray's the only one with sense. I've always believed that.'

'I guess ... Ray ended up getting stuck out on the Eisenhower behind a snow plough. He lost control of the car. He has a restricted license. He wasn't supposed to be on the highway. A State Trooper cited him. We had to wait on the shoulder of the Eisenhower for three hours before AAA came and towed us, and while we were waiting, Ray just started crying like I'd never seen anybody cry before, hitting the steering wheel over and over again.'

Fourteen

Around 2 a.m., I awoke to discover Lori had crept out into the hallway, the door still ajar. I stayed still, trying to make out what she was saying, but couldn't hear. At this hour she was, no doubt, talking to Deb, giving her the summary of how I had received her.

I stayed on the air mattress until Lori snuck back into the apartment. Then, I got up, used the small toilet, and came out into the kitchenette.

Lori was by that time sitting at a small table doing a cross-word puzzle and eating a breakfast pastry I had bought on Sunday morning, along with eggs, bacon and milk, all purchased in a ruse of domestic bliss that I could and would have survived alone.

'I didn't mean to wake you.' She looked toward the hissing radiator. 'It's hot in here.'

'All utilities are included. You could shower for a week and never run out of hot water. We're living on the largesse of the community. There's a monstrous boiler room down below.'

It was still hard making small talk. We had simply fallen asleep in the bedroom, overcome by exhaustion.

Lori averted her gaze to the newspaper on the table as I turned my back to her and reached for the coffee pot.

'I saw something here that might interest you.'

I still had my back to her. 'What's that?'

I heard a rustle of newspaper.

'Didn't you interview some Russian woman for an article?'

I purposely avoided meeting her eyes, but turned and answered in a casual way, 'It was more a summary profile of the troupe.'

Lori kept looking at me with a sudden familiarity, like we had shored things up between us. 'I thought so, and you say I never listen to you.'

She flicked through the paper and handed it to me.

One of the byline stories was circled with a pen – *Brutal Murder of Russian Artist under Investigation*. I felt a sudden wave of sickness pass through me.

Chicago Police are looking for persons who raped and killed a woman and attempted to set her body ablaze in a stolen car.

At 3:30am Friday, police and fire details responded to a report of a car fire at the Cabrini Green Projects. On arrival, officers discovered in the trunk of a car the body of a female. The victim was pronounced dead at the scene.

Personal effects recovered near the scene aided police in identifying the victim as **Marina Kuznetsov, 24**. A Russian national visiting the US, Kuznetsov was a member of an avant-garde street performance troupe and subject of much interest for her provocative nude performance art.

According to statements by troupe members, Kuznetsov left the United Center alone and on foot during Thursday night's Bulls' Game. Unfamiliar with the area, she may have unwittingly wandered into the Cabrini Green Projects.

A tragic footnote to the continuing violence plaguing the Cabrini Green Projects, anonymous accounts suggest Kuznetsov was repeatedly assaulted over a period of hours, by multiple perpetrators in various locations.

As I set the paper aside, Lori said matter-of-factly as if it meant nothing, 'So what was she like?'

I looked at her. My breath was shallow. ' ... *like?*'

'It said in the article she was a nude performance artist. Was she a sleaze?'

A wave of coldness passed through me. I wanted to refrain from fighting with her given what we had just come through, to give in to the uncomplicated blitheness of people like her, where, despite the reality of her own adolescent turmoil, her all-time favorite movies *were* still the escapist, arrested development of *Risky Business*, that and *Pretty Woman*, vapid anti-intellectual, improbable shit that saw a real-life Cruise embrace Scientology, and another actor purportedly shoving a gerbil up his ass before finding solace and atonement with Tibetan monks.

I felt myself forming a diatribe, but betraying nothing, said with a measure of thoughtfulness, nodding, 'I suppose you could have misjudged her as that, as a *sleaze* ... though maybe not in an American way ... more in a *European way.*'

Lori crossed her legs and seemed relatively intrigued. 'What do you mean in a "European way"?'

I shrugged, 'I don't know ... Maybe *campy* would be more like it ... campy in a dreamy idealistic Sixties sort of way. She was at the collapse of the Berlin Wall.'

'So, what does any of that have to do with being naked?'

I said frankly, 'I never got to ask her, Lori. I think in her world, in the world of art, everything was about metaphor. Maybe for her being naked equated with the Truth.'

Lori made an umph sound, like she was finished discussing the matter.

I saw the veins of her leg showing where her nightgown parted.

'I just thought it was, you know, funny, you having interviewed her.'

'It was more the troupe I interviewed than her, really.' Picking up a bear claw, I said, 'Here, have another. They're good, aren't they?'

Lori pulled a fake worried look. 'Are you trying to fatten me?'

'*Me*?' I made my eyes large and playful incredulous. I could only imagine the hell that was Deb's home life, the circumstances that had driven Lori back to me.

Minutes later Lori said, 'I think I'll shower.'

I heard her running the water. We were on top of one another. This was the new reality of our immediate life.

She half-shouted from the bathroom, 'I hope this isn't hard water. Hard water ruins my hair.'

She came to the door, brushing out her hair, already stark naked.

I couldn't help but remember Marina walking with her sign, the indelible image of the perfect V of her pubic hair, the curve of her ribs and small breasts, her sign held aloft, 'I Have Nothing to Sell You.'

Lori kept talking. 'We had hard water growing up.'

I said earnestly, 'Calcium, right?'

'*Lime* . . .' She went back into the bathroom.

I closed my eyes, tried to let Marina's death register at a real level. She no longer existed on this Earth. I sat down at the table, and taking the article, let my finger linger over Marina's name as if touching it could bring some clairvoyant connection to her.

My eyes settled on the time of her murder – *3:30 a.m.*

I read the article again, came to the paragraph, 'A tragic footnote to the continuing violence plaguing the Cabrini Green Projects, anonymous accounts suggest Kuznetsov was repeatedly assaulted over a period of hours, by multiple perpetrators in various locations.'

A sickening feeling curdled in my stomach at what had become of her in the nightmare hours of capture, her political ideology set against the gold-toothed snarl of her captors, in the abhorrent no-man's land of the ghetto.

In the article the race card was subtly dealt, a body removed from the original crime scene, a gangland rape with a trophy victim, a white woman dragged from one place to another.

In the turmoil of my relationship with Lori, I was thankful that despite having called Marina in the last hours of her life, nobody had contacted me. I knew our relationship could not survive her knowing I had pursued a nude performance artist, or that Marina had called me back on what was the most traumatic night in Lori's life, the night Lori learned she would never conceive a child.

What had happened to Marina was all too apparent, her life taken in the sub-culture of a ghetto, a tragedy, the naiveté of a foreigner, drunk and on foot, *walking*, unaccustomed to the subtle nuances of American life, for who can understand but a citizen of this great country the anomaly of setting the United Center, home to the World Champion Bulls, in the midst of a ghetto?

Seemingly not the beautiful, impassioned Marina Kuznetsov, RIP, survivor of the Cold War, witness to the collapse of the Berlin Wall, who died far from home, ignorant of the simple caution we give to our children.

Fifteen

Monday morning, I received a perfunctory call from a detective concerning the calls I had placed to Marina after midnight.

The discussion lasted all of ten minutes. In explaining how I had been commissioned to write an article concerning the troupe for *The Stranger*, I got the sense of a jaded character on the other end of the line, the case open and closed, given where Marina had died.

All I could really offer were the details of our last conversation, how she called me, drunk and disconsolate. I didn't elaborate too much, hedging toward our philosophical and political alignment. I knew the detective had listened to the phone messages. Ultimately it was something that didn't interest him. He cut me off mid-sentence. There was another call he had to take.

My dealings with him ended as abruptly as that, and so, too, my tangential connection to the sad demise of Marina, giving me a stark understanding of the true nature of an overworked police department.

Despite calling me a 'chicken shit husband,' Marina became once more a torch of intellectual candor. Her argumentativeness arose from philosophical intentions, not to undermine, but to inspire her opponent to re-evaluate or defend an opinion. There had been something decidedly mercurial about her, a reckless curiosity that, in the end, led to tragedy.

Through the mid-morning I captured that general sentiment in a quasi-obit piece I appended to the original article about her which I had titled 'I Have Nothing to Sell You'.

I decided to head down to *The Stranger* to see Nate personally, wanting to make sure the article wasn't entirely scuttled, given her passing. I printed off a copy of the article along with a cover sheet, attaching, too, the shot of Marina caught mid-stride, the scissors of long legs wide apart, the V of her trimmed pubic hair like Lenin's goatee.

The refurbished redbrick loft was subtly suggestive of the vastness of the industrial machines that had once churned out products here when things were actually made. It felt like a living museum, capturing the aesthetic of a former time minus the grime and the sweat.

It seemed slightly unreal. Disconcertingly, everybody in the building looked like they were under twenty-five.

On the first floor there had been an urban renaissance of small businesses with brass name plates, coffee shops and a designer tee shirt boutique, along with an advertising agency, a hair salon, a bath and beauty store, an upscale cycle shop, and an organic bakery that gave off the odor of an idealized modern domesticity.

The elevator to *The Stranger* was a glass cube in which the mechanism of how it worked was exposed in a complexity of cogs and pulleys.

A green fluorescent Mohawked late adolescent, dressed in fishnet stockings, and a Sex Pistols tee shirt, stopped me from seeing Nate, who was, according to her, '*indisposed.*'

I said politely, 'When will he become *disposed*?'

She didn't elaborate and went back to her computer screen.

The outfit didn't hide the fact she was plain, her outward belligerence a façade. I smiled, though, since I needed the job.

A nameplate on her desk read, Chastity. I said, 'Is that a name or a statement?'

She just looked up. 'You're old.'

Thankfully, Nate appeared briefly from his vast office, though he was distracted by an advertisement layout for the multi-national, *American Express*. A woman in a business suit, obviously a client from an upscale agency, gave a semblance of legitimacy to the entire enterprise – to what was ostensibly a free weekly. It was hard to imagine there was so much money flowing through the economy that advertisements alone could sustain the magazine, but apparently there was.

In a brief aside on the way to the cube elevator, Nate informed me the Marina article wasn't a priority. He didn't want to complicate an on-going investigation. Also, the assignment had been a bit piece. He couldn't exactly justify the print space, but he was willing to do what he could.

I pointed to the obit piece I had written. Nate smiled in a congenial manner, taking the material from me.

It was all rather rushed. He had the American Express poster mockup in hand. It smelled of Elmer's glue, of real work.

In my outward resolve to change as a husband, I took to rising early, making Lori breakfast. We had found a way back to one another despite everything, offloaded so much stuff to Goodwill in the weeks before leaving the condo. We had literally lessened the burden.

We were like newlyweds. We slept on a mattress without a box spring. It was set beside a low watt lamp with a dented shade. I'd retrieved it from the garbage. It worked! I purchased a small TV which I set on top of the box it came in.

We were saving money by not spending. I impressed that upon her. It was a habit not just us but everybody had gotten away from. We didn't miss most of the things we left behind. Every day I said things like, 'So tell me, what didn't you buy today?'

I made it so it was a game, so that it was like we were winning. We were in the know, outsmarting everyone else. We regained an ease we had once enjoyed. On occasion, in coming out of the shower in the small confines of the apartment, Lori took me in her mouth as she had in the days of our initial courtship, her hair slick as a seal, simply wanting to please me.

The only issue was the unrelenting, sweltering heat of the apartment. The old-style ribbed heater knobs had been painted so they couldn't be regulated. Lori wanted me to get Ivan to fix it.

During the days that followed, I underwent a metamorphosis as profound as Kafka's cockroach, but in reverse, becoming a man again and not the insect I had been for so long.

In staring into the courtyard, into the compartmentalized lives of others, I felt an intimacy that approximated community, something so starkly different from the anonymity of the condo. I had come to refer to that former life as a medical condition, 'The Ivory Tower Syndrome.'

The courtyard reminded me of the one in Hitchcock's *Rear Window*, evoking nostalgia for a time when adults dressed well, when men of distinction like Jimmy Stewart wore tweed and women pearls – when adults acted as such.

The connection to *Rear Window* gave me the illusion of appearing through the aperture of a director's lens, as I arrived each morning onto the set of my own existence. I started speaking in complete sentences, self-conscious, but funny and engaging in that light way of so many fifties style sitcoms. I wanted to do my very best, imagining my entry amidst audience applause, the generous praise of uncomplicated, decent folk, of canned laughter.

I told Lori I wanted to live in the full disclosure of lights and open windows, wanted to hear laughter and sorrow, to eavesdrop, to catch human emotion in its most genuine form. There were, for instance, two gay neighbors who had begun what appeared to be a flirtatious exchange in the early mornings, their respective dogs going potty at the same time.

I pulled her to the window and said, 'Put aside your natural prejudice and tell me, doesn't that remind you of us?'

Seemingly, even here amidst this lifestyle, there were only so many ways to meet. I could see the dogs rutting around, the entanglement of leashes, the two gays unraveling themselves, the little dogs raising their legs, little clouds of smoke rising where they pissed.

It gave pathos to life.

Human longing prevailed in these quiet exchanges, even in places like this.

With Lori's departure each morning, I re-read some of the Fennimore reviews over coffee, to re-capture again that swagger I had experienced when I knew the latent genius of my work had been unearthed. I was done with the indeterminacy of waiting for my agent to call me. I felt I had to push on, to find a way back to a writing life.

I let place be the prevailing metaphor in those first days, writing for writing's sake, trying to capture a voice, sentient to the fall of light and shadows, the lull and swell of noise in the labyrinthine alleys. I committed this new world to memory the way a blind man might learn a new path between his home and the store, as if it was a matter of life and death, which, in a way, it was. I registered experience beyond the visual, beyond the literal, letting all my senses absorb what place meant, the sum total of its true essence – what I considered to be the foundation of Art.

In the early stages of shaping images and scenes into

something coherent, I stood at the window, caught up in a bird's eye view. I had grown accustomed to Ivan's harsh voice. I came to secretly call him 'Ivan the Not-So-Terrible.' He didn't have it all his own way after all, shackled to a babushka barrel of a wife who was now salting the courtyard with the earnestness of a peasant feeding chickens.

She had a habit of spitting like a man into her hands before she shoveled snow. I had seen her do it on more than one occasion.

All in all, they were an improbable lot, an anomaly in the gay neighborhood, and doubly so as a family of immigrants. I developed, too, a curiosity with Ivan's daughter, Elena, observing how she dutifully worked in the hallways after school, vacuuming and wiping down the stairs in the cluster of apartments surrounding our quad.

She had no apparent life outside of school and work.

Her arrival each day coincided with the opportunity I took to retrieve the mail. It was how I came to know her, along with Sergei her brother, an irascible, sickly little moon-faced seven-year-old who looked distinctly like an orphan from the nineteenth century. Sergei was forever playing with his racing cars on the gleaming tiles while Elena worked.

He wouldn't get out of my way when he saw me coming, and on the third day after I had officially moved in I stood on one of his cars, upending myself and nearly breaking my neck, an incident that caused Elena undue fear and concern I would report her.

Born out of this renewed sense of purpose, inhabiting the beginnings of another life, the vein of a narrative voice began to surface again.

I thought, maybe poverty was the natural condition of the artist after all.

In the ensuing days, I tapped an old vein of inspiration. From under a loosened floorboard in the apartment, I retrieved the snuff tape, the disquieting fact Chapman had been involved in a missing persons case at the back of my mind. I knew I should have discarded the tape, but it was a talisman, a revelatory source of inspiration that had enabled me to move beyond the plaintive biography of my father's life. It was the tape that had interested Fennimore, how I had reconstituted it into a parable of modern alienation.

Drawing the curtains closed, I waited. A few moments later a medieval-like script appeared – *The Knight of Infinite Resignation.*

My heart raced at seeing the words.

I knew the tape intimately, anticipating the slow dissolve of the hooded victim emerging, hogtied to a chair in a bare room. It still had a deep impact, the surreal effect of the hood with the crude holes cut for the mouth and eyes.

Not knowing if it was real had always heightened the experience. Now, given the fact that Chapman had been jailed on sex-related crimes, the tape took on a more ominous feel.

At a certain point in the past, I had come to connect the hooded victim with my father's mistress and the act of him strangling her, though paradoxically what the tape also did, was enable me to find a narrative distance from them, from *their* story.

I gained a psychological distance that took me beyond the fields of Michigan to the urban nightmare of Chicago, to some nameless apartment.

Through the afternoon, alone in the sanctum of the apartment, I found that hidden voice again, the perpetrator's thoughts flowing through my consciousness, betraying an abject longing for what had been missing all his life: *Respect.*

In watching the act of slow asphyxiation, I understood the

perpetrator was calling upon the time-honored power of a *laying on of hands*, inducing a euphoric, dream-like effect, a dream catcher stealing the intensity of dying, and with it a conflagration of his victim's regrets and loves, a continent of memory subsiding, consciousness literally collapsing in on itself.

It was the reverse of creation, a slow dissolve toward nothingness making me almost wish I believed in a hereafter.

The intensity of the tape's effect had not diminished. It took me back again to my first dealings with Fennimore. During an early collaborative writing exercise, he had added a subtle plot twist, where his cop, Harry, received, along with a series of snuff tapes through the mail, a ransom-like note asking him to take the K from knight and hang it in a window as acknowledgement of the tapes' receipt.

Literally transforming *Knight* to *Night* ended up a stark metaphor for the novel, hence the title, *Night of Infinite Resignation*, investing the work with an anti-quest motif, the knight turning to night, to darkness and beyond, transforming the esoteric nature of Kierkegaard's fable into something more contemporary and edgy.

It was that subtle change that eventually got the attention of critics and the general reading public alike, a deft stroke of narrative genius that put me in awe of Fennimore's knowledge of the genre, his capacity to work with external influences, to make them his own.

I still remembered the true moment of artistic breakthrough working alone. A particularly brutal snuff murder had just ended. I was in the process of sending my perpetrator down a long hallway toward the toilet. In a languor of sexual release and still wearing the caricature Nixon mask he wore during the murders, he happened past a mirror and stopped dead, raising his hands in that patent Nixon victory salute.

It was then I recognized the unmistakable eyes of my father, those same eyes that had stared at me in the rear-view mirror on the drives North. I had not escaped him, my dark muse.

I heard him piss as he whistled a show tune. He washed his hands in the sink.

I committed it all to memory, typing all the while.

When he came out of the bathroom, he took off the mask and slowly turning toward me said, 'We start out with such high expectations, all of us do, son!'

I looked at him and whispered, 'I'm sorry.' I wanted to say something more, but I couldn't.

He said flatly, 'It's too late for sorry. You gave me no other choice, son!'

Then he pointed a gun to the roof of his mouth and blew his brains out.

Sixteen

Viewing the tape through the course of the afternoon, I sought out my father again, wanting to mine his discontent, to draw him into my current life, to attach his sensibilities to what I had written, to put a voice and perspective to what was reportage and not yet story.

I retrieved the rubbery Nixon mask I'd used as part of method acting and donned it. In the apartment's oppressive heat, I attached a desperation and breathlessness to what I had previously written, typing in a staccato rhythm, feeling a sense of suffocation as I got to the end of a thought.

At times it was too much, and I pulled off the mask to simply breathe. Yet, it was in this way I reworked the isolated passages I'd written in the previous week, placing my father in modern-day Chicago, envisioning him living in my apartment, letting him see through my eyes, hear with my ears, creating within me again that sense of artistic detachment, of clair-voyance, of being other than myself.

As with so much of life, when things went well, they went very well, and so it was in this breakthrough time. I was writing one morning with talk radio in the background, when a listener caught my attention with her hysterics regarding Clinton's evasive deposition in the Clinton-Lewinsky scandal.

I intuitively stopped. I closed my eyes, the voice clear in my head, speaking to me alone. It was a voice drawn from an emerging Christian backlash, the nation caught up in the tawdry soap opera of our President, Lewinsky, and hag confidante, Tripp – all of it underscored by the fact Lewinsky was no Marilyn Monroe, nor this the knightly intrigue of Kennedy's Camelot, but rather *Cum*-a-lot, a sordid frat-boy reality of a President making it with a fat chick in the Oval Office.

Like I said, at the time I was writing well, but one step away from the material that had so captivated Fennimore. And then it struck me – Nixon was passé, the psychosis of my muse, my father, too Cold War, too dated. I had lost an essential connection to modern life.

In a sort of experiment, I ended up shedding one skin for another, purchasing at a costume store a Bill Clinton mask with a cartoon-like bulbous nose.

Of course, it took time abandoning Nixon's zealous right-eousness, his visceral reaction to Communist infiltration. He was, and always will be, a character of the noblest intentions and crudest actions. It was initially difficult tapping into the vacuity of Clinton. He seemed the most debased of presidents, his intentions centered solely on self-preservation, using semantic legalese to lie through his deposition.

What did his popularity ultimately say about us as a people?

I wrote alternately, as Nixon and then as Clinton, reworking the same passages, seeking a cultural register, until I got the voice and perspective just right, using Clinton, not as an examination of our age, but a symptom.

It was a breakthrough that emboldened me to go directly to Fennimore. I felt if I could simply get to him, to speak to him as an artist, I could as yet prevail. What I needed from Fennimore was his honesty, his insight and particular genius with genre fiction – with plot.

Most of all I knew that without his name attached, nothing would come of what I had personally created.

Using a number which inadvertently hadn't been erased from correspondence during the latter stages of our work together, I faxed off a handwritten letter, not to Fennimore, but to his character, Harry, using the persona of our nemesis, Charles Prescott Morton, we had used in the last novel.

The letter smacked of a *catch-me-if-you-can* taunt, a natural prelude to a new novel, and a fresh battle of wits. In referencing the denouement at the end of the previous work, I explained how Charles Morton had improbably survived the warehouse blaze that should have killed him.

I dwelt on the excruciating pain of a series of operations he underwent at a medical facility in Mexico City, where, for the right amount of money, all things were possible, so much so that he emerged a new man.

I made mention of a morphine addiction, of long nights recovering in the sweltering humidity of a rundown Mexican motel, Morton attended by a brown-eyed beauty who dutifully changed a cocoon-like web of gauze as our antagonist literally began living within a new skin.

I went on to describe a move North, borrowing and extending the passages I had written at the apartment, picturing my father, alone and convalescent, reshaping the vignettes of Ivan in tortured drunkenness, the enigmatic specimen of Vladimir, falling eventually upon images of the pubescent Elena toiling with her bucket and mop. A chilling suspense emerged in the unsettling mention of her, but also in the description of little Sergei going *vroom vroom* with his little red cars in the hallway, as he upended Morton.

Sergei would undoubtedly disappear in the opening pages. I was certain of that.

This is where Charles Prescott Morton had resurfaced, in the margins of a new aesthetic of modern love and politics, so totally at odds with the sobering reality of the world Harry, Fennimore's ex-Vietnam cop, inhabited.

In the slow maturation of what I felt was a legitimate novel, I set aside the non-fiction book idea, which had been a non-starter all along, though the soul-destroying nature of my involvement with Goldfarb and the clinical coldness of artificial insemination surfaced in a flotsam of pages.

I was undecided as to how this theme would fit, until one morning, reviewing Fennimore's fifth novel, I came across a minor reference to an estranged daughter, Tiffany.

Fiercely independent and unmarried, and in her thirties, I envisioned Tiffany, re-entering Harry's life, seeking pregnancy through artificial means. I sketched a scene of Morton stalking Harry and Tiffany at a fertility clinic, signing up after they left to become a sperm donor, seeding his evil in a vast legacy only medical technology could facilitate. At the end of the novel, I imagined a stark series of disconnected births, swaddled newborns amassed in hospital nurseries – then a close up of Tiffany and her baby, a natural lead-on to a *Son-of* series.

These were the underlying themes and sub-plots that fermented in the early days of writing, but for most of the time, I focused on the sinewy underpinning of fiction, on mood and pacing, the sights and sounds of this new neighborhood.

It was a pastiche of these sketches, this modern *Rear Window* of observed life I eventually faxed, and then I waited with a quiet confidence I had not experienced in such a long time, feeling I was back in the business of being a writer again.

There is no greater emotion.

Seventeen

Amidst another day of writing, with the radio on in the background, babbling on about yet another chaotic commute home given a predicted six inches of snow, I watched Vladimir working with dutiful Elena playing truant again.

There was something captivating about her. It took time to understand, then it dawned. She reminded me of what a younger Marina might have been like so many years ago in Russia.

Lori called, pulling me back from other thoughts, speaking in the hushed way she always did when making a personal call from her office. I had been there just once, a Dilbert-like cubicle world of institutional intrusion, and yet she had never complained once about her work in our time together, not even during the contentious take-over bid.

Wanting to avoid the rush hour, she was staying on after work to get some stuff done. She had leftover Chinese from lunch to tide her over. She mentioned, too, an independent foreign movie that had been written up in *The New Yorker*. The tacit mention of *The New Yorker* hinted she was trying valiantly to become more cosmopolitan.

We made a tentative plan for Friday night, dinner and a movie.

It seemed so banal and yet so perfect. I said, 'Friday it is!' adding with a solicitous tone, 'Lori, take a taxi home tonight if the weather worsens.'

I set down the phone. There had been no mention of

what had happened between us over the previous five months, eclipsed by a clean slate of re-evaluated life.

It was something I had always admired about her. She could move on.

An hour or so later, in the midst of reviewing some pages I had printed, I heard the whir of the fax machine. A solitary scroll of paper emerged with the words: 'Let's talk . . . Give me your number.'

It was signed, Fennimore.

A mere two days had passed since I sent him the material.

In all our time working together, we had never talked, in person or on the phone. Fennimore was reclusive. He had never released a publicity shot, his identity yet another character I thought I could inhabit back then. Early on there had been the suggestion of my taking over his series, or so my agent had initially intimated, hinting Fennimore's health was failing.

Whatever the mendacity of my agent's assertion, the speed of Fennimore's response indicated at least a degree of desperation.

He had not put out a novel since we had last worked together.

I faxed him a laconic reply, 'I am alone now,' and included my phone number.

He called fifteen minutes later. The number came up as blocked on the LCD.

I was about to pick up, when I suddenly remembered Marina's question about Americans waiting three times before answering to prove they were not alone. I let the phone ring three more times.

Fennimore seemed perturbed. 'I was about to hang up.'

I retained a calm reserve. 'I was lost in thought, writing.'

The subtle rebuke stopped him in his tracks. He began again with a decidedly more friendly tone. 'So you moved . . . Can you see the courtyard you described?'

'It's snowing. The family I wrote about is out shoveling as we speak.'

Fennimore's tone was suddenly reminiscent and quieter. 'I made my first honest two bucks shoveling a driveway! I remember a time when you had to earn an allowance. I had a paper route at the age of eleven. There were no freebies in childhood. I was out in minus twenty in a snowsuit. People wanted their newspapers, no excuses.'

I said, 'Where are you now?'

He stopped abruptly. 'Inside my head . . . where I always am.'

I couldn't quite fathom the evasiveness, why he was still resistant to offering up even this mere detail. I didn't challenge him. I was in a delirium that he had responded at all. It validated what I had written.

I said by way of trying to ingratiate myself to him, 'You must be proud of what you've achieved in life.'

'Proud!' There was an immediate hotness to his voice. 'Don't pull that crap with me. I could just as well hang up right now!'

I said nothing.

'Did you even read the previous five books in the series? One more book they kept saying. That was back with book seven. Six books on and you know what they did to Harry. It was an insult! I was propped up like an old dictator. I never got honest feedback. All I got were conceptual covers from the art department, the backlist rebranded ad infinitum! I've had eleven editors in my career, nine in the last eight years, and you know what the new breed nearly all have in common? They were all married to stockbrokers!'

Our initial conversation went something like that, Fenni-more weaving his own personal history of success and failure.

What came to the fore was his struggle with his creative legacy, his own mortality, something that let me stare into the abyss of another man's failing sense of purpose. He seemed to be on the other side of inspiration, seeking answers to the meaning of his craft, to put his work in context.

He said at the end of a rambling series of non sequiturs, 'You know, I was looking through my grandson's syllabus a few weeks ago, and I uncovered what defines a literary masterpiece: something around a hundred and forty to a hundred and sixty pages long and accessible enough that an eighth grader can write a book report on it. What does that say for us as a society?'

He didn't let me answer.

'I think the great shift for us as a nation came with Salinger's *Catcher in the Rye*, Holden Caulfield auguring the coming of adolescent disaffection. Think about it, a seventeen-year-old kid under institutional care, snubbing the nineteenth century sociological genius of what he calls a "David Copperfield kind of crap" with his own personal story ...'

His voice quieted for a moment. 'Can you think of another country where an adolescent could be soothsayer for the collective conscience? We lost our way somewhere between the Great Wars, or within the Great Depression, maybe that's where it happened, the last time in our history when we had men like Steinbeck able to set out a character like Tom Joad or George in *Of Mice and Men* to do his bidding. There was an ear for that at one point in our history ... That was the genius of our national literature, a language of the people, for the people, by the people. But times changed ...

'Where is our Steinbeck of today? You know the real tragedy, we don't even miss that voice ... We lost it under the sway of McCarthyism, in the polarization of the Cold War. We abandoned the collective sentiment of our founding fathers' motto, *E Pluribus Unum*, Out of Many One. We removed the phrase from our currency, replacing it with "In God We Trust". It tore out the core of what should have been sacrosanct in our constitution, a separation of Church and State. From that point on, we lost a sense of ourselves as political creatures. Our politics became about God and flag. We were cut off from one another, fed a line about individual liberties, about the individualization of the American Dream. We were conditioned to avoid the crowd. If you don't believe me, think how easy it was for Reagan to disband our unions, using the wedge of the Cold War to drive us from the collective bargaining table . . .

'In the so-called greatest democracy in the world, where you could say anything you wanted, nobody was really listening.'

It was a line I could have imagined Marina spouting.

Eventually, he came round to a direct connection to his own work, describing a raid he had participated in on a Vietcong village. A mother with *something* strapped to her back had run out from a hut toward the platoon; his instinctive response, to open fire, cutting her down.

The *something* turned out to be a child.

The incident had changed his life forever. It was something he had included in his first novel, a plaintive story of what one man endured, what he called 'a quasi-autobiographical piece of soul-searching'.

Though, in the novel, the villager had a bomb strapped to her back. There was no child. It had been edited out by his editor.

He kept talking in a quiet, ruminative way. 'When I came home, they told me not to tell the truth about what I saw. That was my biggest failing, just listening to them. I served and fought and watched people die, and I went back again a second time. I wasn't afraid of death! I had been willing to lay down my life for this country, but when it came to the book I let them change the truth. I let them stop me!

'Harry, they told me, had to be something other than me. He had to have his own story. That's how they put it. They didn't outright tell me no, but I knew. There was talk of a series almost from the start. By the time I got the proofs for my first book, it wasn't the book I wanted really. It missed the essential reason I wrote in the first place. I wanted to pay homage to that woman and child I killed. I wanted to acknowledge what had really gone on over there. But you know the irony of it – those goddamn editors were more than likely right about changing the scene. The book sold over two million copies. It gave me everything I ever dreamed possible.'

He stopped and coughed in a rattling loosening of phlegm. 'For years I thought that was enough, the money, or I let myself believe it. I had two ex-wives and a daughter by then.'

It was the first time in my life I had ever talked seriously on the phone for any length of time. It had the import of a deeper meaning. It was getting me closer to what I wanted to do again – write. I was speaking with Perry Fennimore. It seemed real and unreal how things had suddenly changed in my favor.

I listened quietly as Fennimore pressed on, referencing Hemingway's fascination with bullfighting, the ritualistic killing of the bull and the role of the matador as bringing some order to the role of death and cruelty in a meaningless world. He identified with that existential sense of enduring, of confronting what Camus had dubbed *The Absurd*. It was an artistic connection he eventually aligned with Kierkegaard's *Fear and Trembling*, that essential search for meaning, coming to the subject with a faint hint of nostalgia that unnerved and thrilled me.

'Those scenes your agent sent me were extraordinary! Charles Morton's crimes forced Harry to extend his psychological range. He'd lost his moral compass midway through the series. Morton gave Harry a reason to go on living. Vietnam was ancient history, vets transient bums begging on street corners, guys who couldn't move on. There was no youth left in their faces, or hint at what they'd once been. We tire of history in this country.

'I knew Harry was completely lost by book three. I was stuck with the political consciousness of an idealistic kid from the Sixties who had done the right thing and served his country! Now he was just old, full of political venom, full of piss and vinegar. He had become a stereotype of brooding anger, an avenger of a moral order that didn't hold.' He trailed off for a few seconds.

'Do you know what it feels like to find yourself repeating yourself over and over again?'

I wanted to speak but didn't.

'In all my years on earth I've learned one truth. For each of us, the locus of who we are is rooted in some profoundly personal moment. We don't evolve beyond that. We stop growing. That's the essential truth of all our existences. I think history bears me out. Think of the greats, try to understand the social politics of Steinbeck, or Conrad and his relationship to the sea, or Kafka, the stark minimalist empire of his faceless bureaucracy in *The Trial* or *The Castle*, and you'll come to see it is the same story told again and again. In writing, more so than any other profession, you outlive your cultural relevance and, ergo, your usefulness to the world.'

It was a chilling summation of how I truly felt in life.

Toward the end of the conversation, he referred to my two novels, referencing what he felt was the autobiographical nature of the suicide of my father in the novel, a disquieting connection since I had never made mention of my father's suicide in any biographical information. He didn't dwell on the details, tacitly saying he could tell fact from fiction, calling us 'mutual prisoners of perception, compulsory witnesses to life', speaking with a beguiling familiarity that drew me into his sphere of influence.

He spoke of ill-health, again hinting at a personal crisis of faith and a fear of the hereafter. He was unsure if the medal he was given for his service in Vietnam would be seen with such glory in Heaven. That seemed to be where his sensibilities lay.

I envisioned him in my mind with a gaunt face of a life-long smoker, a skeletal figure lost in the shadows of doubt, a recluse with a typewriter awaiting words, entombed in a Floridian paradise, in a place where happiness should have prevailed, but didn't.

Toward the end of the call I broached the issue of money which seemed to disturb him greatly. He said, 'You contacted me.'

I was taken aback. I didn't quite know what to say, though in the end he agreed to send me what he called 'an advance on an advance', a mere four thousand dollars, as he said with a quiet insistence, 'Find me a victim Harry can care about, Karl, someone worth fighting for, someone worth saving.'

It came across as a literal request.

Eighteen

On the back of securing the deal with Fennimore, I called Lori at her office, hinting at what I felt was going to be a pronounced upswing in my career. It was one of the few times when I had something honest to tell her about my writing life.

I didn't go into the particulars.

Lori was quieter than I thought she should have been, given the news.

I said, 'Are you still there?'

She answered, 'Yes.'

'What is it?'

She hesitated. 'I guess you did better waiting for what you wanted. You always know best. I admit it. I was *wrong*.'

I hadn't anticipated this reaction. 'There is no *wrong* or *right* in this, Lori! You were there for me!'

She cut me off. 'This is the big time then?'

'Big time! There is no big time in writing. You know that! Come on, this is all good, isn't it?'

She said quietly, 'Yes,' but she didn't seem convinced. 'It's just ...'

'It's just what?'

I heard the rush of her breath. 'This is selfishness talking. It's going to make you hate me. I've always been afraid that once you made it, you would leave me! Does it make you hate me?'

I said quietly, 'No, it doesn't. I want us to go out and celebrate tonight. This is a turning point for us.'

Through the late afternoon I continued writing, stopping what I was doing only when I heard the sound of Elena and Sergei in the hallway.

I descended the stairs.

Sergei was petulant about not being allowed to get a new toy car. He was speaking in English, fighting with Elena who was mopping the floor. She spoke back to him in Russian.

When I passed them to get my mail, Sergei boldly pulled at my arm and asked me to buy him a new car. He began to explain it. It was being advertised all over the TV. He was sure I must have seen it. He had his hand out waiting for the money.

Mortified, Elena said something abrupt in Russian, while Sergei vigorously shook his head. He still had his hand out.

I looked crossly at Elena. 'Shoosh! I want to speak with Sergei.'

She said flatly in English, 'He has a car! He has lots of cars!' Her face was red.

I looked gravely at Sergei. 'Elena tells me you already have a car.' I pointed at the car in his hand.

Sergei stomped his foot like a spoiled brat and shouted, 'No, I want a *new* car!'

'Listen to me, if you want a new car, then you'll have to work hard. That's the way it works here. So what do you think you could do to earn the money?'

Sergei kept staring at me with a defiant look in his eyes.

I said, 'OK, if you can't think of anything, how about you hop on one leg for one whole minute.'

Elena piped up hotly, 'That's not work!'

I made a serious face at her. 'Obviously you don't know what passes for work these days. Life is not all buckets and mops,

Cinderella.' Then I turned toward Sergei and said, 'OK, count to sixty, start hopping.'

As he hopped and counted, I said matter-of-factly, without directly looking at Elena, 'So what do you wish for?'

She stubbornly refused to answer.

I said in a goading way, 'I see, you have no imagination! Is that it? Are you a girl with no dreams? Are you a peasant?'

Before she could answer, I said, 'Keep counting, Sergei!'

Going behind her, I put my hands over her eyes. Her body went rigid as I put my mouth close to her ear and whispered, 'Here's a secret, Elena. It's not the most deserving who necessarily get what they want in life, but the most insistent. Remember that.'

I was jolted in that instant, experiencing a déjà vu of Aleksey putting his hands over my eyes, Marina surging in my mind.

Elena let out a squeal.

I had reflexively tightened my hold on her.

I tried to recover, and looked toward Sergei, intent on making him the focus of attention, when to my horror I saw Dasha, standing outside the glass paneled hallway door.

I let go of Elena.

I said with a dismissive laugh, while beginning to fumble in my pocket for money, 'We were all playing a silly game.'

Dasha pushed past me.

In the most violent of ways she took Elena by the hair, slapped her across the face, and dragged her across the courtyard.

I stood frozen as Sergei looked on and then snatched the money from my hand, before scurrying like a rat after them.

By the time Lori arrived home, the discussion with Fennimore had receded in the wake of what happened with Elena.

She thought my melancholy was because of how she had reacted on the phone.

I was at pains to make her think otherwise. She had rushed home to be with me.

I watched her change out of her office clothes into jeans and a sweatshirt, donning her over-sized parka that looked like a sleeping bag.

I was almost prompted to ask her to put something else on, but it was snowing and cold, and it didn't really matter.

We left almost immediately.

In a small barred basement window facing onto the courtyard, I saw lights on in the apartment where Elena slept, and I had the strangest of thoughts. In another time and place, at the age of almost thirteen, Elena could have been of marrying age, a chattel in some agrarian arrangement with an older man of means, her worth tied to her family's dowry, a transaction outside the domain of love or courtship.

It put into perspective Dasha's violence. How was one's worth established in this new world? What price could one put on Elena?

I must have hesitated, because Lori tugged at my arm. 'Are you OK?'

I nodded, pulled back from my thoughts.

Beyond the courtyard, the snow cast a faint luminescence that made everything seem like a postcard.

We passed a flower shop, a hair salon, a herbal remedy store – all small, discreet enclaves eschewing cutthroat consumerism for a more personal touch.

It was almost Dickensian in a stylized Hollywood way, though my thoughts were still with Elena as Lori stopped outside a travel agency.

In the window, a neon sign blinked invitingly like a Christmas decoration, asking a tired, adolescent joke – What is long and hard and full of sea men?

The answer shone intermittently, revealing a miniature model of a cruise ship sailing silently on an azure sea. Faces looked out from portal windows, while on an upper promenade bathers lay on towels. The figurines were all tiny naked men.

It was an advertisement for a gay cruise.

Lori squeezed my arm and said in a conspiratorial way, 'Oh my God ... It's so *sick*.'

I thought of fighting against her. I found it hard maintaining the façade of being a decent, normal human being. I said, 'I don't know. Is it? This is the logical extension of lifestyle choices, Lori ... Tell me, how many rainforests and innumerable species do you think have gone extinct because of the disposable diaper?'

Lori moved a step back from me.

I continued, 'Is there anything more truly abject than the emasculating sight of men pushing strollers? It makes me want to hold up a sign that says something like "Men! Follow me. Let's go hunting! Let's kill a deer!"'

Lori self-consciously looked around to see if anybody was within earshot, then looked at me again. 'You're joking ... right? You're just being the *writer*!'

I said, 'Of course I am ...' and taking her arm, I led her through the veil of falling snow.

The restaurant we chose turned out to be an intimate Italian restaurant, all of nine tables beyond a velvet-curtained façade. It felt like entering a secret society. All the couples were males, except for one.

Within lay a certain romance, the starry-eyed gaze of infatuation and mystique, hand holding and quiet laughter, a drinks menu offering Velvet Hammers, Old-Fashioneds, Mint Juleps and Chocolate Martinis.

I saw Lori hesitate despite her best front, but, in the complicated Rubik's cube of table and chair maneuvers to get us seated, we were almost immediately trapped against a wall.

We were stared at for the first time in our lives as a minority, the pejorative term for our kind, '*breeders*', ironic, given our circumstances.

Disconcertingly, we had nothing to talk about, our heads buried almost immediately in the menus to avoid staring at the coy exchange and hand holding at the other tables.

To put it bluntly, we were dressed like crap, and maybe the true representatives of heterosexual jadedness. We took our relationships for granted, whereas gay life was still decidedly romantic and showy.

For a sense of solidarity I looked at the other heterosexual couple, the woman strikingly statuesque and refined in an Amazonian way, with a chic beauty that made me slightly embarrassed for Lori, who caught me looking.

I smiled feebly at the woman, who graciously returned the smile. She had the milky grey eyes of a wolf, undoubtedly contact lenses that made her strangely alluring and erotic, until suddenly I realized I knew her.

I shrank into my seat, withdrawing my stare immediately.

Lori leaned forward and said suspiciously, 'Do you know her?'

I said, 'No ...' under my breath, scared as hell the woman was going to come over. If we'd been in a restaurant of real proportions, I would have insisted we left, but in such intimate confines there was no escape.

The woman was really a man, Glen Watson, a.k.a. *Hermaphrodite*, a gender confused transvestite enigma. He had appeared in a series of glossy fetish transsexual magazines at

The Portal, featuring his trawl of heterosexual hangouts, sports bars mostly, his bounty jocks and married men, where inevitably the latter sequence of stills always focused on the sudden shock of guys confronting the coiled meat of his cock in nylons.

Lori kept stealing glances.

I knew Glen was in his element. He had asked me out while at *The Portal*. He'd said to Max he could change me. That was his essential mission in life, what he called 'Uncovering the Truth beneath the Lie.'

I could tell he recognized me. I just prayed to God he wouldn't come over to our table.

I had never revealed to Lori I'd worked at *The Portal*.

I delved again into the menu. 'So what looks good?'

Lori was still drawn to Glen. She whispered, 'She's looking at you . . . She knows you . . .'

I reached across the table for her hand, but it took only a few more glances for Lori to *get* what she was really seeing, given where we were. 'That's a *man* . . .'

I said, 'She . . . He was one of those interviews I did in the past for *The Stranger.*'

Lori fixed her eyes on me. 'That same magazine you were supposed to write for about that Russian *sleaze*?' Lori shook her head. 'Why do you write for rags like that?' There was a hint of accusation in her voice.

I said, 'It's what a writer does between books, nothing more than that.'

In a desperate attempt to change the subject, I told her about what had happened with Elena, referring back to my hesitation in the courtyard as we left.

I said, 'If there had been a child, would you have been inclined toward discipline?'

Almost immediately Lori took the bait and launched into a complicated story about her upbringing, something about

Deb, a fat joint and box of tampons. It was like a bad joke awaiting a punch line, but I listened with a strained enthusiasm, trying to keep her preoccupied.

I kept nodding.

Apparently, Deb had been locked up for an entire weekend in the attic to make her confess to owning the joint, given only a jailer's ration of bread and water, yet she admitted nothing. In the end, she was beaten by their father in a domestic nightmare of blood-curdling screams.

Lori stopped. She looked at me in a self-conscious way. 'Go on, say it. We were trash, right?'

I shook my head. 'Why are you trying to fight with me?' I had Glen in my peripheral vision all the time.

She pressed on. 'You know, the thing is, I envied Deb's relationship with Dad. At least he tried with her.'

I saw Glen rise to leave with his date. He said, 'Toodles,' to the waiter.

He smiled right at me as I looked away.

Lori tracked him with her eyes and said with a hint of condemnation, 'Sometimes I think there is such a thing as too much choice. Maybe I'm hopelessly old-fashioned.'

Glen was thankfully out of earshot, or just pretended not to hear.

When he was gone Lori looked at me again, unperturbed, and got back to her story. She said, 'I wish my father had taken the courage to hit me before everything happened with Don.'

When she blinked, tears rolled down her face. 'You know, I feel so in love and lost at the same time . . .'

I leaned forward. 'That's the nature of adult life. Nothing is easy.'

She kept talking. 'I know you think I'm an idiot . . . but I'm not. I never get to say these things . . . At work and on the commute I find myself having conversations with you in my head. I want to say the right things.'

I let her talk. A waiter stood nearby, and I averted my eyes so we were not disturbed.

She looked directly at me. 'Can I tell you something important, something about me? It's good news.'

I felt the pulse of my wrists in her hands as she took and kissed them.

'It wasn't my eggs. They found out the problem. It was my uterus. We *can* have a child ... All we do is hire a woman to carry the fertilized egg to term. It's called gestational surrogacy. The beauty of it is, genetically, the child is still *us*.'

There was literally nothing I could say.

Nineteen

The general idea of a child didn't seem as burdensome with the prospect of money and security, or maybe it was the overall shock that made me immune from feeling anything else.

There was also closure to the surrogacy, which was vastly different from the indeterminacy of Lori trying to become pregnant. In my mind I had this vision of baby Frank Klein as a tangible piece of medical handiwork. Denise Klein had achieved this legacy after death.

The surrogacy dovetailed with my continued work on Fennimore's next novel, the process of medically assisted birth taking on a greater import in the overall theme. I felt our experience becoming a subplot within a far grander project, looking toward a philosophical understanding of the meaning of life.

In agreement with Lori, we committed further to economic frugality. I hedged and put off the actual date of my huge advance. I was in the end stages of *delivery*, double-entendre not lost on her.

I outlined a strategy my mother had used to stretch my father's paycheck, shopping every eighth day, so that in the course of seven weeks we saved a week's worth of grocery money. It was an old-world anecdote that defined how people survived not so long ago and led me to explain to Lori the nature of my commitment to my mother and why I had sent off the better part of the advance from Fennimore toward her continued care at PALS.

For the first time in our relationship I spoke about the nomadic days of my life after my father's murder of his mistress and his suicide, how my mother endured, setting aside his betrayal, looking always to the future and my advancement. I put her sacrifice into the context of the implicit oath a parent takes when bringing forth a child, an oath that garners no great honors, no public notices or written commendations, where untold dreams and aspirations are set aside in the service of a greater good.

It was a conversation that was met with an understanding I would not have thought possible, but then I had never tried to tell Lori before.

It was with this newfound contentment that I stole almost three hours a day, rising in the early hours of the morning, leaving Lori's side to write in my boxers at the computer.

By first light, I faxed off brief character sketches and scenes to Fennimore, the scenes not yet a story, but written with a view toward extending the voice of the letter we had mutually agreed would form the prologue to the new novel.

It was the most perfect of circumstances, a honed-down existence, giving me a renewed sense of purpose.

During the second week of this morning routine, I heard the clank of an iron gate in the courtyard. Going to the window, I observed Glen down below fumbling with a key in the foyer of the quad across from us. He was returning with a guy in a business suit.

We were neighbors. The dragnet of life widened in the intrigue of so many other lives, so that over the following days, I began to await Glen's arrival home in the early morning, his nocturnal wanderings finding their way into numerous set pieces I wrote. I had this distinct sense of parallel existences going on in the city, bringing a multiplicity of voices to my work that had not previously been there, eclipsing the singularity of The Opus.

I had Fennimore's cop, Harry, in mind always; sensing his want, his sleeplessness, in bars and diners, eating anti-acid pills, reading again and again the letter that had been sent to him, brooding over it, nervously awaiting the entry of Charles Morton.

I was anticipating Fennimore's midmorning discussion when Lori called. She had finalized our appointment with Goldfarb and a surrogacy agency. A surge of tension passed through me.

She sounded apprehensive.

I knew she was waiting for me to reassure her we were doing the right thing. I said, 'We are,' in a way that didn't reassure her.

She asked if I had spoken to Ivan about fixing the heat in our apartment.

I lied, wanting to get her off the phone so I wouldn't miss the call from Fennimore.

She told me she was calling from the cafeteria pay phone for the sake of privacy.

I said in an upbeat way, 'Look, why don't you get something to eat at the cafeteria. Forget the brown bag austerity measures. Get the works, mashed potato, meatloaf, apple pie à la mode. You're going to need to keep your strength up.'

'Why?' She waited a moment. 'I won't be carrying, or had you forgotten?'

I had forgotten.

This was the core of her melancholy, why she had called in the first place.

I said, 'Who remembers the womb, Lori? Who remembers birth? Look at this in a democratic way: you're going to be *not* experiencing what I'm going to be not experiencing.'

She said, 'You're right . . .' but without a sense of conviction.

I was already distracted, wanting to get back to work. 'I'm not trying to minimize what you're feeling . . . I'm not.'

There was again a silence of indecision. She had more to say.

'I read sometimes the surrogates don't give the babies up . . . It happens. They get attached. They become the mothers.'

'Then we choose carefully, Lori. We interview as many women as we can until we're satisfied.'

She breathed into the phone. 'There's just one other thing. We're going to have to decide whether I'll wear a pregnancy belly or not . . . if we want to pretend I'm carrying. It can have a bearing on how we adapt as parents.'

I said, 'Maybe *we* should research the literature, see what it says.' I imagined her cradling the phone, trying to suppress her true emotions.

She said quietly, 'I've got to get back to work, Karl. Just take care of the heating, promise me, OK?'

A few minutes later I descended the utility access stairs of our apartment building to confront Ivan.

The dark basement looked like the bowels of a submarine. A string of exposed bulbs cast shadows on a phantasmagoria of serpentine pipes reminiscent of a Freddy Krueger nightmare. Such places still existed in these old-world buildings, the network of passageways leading to a laundry facility and a communal storage area next to the building's monstrous boiler which sat squat and black behind an iron door.

The temperature approximated what I thought Hell would be like.

I was apprehensive of running into Ivan's wife Dasha, given the misunderstanding with Elena, and who answered the door but Dasha.

She took up the entirety of the frame, her arms folded with a peasant's obstinacy. She had huge breasts and a plump face riddled with spidery veins.

I quickly mentioned the problem with the heat. Like Ivan, she pretended not to understand me. While I was mid-sentence, she shouted out in Russian and turned and walked away toward a steaming stove with two pots.

The apartment reeked of a sour cabbage smell, a sweltering hovel with a low slung ceiling with insulated pipes hissing and clanking. Then I spotted sweet Elena sitting at a table in an alcove. The miserable brat Sergei was there too. He immediately stuck out his tongue at me.

Ignoring his provocation, I continued to stare at Elena, an incongruous hothouse flower down here in the vapid heat among this troll-like family, contrasting so with Dasha, her skin an alabaster perfection youth bestowed and time ruined. I wondered, had Dasha ever looked like this? Was Elena's genetic fate tied to that of her mother?

Again I thought about what a child like Elena offered once upon a time, an investment against hard times. In my mind's eye I pictured the rotundity of Dasha's belly, like one of those Russian nesting dolls, opening up to reveal another and yet another little Sergei or Elena.

I nodded civilly at Elena, still pained at how things had developed.

She looked nervously at me for an instant, before looking away.

Dasha shouted in her guttural Russian, startling me. I watched her ladle soup into four bowls before stabbing at a coiled link of blanched sausage which she set on a huge platter.

The sausage brought immediate protests from Sergei, who climbed onto a counter and, defying Dasha, took down a box of Count Chocula cereal. Dasha rushed him, lifting him by his arm so he appeared to levitate, his legs wheeling in the air in a Currier and Ives scene from another century, *Mother's Admonishment*, Dasha in her apron, Sergei wailing.

Elena rose quickly under Dasha's instruction and tried to pry the Count Chocula box from Sergei's small hands as he thrashed and kicked wildly at her.

Amidst the commotion, Vladimir appeared from a bedroom in a tank top. He said something conciliatory, tousling Sergei's hair, suddenly quieting him, restoring order. He was a physical presence, especially down here in this hovel.

Moments later Sergei was arm-wrestling Vladimir at the table.

What struck me was the natural ease Vladimir assumed in this adopted life, taking a fat sausage link from Dasha, while little Sergei continued to struggle with both hands to budge Vladimir's arm.

The scene got even the boorish Dasha laughing as she stood swayback in her slippers, her feet set apart.

It was a claustrophobic closeness I knew no American twenty-year-old would have endured, and yet this was how the American dream lived on, in basement dwellings such as this, a distant relative extending the security of a foothold in a far-off city. In this instance, a city called Chicago.

It contrasted starkly with the essential fraud of what I had witnessed at the boutique hotel with the troupe, their so-called anarchy and protest incongruous with getting loaded on twelve dollar vodkas. This was the heart of true émigrés, a clan set adrift of their homeland, making do without resort to political agitation, advancing by small measures, seeking merely to survive.

Almost on cue, Ivan, the shambling patriarch, the great benefactor, appeared, reeking of cheap vodka.

Out of his usual anorak, he looked diminished, like a

tortoise without its shell, and his eye sockets looked painfully puffy.

I said his name aloud, trying to catch his attention, trying to explain again the problem with the heat.

He spoke to me from across the room, stonewalling me with his usual evasiveness, feigning a lack of understanding. He stopped by a small table with a chessboard, stared at it, directed some comment to Vladimir, then took up a piece and rolled it back and forth in his fingers before making his move.

Then he sat down at the table, attended by Dasha, who, with the lavish servitude of some bygone era, jabbed a sausage and set it before him along with a bowl of soup and bread, prompting Ivan to say dismissively, 'Mr Karl, we are eating now. Please go!'

In the end, it was an exercise in futility, arguing further, the family gathered around the table as Ivan lowered his head in silent prayer.

I was the outsider, the lost American inside America.

Back in my apartment, I checked for a fax from Fennimore. There was none, which set me at ill-ease, the weekend yawning like a chasm. I had been dissatisfied with the initial sum he sent me, given his sense of desperation. I wanted to renegotiate.

I faxed him a laconic one liner, 'We need to talk!'

Looking toward the floorboard, I tried to rouse a sense of purpose for retrieving the tape with a dutiful sense of commitment if I was going to push him for more money, but felt no real compulsion to draw my father to the fore right then. There seemed something fundamentally pointless in trying to capture yet again the eternal suffering of the nameless victim.

I had suddenly lost the essential connection it represented at a real or artistic level.

Instead, I sat at the computer again, writing without the Clinton mask, trying to simply capture what I had experienced below in the basement, the serpentine pipes and smell of scorched dust, yet after a time, I found myself drawn toward the contrasting life of Vladimir and Sergei in their absurd arm-wrestling match.

It was a preoccupation that caught me unawares with a sudden heartfelt sense of what my future potentially held – fatherhood, and the sort of unconditional intimacy one human could bestow on another human being.

Against Fennimore's morning silence and the continued pressure of what had slowly become anathema to me despite my best intentions to fight it, this writing life, I thought, maybe in the footing of fatherhood, I could invest a redemptive sense of purpose as stay-at-home father.

I imagined Frank Klein at some point in the future, attending Frank Junior's graduation ceremony and weeping silently for what had been created in the last gasp of his wife's want.

Frank had made a deep impression on me, a contradiction. He seemed noble and trapped, and yet I respected him maybe more than anybody I had met in a long time. He had shown me something worth living for – another human being, little Frank. Who knew what Little Frank might end up becoming, this Frankenstein creation of Denise Klein, maybe president? Wasn't that what all parents secretly wished for?

I thought about calling Frank just to talk, to see how he was doing, knowing it was simply a distraction at this stage.

I turned toward the computer and wrote again, then stopped, preoccupied with what I had seen with Vladimir and Sergei, that familiarity and love.

All I needed to learn was how to set aside personal ambition in its truest sense, do what my mother and so many like her had heroically done, re-direct my ambitions, invest what I had learned into my own child.

This was the natural order of generations.

I put my hands to my face, leaned forward and let out a long breath, suddenly aware of my mother's parallel life continuing in the long shadow of so many lost years, dying alone at PALS.

I thought, maybe with the arrival of a child, I could set my personal sacrifice as stay-at-home father as a legitimate reason I couldn't continue paying for PALS, foisting on Lori the need for my mother to come live with us, setting her up in something like an annex over a garage. She could give an added depth to our child's life.

Outside of this age, that had been the natural course of relations. What was bestowed so lavishly on one during youth was simply returned in kind in later life. It seemed the most natural and equitable of exchanges. Who knew the particulars of what passed between a parent and a child, but the two of them alone.

Looking up from the computer, I heard the gate in the courtyard clank, drawn to the window by the laughter of Sergei and Elena cutting the midday quiet of a pale sunlight with their mere presence.

This was the music of angels. I stood up to watch them.

Across the courtyard, I knew Glen was asleep in his daytime sarcophagus after his night on the prowl, his blinds drawn as always until late afternoon in a nocturnal urban existence few outside the gay neighborhood could ever really hope to comprehend.

Lori called again in the late afternoon. She still sounded down. She complained, 'I know you're not listening. I can hear you typing!'

I stopped mid-keystroke. I had not actually heard what she'd previously said.

She told me Deb was taking her out for dinner. Just hearing the name Deb made me wince. As we talked, there was no suggestion I should join them. She said she might spend the night with Deb.

I closed my eyes at Deb's continuing interference and said, 'Let me read something to you.' I had just finished the piece about Sergei and Vladimir, wanting to intimate my greater understanding of where we were heading, but in the background I heard Deb say something, then the muffled sound of the receiver being covered.

It was an outright betrayal of our agreement to live our own lives. I said loudly, 'Deb's there with you now, isn't she?' for the benefit of Deb mostly.

Lori answered. 'Yes.'

I took a deep breath and closed my eyes. 'I'm just following your lead, Lori. Why is she there?'

Lori said out of left field, 'Do you believe in Love at First Sight?'

I put the phone to the other ear. 'What's wrong?'

She spoke with a rush of emotion. 'I saw your *Russian Sleaze* made it to the cover of *The Stranger*! They used your photograph, the *nudey* one you took of her.'

I said incredulously, 'Is that what this is about? Jesus Christ, listen to me! I took the shot in a hotel lobby! There was nothing untoward about it. It was a fucking assignment, nothing else! Why do you do this to yourself ... to *us*?'

She started shouting over me, hysterical. 'You were the last person she called! I lost my pregnancy and you called her ... goddamn you ... you called and you talked and flirted with her while I was passed out. It's right there in the article, everything ... you calling her, her calling you back.'

I felt sucker punched. It wasn't the story I submitted.

She sobbed for the longest time.

I heard Deb shouting she wanted to talk to me, but Lori wouldn't let her. She said with uncharacteristic sharpness, 'This is my problem, Deb! Don't!'

I shouted, 'Lori, listen to me,' but she didn't.

Her voice became alarmingly cold, defiant and direct. It didn't sound like her.

'You must have made a big impression on her, right, Karl? Maybe I should be flattered a woman like that was interested in my husband! I should be pleased you came home at all!'

I cut her off. 'She was lost in a foreign country and drunk. She wanted to understand who we are ... That's all it was about, nothing more.'

Her voice faltered. 'Stop lying ... just *stop* ... I read the article. I know she wasn't Russian! Why did you marry me, tell me? I was never good enough for you. You were never satisfied with me, never! I always knew it, but never let myself believe it until now. That's what you've wanted all along, some East Coast bitch with money to burn!'

I didn't get to respond. I had no idea what she was talking about.

In the background Deb was shouting. Lori evidently dropped the phone.

I heard the sound of the receiver hitting the ground, Deb's voice growing distant, before the line suddenly went dead.

Twenty

Surging waves of adrenalin coursed through me as I pulled a copy of *The Stranger* from a bin of free weeklies at *Caribou*, Marina on the cover, her hands aloft, holding her sign – I Have Nothing To Sell You!

Beneath was a heading: Murdered Yale Debutante Faked Russian Persona.

I couldn't believe any of this was truly happening. It felt dreamlike, the centerfold of the paper done in a collage of images of the troupe, along with the crime scene, including a stark shot of the burned car in Cabrini Green where Marina's body had been recovered.

Frantically scanning the article, I saw that Marina's true identity hadn't been uncovered until almost a week after her murder, purposely hidden by Aleksey.

Then I came across the reference to my calling Marina, the extract of our conversation in italics, listing me as the last known person to speak with her.

Back at the apartment, in the unsettling aftermath of what had happened with Lori, I looked at the answering machine to see if she had called back. She hadn't.

I thought of calling her at work, then didn't. More than likely she hadn't called from her office. In fact, I knew she wouldn't have behaved like that, not in the cubicle nightmare of eavesdropping. She was off with Deb somewhere.

I sat down. I stared at the cover photograph of Marina. It

was the amateur color image I had taken, but manipulated, overexposed. Striding in her military boots, she looked like a chic mercenary in search of a war.

In a strange way, the revelation about her death, and now knowing her true identity, renewed within me a clawing feeling for what might have been. Intuitively, Lori was right. This Yale debutante was the sort of woman I had been searching for all my life. To be tangentially associated with her, to have been the last person she had reached out to hours before her death, validated something about her instincts toward me.

There was something vaguely noble holding that honor, being the last person to have ever spoken meaningfully with her.

It connected us in a way that ran deeper than I would have expected.

I felt a trembling intimacy in staring at her photograph.

The shock of her death had passed a week earlier, but it came back to me again as I ran my finger along her face and touched her lips. I could feel her presence even still, even more so now.

A bio note briefly outlined the particulars of her life, not that it mattered really, but I read it all the same, forming the words as I read the small text font.

> 24-year-old Emily Piper Hampton was a native of Montauk, Long Island. Affectionately referred to as 'M' by friends and family, she was described as a student of distinction, remembered fondly by her Harbor Country Day life-long classmates as 'free-spirited and generous.'
>
> Her scholastic merits included graduating *Cum Laude* with a double-major in Political Science and Russian Studies from

Yale in 1997. She had been accepted and deferred enrollment to Yale Law School, electing to travel with a political theater group, *The Revolting Bolsheviks*, she had co-founded with her partner, Eric Brandt, Ph.D., a.k.a. Aleksey Romanoff.

The troupe had been engaged in a Mock-umentary on the apolitical nature of American society, revealing the social and political arrogance of American domestic and foreign policy.

Estranged from her family through college, Hampton was an only child, survived by her mother Grace Heath-Hampton and father, Timothy Hampton III, a noted Wall Street financier and CEO of Sterling Wealth Management, Inc.

Despite the incongruity of her bio, it changed nothing. All it did was further validate what I felt about her.

I remembered a professor in college talking about how most social agitations started, not with the underclass, but with the empathy of a few renegade upper-class eschewing wealth and privilege, so much so that when the Soviet revolution eventually broke out, Lenin was allegedly overheard asking of his cohort intelligentsia about the revolutionary masses, 'Who are these people?'

The two-page spread also featured an interview with Brandt centering on the controversy surrounding his concealing Marina's true identity. He had withheld her identity on what he called philosophical and political grounds, arguing identifying her as the offspring of a wealthy East Coast family was not representative of her political beliefs.

It was a macabre and almost borderline psychotic justification.

In an inset photograph, Brandt was in the same John Lennon glasses, wearing a teeshirt with the words *I Have Nothing to Sell You* – the line attributed to an essay Marina wrote during her sophomore year, a personal manifesto, and something Brandt had copyrighted as the provisional title of an on-going documentary, with an associated website, www.ihavenothingtosellyou.com.

In reading again and again through the article, I thought: what if unbeknownst to me the exchange at the hotel had been filmed, my actions destined to make some director's final cut, tied to the messages I had left at the hotel?

I had met Brandt. I knew what he was capable of doing. Did he have footage of that last encounter in the hotel lobby? An opportunist like him was liable to have done anything.

All I could imagine was Lori, witnessing my undeniable interest in Marina.

I cringed at the prospect of her seeing me handing Marina my business card.

Twenty-one

Heroically, against the encroaching dark I pulled up Word and tried to set aside thoughts of Marina and Lori. There was work to be done.

I set about refining some of the Fennimore scenes for close on two hours, during which all I did was revise the initial letter I had sent him, changing tenses, lengthening and then shortening sentences.

I was hoping Lori would call.

Distracted, I looked again at the cover image of Marina.

For some stupid reason I called Nate, out of indecision and distraction.

The Stranger's office was closed. I selected Nate's extension and left a message on his answering machine. I said, 'Thanks for cutting me out of the story, Nate, you son-of-a-bitch! You could have fucking called me!' My voice suddenly escalated. I hadn't planned on cursing. 'I've a good mind to sue your fucking ass for mentioning me in connection with Marina. My wife's walked out on me because of you! Who the hell gave you the authority to reference me in any fucking way? You don't know the first thing about journalistic integrity. You run a fucking rag is all you run. You're a joke, you hear me, Nate? A fucking ...'

The answering machine beeped, cutting me off.

I felt better for a moment, then didn't. The heat was gone out of what I wanted to say to him. I called back and said, 'I'd appreciate if you'd send me my check, Nate. I apologize for the previous message. It's just . . . My wife miscarried the night I met Marina. It's one of those unfortunate coincidences. I'm dealing with the fallout of it is all. I just wanted you to know.'

I hung up, still lost to indecision.

The Fennimore material had dried up for the night.

I paged again through *The Stranger* until I came across the reference to the website Brandt had created, prompting me to leave the apartment and buy a 56k modem at Radio Shack along Broadway.

On the way back to the apartment, I lined up outside a crowded Thai restaurant. I hadn't eaten all day. I wasn't hungry really. I just didn't want to go home, but then decided against eating in, and ordered off their take-out menu instead.

In the fifteen-minute wait I bought two oil-can-sized Foster's beers at a hole-in-the-wall convenience store run by a Chinese family, the owner's ten-year-old son sitting by his father on a stool doing his homework. Behind the counter were racks of gay magazines, and XXX-rated videos, along with cigarettes, Michael Jackson's *Billie Jean* playing loudly through a dated Eighties boom box. I saw a TV on at the end of a narrow passageway and an older woman, undoubtedly the grandmother, shuffling forward in the deep blue Maoist outfit of a field laborer.

It was yet another version of the Ivan story, immigrant life finding prospects in the most unlikely of places, doing what my father had failed to do – survive.

Heading back amidst the pulse of nightlife, it was strange to be so removed from those around me, to be unmoved by human attraction, by the sight of what I suppose were hunks, bears and studs. I felt there was something lacking within me, as if this culture was the natural order of human existence and love.

*

Back in the apartment, I ate at the table with the lights turned off. I finished off the first beer, started in on the second, wanting the release of sleep, the world outside alive with the resounding bass from a weekend club called 'The Manhole'.

I was waiting for the alcohol to take me under, but it didn't in the way I had hoped.

Melancholy beset me, so much so that I paged Lori. I felt weak in doing it, but couldn't help myself.

This was freedom, and yet I was here alone, a Friday night passing in the uproarious noise of human life.

I lowered my head, met Marina staring back at me from the cover of *The Stranger*.

In a slow release of inebriation, I went to the bathroom and came back and sat and waited.

I kept looking at Marina like she was a date who had stopped talking. I felt suddenly uncomfortable, looked away and then back at her and drank some more.

This was my shot of her, my image, and yet in looking at her she receded at certain moments. She was lost to me. The graphics department at *The Stranger* had rendered the shot into something more stark, more politically charged. I was again a ghost contributor, this time of a negative, the obscure originator behind the lens of a camera.

I couldn't help but make the connection to the work I had done for Fennimore, the ghost of my work in there somewhere, but less apparent, lost in the pages we exchanged.

It took almost an hour to hook up the modem and to install the AOL software. I typed in a search for Marina's real name, 'Emily Hampton.'

What came up was a hit to a virtual memorial site set up by her family, featuring a picture of her taken the spring of her junior year at Yale. It was an unselfconscious shot of her sitting, legs akimbo, studying in her dorm room, the image catching a last flush of innocence and youth, her outward self not yet aligned with what lay deep within her. Though above her on a slanted ceiling was a collage of images featuring Gandhi, Mandela, Bob Marley, Che Guevara, along with The Clash's seminal anthem poster, 'London Calling'.

A stark statement under the photograph read, 'Our beloved, free-spirited daughter, M, stolen from us too soon!'

It was signed, 'Lovingly, Mom and Dad!'

Most of the initial postings on the site bore testimony to the corrupting influence of 43-year-old Brandt, entries describing him as an 'ego-maniac, manipulator', a post-doctorate adjunct who had purportedly influenced numerous students with his quasi-socialist spiels, having siphoned off literally tens of thousands of dollars for his vanity press publications, left-wing freebie newspapers, and a documentary he had been intent on making in the Soviet Union, a project that had morphed after the fall of the Berlin Wall into the idea of a *mock*umentary, filming a fake Soviet troupe crossing America.

In further scrolling down the site there were remarks by other disgruntled troupe members, describing the spiraling events prior to Hampton's murder. There had apparently been a struggle within the troupe, Hampton openly leading a challenge against Brandt's artistic aimlessness, confronting him over the lavish expenditure of the project.

In staring again at her debutante image, I understood the willful strength it had taken for her to rebel against such ease and privilege, to challenge even the likes of Brandt in the end.

I dwelt on the term 'free-spirited' in the single line entry under the photograph, her parents obliquely referencing what undoubtedly had been her predisposition all her life toward leftist causes, begging the question, where might her destiny have lain if she had never come under the influence of Brandt?

It was a thought that made me mindful of Frank Klein's question regarding Keith Richards and Jagger, about how lives can be changed through chance meetings, how two people can become a third entity.

I think her parents had fallen upon that same notion, firmly placing the blame with Brandt, especially aggrieved at his willful misleading of the police in the early stages of the investigation.

In a continued trawl of the Internet, I did a search on the quote 'I Have Nothing to Sell You', coming up with over three hundred hits in the emerging world of second wave Internet sites, almost exclusively in the domain of college life and Mac aficionados.

On most of the linked sites, college kids were pictured, as per Brandt's request, wearing their makeshift protest *I Have Nothing to Sell You* T-shirts, marker pens held defiantly aloft.

In death, Marina had gained cult status.

Finally, I entered Brandt's site. The banner featured an animated gif of a scene culled from his *mock*umentary – the grubs being beaten, with a slow dissolve to the image of Hampton at Yale on through to her incarnation as kitsch Russian performance artist that ended with the stark black letters RIP.

I reloaded the page, watched the transformation happen before my eyes again and again. It was difficult reconciling the two images as one and the same person; the apparent innocence in her at the dorm room at Yale, to the dominatrix in the military boots and trimmed box at the hotel in Chicago.

Despite having been duped by Brandt and knowing at a gut level he had used Marina, I thought appealing to him online might grant me some measure of control over the footage he had of me.

I added my own postscript to her life, typing into a scrolling field part of what I'd written for *The Stranger*, likening her to Lady Godiva.

In exiting the site, I knew, despite knowing her real name, and everything about her, I would never bring myself to use it. To me she would always be Marina Kuznetsov from Russia.

Twenty-two

In the middle of the night I awoke into complete darkness hearing voices. I thought it was a dream, before I realized it was coming from outside my window.

Glen Watson was drunk, loud and alone, struggling to open the apartment foyer door.

I watched him enter the building.

I went into the kitchen, put down a pot of coffee, and drank it black. I turned on my computer, trying to muster a sense of confidence to push on with Fennimore's material.

I got nowhere.

Instead, I logged back on the net, navigating to Marina's memorial site again.

It had become a perpetual digital procession of strangers drawn in a similar way to the lugubrious public mourning displayed in the wake of Princess Diana's death, Elton John swapping out his ode to Marilyn Monroe for Diana, as if the same tired emotion fit all such occasions. I watched the hit count rise on the page, even as I was logged on, a silent vigil honoring her passing, disparate strangers adding to an online digital remembrance book.

I was about to log off, when I decided to do a search on Glen Watson. Nothing came up.

I put the word 'Hermaphrodite.' It came up as a hit.

I clicked the link, a page slowly loading in a looping five second postage stamp video of Glen in a wedding dress and garter belt, jerking off, his hand going back and forth on what turned out to be an unusually large cock, even for a man.

The site was linked to other sites – from sexual fetishes, dominatrix and S&M sites, to ass-worshiping and ass-flogging, anal-gaping and fisting, to caning and bondage.

Despite the second wave of legitimate college student sites, the Internet was still a vast uncharted wilderness, a predominantly male frontier of inarticulate longing, outcasts willing to tolerate dial-up services, to make do on the edge of nothingness; a discontent reaching back to an innate male need to explore – maybe no different than how all new frontiers were explored.

Had anybody ever considered Columbus' real motives for exploration, for who sailed away from the comforts of home and family who had not rejected society? Who dared take their chances in the unknown rather than the known world?

Internet porn was a continuation of that age-old male yearning, a journey into uncharted waters, into what was now a post-modern pixelated wilderness, an unregulated territory of bits and bytes, men drawn as ever by the lure of sex, by the mystical call of sirens.

I came back to Glen's site through a series of links given to a sub-category called Shemales, or Chicks with Dicks, the models arrestingly female from the waist up. They seemed like a mystical third sex, bringing to mind something I had read in Plato's *Symposium* concerning the supposed origin of Love. He described the true nature of humanity as hermaphroditic, humans in ancient times possessing both male and female sexual organs. In this hermaphroditic state, humans had enjoyed twice the power of contemporary humans. It had been a situation that so troubled the Gods that Zeus tore humanity apart, yet to his surprise he discovered that all the separated sexes did was spend their time trying to conjoin.

Plato contended this was the origin of love, nostalgia for that former state of wholeness.

Glen seemed the embodiment of that idea.

In scrolling down the page I saw it was state of the art in terms of pushing online content. Save for a few static teaser images from her magazine spreads, the site was driven by a pay multimedia engine, where for a basic $69 a month you gained access to another world.

A ruffled velvet curtain suggested what lay just a few clicks away.

I signed up.

What materialized was the image of a small apartment in a digital choppiness of buffered content in what ultimately proved to be a feed devoid of sexual content.

Of course there was no refund.

Into the early morning as I tried valiantly to continue working on Fennimore's series, I kept coming back to Glen's site, struck by the perpetual gray feed panning back and forth, bringing to mind the omniscience I supposed God endures, tracks of existence eerily signifying nothing.

In a concatenation of time that had spun itself out in an endless procession of hours I fell asleep at some point at the computer, only to awaken again to the sound of my fax machine.

The message contained a single line: 'I've been sick. Are you free to talk?'

I faxed back a scrawled Yes.

Fennimore monopolized the conversation as he always did, a voice in my head relieving me of the burden of my problems for a time.

What came to the fore again was his struggle with his creative legacy, his own mortality.

I roused but couldn't feel any real emotion other than

understanding this was maybe the inevitable legacy of the writing life, a growing solipsism of discontent and last words for even someone like him.

He said, 'I don't have much time, Karl. Have you been working? Have you found me a victim yet?'

I hesitated.

'I knew providing you with money hadn't been the right thing to do. It went against my better instincts.'

I had my hand to my head. 'I'm trying, honest to God, I am.'

'So what is it?'

I struggled to find an answer, before saying quietly, 'I lost the context of why I write.'

Fennimore settled, appealing with quiet insistence. 'We've come so far, Karl, you and I. Let's not fail each other, okay?'

I answered like a penitent. 'I don't want to let you down, Perry.'

'All writers go through this, Karl. The point is to not give up.'

I had my hand to my forehead. I could feel the pressure of my eyes burning. 'I wish I could be what you want me to be.'

'All you've lost is a sense of perspective, Karl, a point from which to look back on things. Everything that is *you* is still within you.'

I could almost feel the stirring of ideas and memories as he talked. It was good having that voice to listen to again.

I began to say something, but he preempted me. He was off on one of his monologues.

'You know what drew me to you initially was your evolution as an artist, your work lying between the politics of Steinbeck and the irreverence of Salinger ... How many writers can co-exist in two stories, in two realities? But you did. I remember reading the descriptions of the landscape and rural farm life in those first novels of yours, and I knew you had *lived* this in your heart, that longing for land and security. That would have been enough of a story, compelling in its own right, but I saw where you wanted to go even early on … I think it was there all along, in the way you used "the boy" throughout your first novel … the boy's eyes meeting the eyes of his father in the rear-view mirror, his father daring him to speak. "Who wants their father to be anything other than their father, other than someone to talk to on the simplest and most honest of terms?" That was the boy's lament …'

It was a line verbatim from my first novel. I had never been addressed with such candor.

Fennimore said softly, 'You see, Karl, I know you better than you know yourself … That is one of your more authentic lines, written from the heart, no doubt.'

He pushed on. 'I don't expect you to answer me. I just want you to listen. What your agent gave me that first time over lunch was chilling; the snuff tape vignette unnervingly brilliant. But it wasn't until I read your earlier work that I put everything in context … that I saw your range, where you had been and arrived at in the passage of intervening years. There was a story of untold loss there, a middle story of self-doubt.

'I can still remember reading in your first novel, in the context of having seen the tapes, that sequence of "the boy" arriving at the house of his father's mistress, skulking around the perimeter, edging closer, finding his father and the woman just sitting and talking in the parlor … It was so devastatingly mundane. There was genuine pathos between the father and the woman. They were playing cards. That's how the boy came upon them.

'That's what unhinged the boy of course, the anti-climax of what he eventually confronted … absolute ordinariness. It's what legitimized his loading the chamber of a shotgun outside the house.

'Of course, from the boy's point of view, it was the woman's fault. I got that. If only she could be removed from the father's life. Logically, and thematically, it would have worked, the boy killing her . . . a *mere* boy with that single-minded intensity of youth trying to establish a code of honor in a world he didn't fully comprehend . . . It could have ended there, with her murder, the boy forcing his father into complicity in covering up the murder. What a trap the boy had set. What father would ever give up on his son?

'I watched it all unfold toward her murder, the way the mistress made a move toward the boy, seeking understanding, or simply wanting to live . . . and the father grabbing at her, pulling her to the ground, his hand over her mouth, stopping her screams as the boy fired the gun again. In that moment, the woman lost faith in the father. There was nothing between them, the father suddenly fighting for his son's survival. As a reader, I understood it was over for her. I know she did, too. This was about a father reclaiming his son. It had all moved beyond a point where there could be any reconciliation. Something would have to be done.

'Life happens in such moments of revelation, Karl. I remember thinking at the time: Let the boy turn now in the stony silence of indecision, let him leave them and us to contemplate where things might go . . . The trick in fiction is to know when to end a story, where to stop, to let the imagination roam. The narrative instincts were all there for the scene to simply end, but then it didn't and I knew right then this is most probably how it happened in real life. The craft had been overtaken.

'I still remember your description of the boy after he shot the mistress, then glumly handing the gun over to his father, "with the look of a boy who had just shot a bird with a slingshot, looking to his father to right things" and the way the father spoke, taking the weight of the shotgun, relieving the boy of the coming burden, pretending some solution could be found, easing the boy out of the house, and onto his bicycle … the boy starting toward the glow of lights in the distance, hearing moments later the peal of a single gunshot. That's how it happened, isn't it?'

I hesitated to answer so directly, to admit to having killed my father's lover.

Fennimore sensed it. 'I don't care about the mistress, Karl. I'm talking about something different, something more essential to you. Your father's suicide was the only way he could escape you, right?'

I found it hard to form the words to speak. I was shaking. 'What do you want from me?'

'Want? This is a triumph, Karl, not something to despair over. Give up any fears about me bringing the law into this. We are talking about other matters. She's an incidental character in a grander story of you, Karl.'

He kept leading me away from that initial anxiety, appealing again to me.

'I want us to be equals. Isn't the dream of every artist to be read, but more importantly, to be understood? Your work straddles a divide between the nostalgic naiveté of blind faith in the boy, through to the psychotic searching of an agnostic in those vignettes your agent sent me, the boy, now a man, taking the life of his victims for no apparent purpose other than to understand what struggle might feel like.

'You described a loss of faith, tapped the emptiness it can bring to a soul. You know, in my time in Vietnam, I used to think about the life of Jesus Christ and those forty days and forty nights he spent alone being tempted by the devil. I used to ask myself, what if he'd found nothing, no salvation? I think it's a real possibility. It would explain our world more than the gospels do. What if his sacrifice was simply keeping us from that truth? Maybe that is the great triumph of ordinariness. It keeps us away from *Truth*. It occupies us with other things …'

I tried to say something, but Fennimore persisted. 'Let me finish … please … That is what I want Harry to confront, Karl: the impasse of faithlessness in the persona of the boy, of what he became in later life. I know the desperation of how badly you wanted to succeed. I understand what might or might not have transpired under the stress of life at that time, Karl. We have to find our way toward destiny. At times we have to create inspiration. It's not every day you arrive in the jungle of Vietnam and kill a woman and a child. At times to get back to that intensity, you invent or you recreate …'

I cut him off. 'I don't think I want to continue this conversation.'

But he persisted. 'We are one, you and I, deep down we are. We see with the same vision. We were inspired by tragedy, by circumstances beyond our control. Art is not choice, it is compunction. It's an affliction of the soul …'

I shouted, 'Leave me alone, goddamn you! Stop talking!'

Fennimore was quiet for a time. 'You contacted me that first time, Karl.'

I said, 'It's over.'

'It can be, if it's for the right reasons, or are you just at an impasse? That's all it is, Karl, an impasse.'

'What do you want me to do?'

'I already asked you: find us a victim, someone worth saving.'

Twenty-three

Light was just showing in the East as the call ended. I felt as close to a nervous breakdown as one could get, and then I considered the Catch-22 of the situation, that to be truly crazy you would not necessarily know you were crazy.

I took it as a measure of sanity or of further delusion. It was hard deciding really.

I was, though, relieved to have finally achieved a level of parity with Fennimore.

The tremulous effects of his words inspired me in the way that only he could. He validated what I had given him. He was asking me to continue.

Standing in the kitchen, I made a cup of coffee, letting the aroma filter through the apartment.

Across the way, I stared at Glen's apartment, at the close quarters we all shared. I was coming to inhabit this place more and more. It was becoming home.

As I poured the coffee I dwelt again on Fennimore's deep connection to me, for if he understood the context of my work, I, too, had read and understood him as well. We were born of the same crisis.

In his first novel, *The Watchman*, I had come upon an autobiographical hint that his wife had left him in real life, his protagonist, Harry, driving around at night to where his wife had moved simply to catch a glimpse of his only son.

He described the feeling as one step removed from

normal life, speaking of himself in the third person as 'The Watchman.'

It was a throwaway scene between plot elements and yet it had clued me in to the reason he wrote, the surveillance scenes born of real experience. There was a poignant passage midway through the novel, Harry alone in his car watching his wife, when he cast back to his first tour in Vietnam. As a nineteen-year-old watchman at a base outpost, high on hash, he recalled for a fellow soldier an event which, up to a mere six months previous, had been the most significant event of his life – prom night in his old man's station wagon when he had tremulously gotten to third base with his date, a girl he had known since the fourth grade, since that's what was expected on prom night.

Delivered with the solemnity of an older voice, the watchman's memory hinted at a narrative level what terrible things had happened in the interim, how innocence can be lost anywhere along the way – in his case, the act of a nation going to war, in calling forth what otherwise might have been normal souls to the far reaches of the globe.

The voice had a subtle rage that had instilled the entire novel with the foreboding sense of what Harry was capable of doing, and indeed, what he had already done to a young woman with a child strapped to her back.

I knew intuitively without all the events he described aligning as they did in his life, he would never have become 'the Watchman,' remaining in real life just a cop investigator.

In many ways his life was not unlike Lori's, or anybody else's, in as much as we all, if pushed, could define our life around one single event or period. I think this shock of self-awareness can yield a work of genius if faithfully captured. It had happened for Fennimore in his first novel, awakening into consciousness in the grim surveillance of his wife in a car in the dark. It provided a point of dramatic reference to who he was, pre- and post-Vietnam.

There was an exercise I used to give students, adding the line 'In the days before my death' at the beginning of their work. A simple point of reference could fundamentally change a story, giving it a sudden immediacy and tension, capturing what happened at a subconscious level when the entirety of a life came into revelatory focus.

Of course, the problem came with the second and the third work, in the cold reality of self-analysis, in the diminishing return of mining an old vein, for the truth is, the intellectual range of what we truly understand may be but one shrill note, one song. In the quiet of my own professional failure, I had confronted that dilemma as I struggled beyond my second novel, bogged down with The Opus, trying to move beyond the precinct of my own immediate experience.

In a sobering way, in the cool pale light of the rising morning, I summoned such thoughts, for in time I would tell Fennimore such things, speak as his equal. We would need the shoulder of each other's faith.

Our relationship would span one last novel. If this was Fennimore's swan-song, it was also mine. I was not so much being saved, as being given one last chance to attach the right voice and tone to a mutual sense of failure, to exit a career on my own terms, to deliver my own eulogy.

Despite the inspiring praise of his compliments, I was still unsure if a protracted, mutual academic understanding of our own creative purpose wasn't a poor substitute for the authenticity of the subconscious, for what arose from spontaneity.

Could we again resurrect a working relationship?

What we were trying to do this time around was re-create something that had organically happened between us. Now, we had the expectation of the past as a burden. We would judge our progress against Fennimore's plot twist with knight and night, always mindful of that initial success, at how easily our relationship had developed considering we had never talked.

I was aware whatever we created between us would always be one step removed from who we really were as artists, that the artifice of story and character would be evident to a discerning eye, but then, who read that closely anymore, who sought answers in books?

Setting aside such stalling questions, and in the continued absence of Lori, I turned once again to my computer, settling on the more immediate question Fennimore had squarely set before me, whom to murder?

A half-hour later, I found myself descending into the basement to the coin-operated laundry machines. Passing a makeshift weight-room, I spied Vladimir already up and working out, benching weights the size of locomotive wheels, a cassette tape of classical Russian music incongruously playing in the background.

I would have figured something like 'The Eye of the Tiger', a *Rocky* style self-centeredness.

Almost immediately, I imagined a scene early on for the book, Charles Morton coming upon Vladimir, a first, and then a second time, descending into the basement armed with his Clinton mask, observing the tremulous count of a bench-press set, entering on the straining count of say eight or nine, pushing ever so slightly against the bar, Vladimir's muscles spent, incapacitated, his windpipe crushed, dying, staring into Morton's eyes.

Back upstairs, I committed to Word what I had seen and envisioned in the basement, feeling something take shape in the recess of my mind, attaching a silent movie of images to a voice, the composite parts slowly coming together in the unfolding of a legitimate plot.

It was there just beyond my grasp, and yet it was hard justifying why exactly Vladimir would die.

I took to closing and then opening my eyes, looking inward and then out again, jabbing at the keys, snatching details.

Sometime later my concentration was broken by the sound of Elena vacuuming in the hallway.

I regretted how things had turned out between us.

For a time I did nothing but listen to her working. The vacuum cleaner was suddenly switched off. I heard the slosh of a mop in a bucket of water and a scent of pine cleaner hung in the air.

Picking up a pack of gum from my desk, I went over to the peephole. I pushed a stick of gum under the door and waited.

A moment passed before she stopped and took it.

'You know, of course, Mr Karl, I will need a second piece for Sergei.'

It felt like a small triumph, the ease of forgiveness from someone like her.

I passed under another stick, and listened to her retrieve it.

She said directly, 'You know, it hurt what you said about me, that I have no dreams.'

I could see her in the fisheye lens. I said contritely, 'I didn't mean it. I'm sorry.'

'My mother says you live off your wife. You do nothing with your life.'

I laughed with an audible disdain. I wanted to keep her engaged. 'What would that *peasant* know about anything in America? You know, I'm surprised they even let her into America.'

Elena answered, 'They let anybody in.'

'Well maybe they do, but when those people get here, they have to obey our laws. I should tell the authorities what she is doing to you. In America children have more rights than adults. She could be arrested for hitting you.'

Elena giggled at the mere suggestion.

'And you should demand to be paid for the work you are doing here.'

I heard the snap of the gum in her mouth. 'Mr Karl, please, you are being so ridiculous.'

I said, 'Yes, I am being ridiculous.'

My eye was to the peephole. I could see she wanted to ask me something. 'Is there anything else?'

She answered, 'Do you have a TV?'

'Does this mean we are friends again, Elena?'

I could see her eyes moving toward the lens, trying to look back at me.

'Could you please record *The General Hospital* on the ABC Channel 7 for me?'

'*General Hospital*?' A smile spread across my face. 'Don't tell me you are planning on becoming a doctor?'

She answered with a strident formality. 'No! I want to learn how to marry a doctor.'

My heart ached for her. 'You know, in America you could become a doctor. All things are possible, even for you.'

'Yes, but I would prefer not to work, just like you, Mr Karl.'

The candor of her answer stung me. I didn't know if it was meant to be a compliment.

I heard Sergei in the background, and Elena call back in an animated way, 'Look, Sergei, I found a stick of gum.'

She said in a hushed voice, '*The General Hospital* on the ABC Channel 7 if you please, Mr Karl. I will be very happy with you.'

*

Holed up in my tiny bedroom, I wrote straight through into darkness, blanking out the fact Lori had not called. It was, I supposed, well and truly over.

I used the reality of my circumstances to spur me onward, so that by early afternoon, with almost seven hours of writing accomplished, I felt things coalescing for the first time toward a sense of what I was after really. I threaded the disparate narratives of Ivan, Elena, Sergei, Marina, Lori and Glen into a novel of sexual dystopia, multiple lives tied together in the hunt for a serial murderer.

As my energy flagged, I eventually closed Word, ready for sleep, but not before revisiting Brandt's site. I wanted to see if he had posted my eulogy, comparing Marina to Lady Godiva. It wasn't there.

Below the animated gif of Marina's two personalities fading in and out was a flashing link to a piece on the two suspects in custody for her murder.

Of the two, DeShawn R. Tate's biography at age fifteen proved the more horrific, dehumanizing and yet predictable. We had grown accustomed to the nightmare plight of such animals. Born with medical indications of fetal alcoholism and a crack cocaine addiction to a mother with HIV-AIDS, DeShawn was the last of eight children and had spent the entirety of his childhood in state care, shuffled through a series of foster homes. At age nine, he was diagnosed with Attention-Deficit Hyperactivity Disorder (ADHD) and medicated on Ritalin. Age eleven, he ran away from the County foster facility and began life on the street as a petty drug runner for the notorious *Gangster Disciples*. Before his twelfth birthday he had fathered three children by girls all under the age of fourteen. The mothers and babies were on welfare.

His accomplice, Antonio Jones, age seventeen, had fared no better in life, his life less tragic, but riddled with a criminal record related to drug dealing and weapons charges. He had been arrested eleven times and served two jail terms. At the time of his arrest he was found to be carrying an unregistered .44 Magnum, along with two grams of crack cocaine. He was listed as the father of six children.

He had entered a plea-bargain with the state's attorney admitting to being an accessory to aggravated assault, rape and kidnapping, stating he and Tate had found the victim, disoriented, drunk and lost in the ghetto, where they had both raped her in a nearby alleyway, before leaving for a period of two hours, in which time they stole a car, got high, then returned to rape her again with four accomplices. Eventually, Tate slit Marina's throat before her body was dragged to the stolen car which they set ablaze.

It was a chilling summary of her last hours.

As I was about to log off, an updated scrolling marquis titled 'Breaking News' announced Brandt was coming to Chicago to film a segment on Cabrini Green for his current documentary. He was soliciting volunteers for a shoot, the event coordinated with the reconciliation vigil hosted by *The Stranger* to highlight conditions at the projects. Brandt's site linked to that of *The Stranger*.

It was a further affront – this alliance between Brandt and *The Stranger*. I had been there at the close of her life. She had called me in the hours before she died. I felt a wave of anxiety fill me. I knew I should have kept myself from following the story, simply let it go, but I couldn't. It was the sort of distraction that could sidetrack my work with Fennimore, keep me from inhabiting our story completely, and yet I couldn't stop myself.

Instead, I entered Marina's memorial site.

Her parents had posted a collage of Polaroid scans of her, depicting what must have been the most perfect existence of prep schools, European vacations and pony rides.

I scrolled through them, struck particularly with an image of her as an eleven-year-old with her father at the changing of the guards at Buckingham Palace.

In wellingtons and a mackintosh, she was sticking out her tongue at an impervious Grenadier guard – an innocent image foreshadowing her anarchist tendencies, what she would become in less than a decade.

Twenty-four

Lori called just before eleven o'clock. She didn't reference Marina or *The Stranger*. She was 'holed up' as she put it at Deb's as she talked in a furtive whisper that made me wonder if I was simply insane.

I didn't dare reference what had gone on between us.

Apparently she and Deb had dined the previous evening on an early bird special two-for-one coupon at Deb's all-time favorite restaurant, Red Lobster.

I said just so I could enter the conversation, 'I've always said they have good food there for people who don't know what seafood *is*.'

Lori's voice faltered. 'You don't want me back, is that it?' then it trailed off. I could hear an undertow of fragility.

I pushed, not willing to give in. 'It must really suck out at Deb's if I'm the alternative, right?'

'It's never the same without you.'

'Is that a canned phrase from one of Deb's greeting cards?'

'It's from the heart.'

I closed my eyes. I thought I had moved past needing to speak to her. I said, 'That sounds like co-dependency to me, Lori. I read about it. It's real dangerous. You never want to get caught living through somebody else. They used to have an old-fashioned name for it: Love.'

'Don't! Just don't be like that right now. This is me ... not you, I admit it. I dragged you into this.'

I said, 'I'm done.' It was the first time I had asserted any general control over a situation with her. And then of course, I somehow regretted it. I said, 'So what's really wrong?'

It gave her an opening.

She began talking in her usual rambling way. 'I'm looking at this from the point of view of how old we will be. I don't know if I have it in me to chase a toddler at forty-five years of age. Last night there was trouble, Deb was up half the night waiting on Misty. Ray and I stayed up with her. Ray tried to calm Deb and got out some old albums of Misty as a kid, a book of firsts, locks of hair from a haircut and her first nail trim, her first tooth ... Ray's good that way, level-headed. He balances Deb.

'I ended up making cocoa for Deb as Ray managed things as best he could. All Deb did was cry and then scream and bang the table with her fists. Two o'clock came and went. It got crazy. Deb started calling Misty's friends. She was making a show of herself, but you couldn't stop her. She was demanding Misty's friends tell her who Misty was with.'

I interrupted her. 'That was Deb's first big mistake, naming a daughter Misty. It's a name for a pole dancer.'

Lori barely broke stride, just kept on talking. 'I tried to stop Deb, but there was no stopping her. Misty is a version of Deb. I told Deb, the more she confronted Misty, the more things were going to escalate. Deb was just getting back what she had dished out to Dad years ago, but Deb couldn't take it. She didn't want to hear about the past. I tried to explain things to her. She told me to get out of her house.

'Ray ended up taking me aside. He said the last thing she needed to hear was common sense. I sat down with the photo albums. Deb was still making calls. Someone cut her off for calling so late, and she started screaming and went upstairs and dragged Misty's clothes out of the closet. She flung them to the bottom of the stairs. I stayed with Ray in the kitchen, stopping on a picture of Misty at her ninth birthday party at Chuck E. Cheese. She stumbled in drunk after 3 a.m. Her boyfriend dropped her off. He didn't even wait to make sure she got into the house.

'Deb overpowered Misty, dragged her to the floor. She had Misty's arms pinned like on that show *Cops*. Deb started screaming, "This ends now!"'

I cut in, 'So how did it end?'

'Deb's contacting some crisis intervention boot camp for angry teens, run by some Gulf War drill sergeant.'

Just hearing Lori parroting the phrase 'crisis intervention' made me roll my eyes. We were all using the new lingo of daytime pop psychology, and yet the wearisome encroachment of this juvenile slut granted me a psychological reprieve from the solipsism of the previous nights. In just listening to the trials and tribulations of this suburban drama, I suddenly felt better about my own life, or it connected me to something larger but ultimately inconsequential.

I went to the toilet, the cordless receiver cradled between my shoulder and ear, listening.

Schwartzy came to mind as Lori kept talking. The reference to *gulf*, as in Gulf War, had a nice double entendre of estrangement. I could see the blurb on a newsstand rag, 'Gulf War – *Tactical Strategies from the Front Lines of Parenting*' – I wrote it down on a piece of paper as Lori kept talking.

There were still even more forthcoming details about Misty, all bad, a tattoo and an STD that had to be discreetly taken care of the previous summer. Deb was at her wits' end.

I said, cutting in, 'You know what Misty really needs, and I'm not just saying this either! Get Ray to drop her off at the edge of a ghetto and have the fear of God put into her that she'll get gang raped. That would be my God's honest idea of crisis intervention.'

By the time I had it said, the allusion to Marina was already made.

We were both silent.

I tried to say sorry, but Lori said, 'I'm over that. ... OK? I overreacted. It was work-related. Deb brought the article to me at work.'

I thought: This is all good, make Deb the bad guy.

Then her tone and the subject changed. She mentioned, among other things, a sale on Men's *Gold Toe* Windsor Wool Blend socks at an outlet mall, something apparently warranting a sixty mile drive to the middle of nowhere. She was considering heading out there to make a day of it with Deb. Misty might go with them as well if Lori could get the better of her.

It was information delivered like it wasn't exactly for my benefit. She would be home later that evening, if that was OK with me, which, of course, it was.

Then I heard Deb's voice in the background. She said my name.

I shouted, 'You reap what you sow, Deb!'

Lori hung up.

For a time I did nothing, just stood in the warmth of the sun's rays with a reptilian bliss.

It was midmorning of the Sabbath, a day of rest, and I did just that.

Twenty-five

I slept until the afternoon, awakening to rain softening the edges of the world. There were lights on in most of the apartments, the street slick and emptied of life, the sky backlit by the city centre miles downtown.

The Stranger's reconciliation vigil at Cabrini Green was two hours away. Undecided if I would go, I took a shower for over half an hour, letting the apartment steam up like a Turkish bathhouse.

I had put off the inevitable for too long. I picked up the phone and called PALS, intent on breaking through the protracted bureaucracy I inevitably encountered when calling outside the prescribed time.

A caregiver answered.

I learned my mother had taken a turn for the worse. She had pneumonia and was in a local hospital. The caregiver advised me the home had tried to call on numerous occasions, leaving messages on my answering machine. I had received no such calls, but then Cantwell got on the phone, insisting she had left five messages in the previous week. They were all assiduously documented, since she got to charge for her time as intermediary. She read off the dates and times.

'I'll check the machine, Jane. I'm not good with technology.' I was overly appreciative, in the way I always was when it came to Jane Cantwell. 'You're doing the Lord's work up there, Jane. God bless you.'

Jane replied in a curt way. She wanted to know if I was

coming up and gave me the hospital contact details with an efficiency that suggested, well, *efficiency*. There was also the hint that, now that my mother was out of PALS, she would probably not be accepted back. PALS didn't have the medical facilities to manage her care. There was no discussion regarding my mother as anything other than a client, no reference to her personally. She had been with them for over a decade.

I said, 'Jane, may I ask you something? What color are my mother's eyes?'

She hung up on me.

I decided against venturing into the minefield of my mother's failing health. There was little I could do for her. In the year and a half since my last visit to her, I had come to see her as other than she was now, inhabiting instead that roadside picture taken after my father's suicide, standing in her gingham dress. It was how I wanted to remember her, as decidedly pretty, her hair pulled back with a stray wisp of hair touching her cheek. I could see the allure in her, what she had been in the eyes of men, the eyes of my father.

I think beyond physical birth or death, there are other more important moments that define us. We come into consciousness under the sway of circumstances, under the influence of nature, but also nurture. I wanted to remember my mother as she was at some remote time in the past, not as she was now. It didn't define who she was to me.

There lay another story behind my mother's past, before she married my father, before I entered her life.

I'd learned about it from a first cousin of my mother, Louise, a bookish woman who tracked my early success. Older than my mother by a matter of half a decade, Louise had kept in touch through a series of dime postcards giving brief accounts of her home life, acknowledging, too, the passing of my birthday each year with a card addressed to me containing a crisp $10 bill.

In later years, Louise sent me a handwritten note with a clipping of a review that had been published in the *Milwaukee Journal Sentinel*. She saw I was passing through on a reading tour and wanted to meet and accompany me to visit my mother.

Her letter rounded out a general sense of accomplishment that my family, however distant, felt involved in my initial success. I made the journey North in a full size rental, stopping off near the place where my mother was born to pick up Louise.

She emerged in a fox stole, carrying a black purse that looked like an anvil. Travel was something special for her, making me smile and suddenly appreciate the luxury of the automobile. She smelled of moth balls.

We spent the day together in that fall of 1985, one of the few times I ever took my mother out of PALS. She had suffered a series of mild strokes. At sixty, she was one of the younger residents, her former beauty still evident on the right side of her face. Palsy had slackened the other side, the eye perpetually weeping and moist.

Even then, my mother moved between states of understanding and confusion. This was the woman who had emboldened me with the desire to achieve and I wanted to care for her in a way she deserved. At the time PALS had seemed the most humane decision, with its expanse of lawn and pastoral surroundings. I was looking toward fame.

Over ruby port in the art deco interior of the Milwaukee Astoria, Louise kept showing my book to a series of waiters and guests. The hotel was by then part of the Best Western chain, its grandeur diminished. I felt vaguely self-conscious, like John Boy Walton accompanying the sloshed sisters of Walton Mountain who had brewed Daddy's recipe.

Louise got hammered in a way that only old people got hammered; she became sentimental and nostalgic, hiccupping and putting her gloved hand with the mother of pearl button to her mouth. She regaled us with a history of the heady years of World War II, when she and my mother came into their own, my mother plucked from the obscurity of a backwoods life to work at a munitions factory in Sauk Prairie, Wisconsin. My mother's twin brother Karl, after whom I was named, had died in the Pacific two months earlier.

This was not something my mother really wanted to hear about, and yet she hadn't the power to stop Louise, nor I the compassion to prevent her. I wanted to hear this story.

The good side of my mother's face registered emotion but it was hard to tell exactly what she was feeling.

The reconstituted version of Louise's story re-emerged the next day in the flair of a hangover, as I visited the place Louise had talked about, her words a backdrop as I stood where my mother had once stood.

As I drove out to my mother's old home, I had a moment of clairvoyance, watching as a car appeared, trailing across a hillside on one of those scudding cloudy days. I saw my mother's hands pink and withered from the washing of clothes; watched her put her hands to her face. She knew something terrible was coming, instinctively turning toward the house as the engine grew louder, seeing her father in the door of his barn, the breath of horses at his back.

For her entire life, up to that point, she had lived according to the seasons, mushrooms and cornbread in the fall with venison and game birds; through the winter months of smoked meat and cold stored squash and rutabaga. She had never been more than ten miles from her town in her nineteen years of life.

Less than two months on, after Karl's death, she left home with butterflies in her stomach and her head a turmoil of sadness, duty and patriotism. She had her picture taken on the day she left. Louise was invited.

Louise had shown me the photograph the previous afternoon at the Astoria, a picture that troubled my mother greatly. It was a stylized sepia shot, 1944 scrawled on the back in a blotted inky blue. My mother looked purposefully older in the way it was back then, when movie stars were older, when maturity and security meant everything.

But there was something else about the photograph Louise wanted us to see. Beyond the focus of the portrait was a blurred eerie image, what looked like a human form passing through the photograph, a face turned toward the camera. For Louise, there was no doubt it was my mother's brother, Karl. She believed in the transmigration of the soul.

Later that same day, after having her photograph taken, my mother left home for good. She had been advanced a small sum of money for travel to Sauk Prairie, which she picked up at the post office. A week prior to leaving she had answered a classified listing by two women seeking a third roommate. My mother intimated it was only the second time she had spoken into a phone.

The story advanced by degrees, the women speaking in turns to her, one and then the other. Both worked at the munitions plant. They were home when she called only because they were working the night shift that week, as there was more money to be made on the night shift. They could arrange it. Helen, that was the more forward of the two, had an arrangement with one of the bosses. It was all discussed with the faint hysteria of two innocents fast becoming wise to the ways of the world, though not corrupted yet, for men were dying on various continents after all, and amorous glances were all that could be expected.

With the money advanced her, my mother bought a coat and hat. She had her hair done. She offered up those facts in the quiet of the Astoria, remembering Helen as a gorgeous blonde with a penchant for married men.

She remembered, too, buying a copy of *Calling all Girls*, a magazine that never fully decided on how it felt about its readership or the role of women in general. I checked out issues of the magazine years later, the articles written in a confluence of patriotism, pragmatism, and sublimated misogyny, and titled accordingly – 'When Duty Calls,' 'Miss Always Available,' 'Plan for a Husband,' 'No Proposal By Moonlight,' and 'It's Smart to be Stupid.'

My mother ate her first meal alone in a diner.

Louise had a stack of postcards my mother had written to her over the years, a correspondence she let me photocopy. She held them out like a royal flush at the Astoria. According to the postcards, my mother ate the daily special, liver and onions.

I imagined my mother looking out into a world that hurt if she stared too long.

In the slush of passing cars, she watches a squat store owner roll out two barrels of winter apples. There was a general store that had gone out of business across from the diner. I sat where I felt she would have sat, away from other people.

It is during the meal she notices him, a kid in an ill-fitting, hand-me-down three piece suit, wiping clean a bowl of stew with a heel of bread. He makes eye contact with my mother and smiles, says something to her across the diner. They are about the same age. My mother instinctively looks down and blushes. This is when she sees the tattered leather case. Here is another enlistee from the farms.

I can only imagine her thoughts were with her brother, the loss still fresh and deep.

The kid's attention drifts as my mother looks up again. I see him harassing the waitress, pointing at some custard pie in a mirrored case. As the waitress bends over, the kid smacks her on the ass, and the middle-aged men laugh. The waitress keeps a straight face, like she doesn't know exactly what's going on, and the kid keeps asking to see this or that pie. Even my mother is smiling.

These are the quiet ways everybody deals with a world at war.

And so it goes, through the lunch hour, the ping of the bell over the door, men in overalls bellying up to the long counter, drinking coffee, smoking cigarettes, listening to a radio. An old fashioned voice speaks of fluctuating futures for hogs, wheat, and corn. Then comes the war news, a major offensive on a Japanese island, resistance fierce, mounting casualties. My mother mentions it in the postcard she is writing.

I imagine the kid growing quiet, my mother closing her eyes. If not for the war, she would have been at home now, in the murky flicker of a kerosene flame in the barn, seated with the side of her face against the warm barrel stomach of a cow. This was what she knew, nothing else.

She opens her eyes again, adjusts to the light streaming through the window, and tries to make do as best she can.

On Main Street, the low winter sun is skewered by the bayonet of a young Union soldier atop a Civil War memorial. The soldier could be her brother, or the kid in the diner, so much so she turns, but the kid is gone.

In a store, there are no nylons because of the war, so she pays to get eye liner etched up the back of her legs, all the time thinking of her roommates, of a question they asked her on the phone, whether she has a sweetheart. She is breathless with anticipation, moving toward adulthood, toward the vast expanse of a world where she will know nobody. The war has done this to her. She is moving closer to my father, to a man who will turn and take a second look at her in years to come, because she will hold his gaze absolutely, if only for a moment.

All this was laid out in the tarot of cards Louise had kept through the years. It was just a matter of aligning the cards with an understanding of who my mother was.

For now, the bus is an hour off yet. My mother doesn't feel much like going out into the cold so she returns to the diner for a slice of pie. Someone puts their head round the door, says it is snowing hard out in the county.

It grows dark. Snow falls. My mother waits. She drinks what they call a bottomless cup of coffee, which gives her the jitters.

She leaves the diner and makes her way to the bus depot. It is shut. A simple handwritten sign says, 'Service Cancelled.'

Snow melt runs down her neck. She feels cold and her feet are numb. The eye liner seams are a smudge of ink. She has wasted money, given in to vanity, and feels deeply ashamed and stupid.

What do people do when they have no money, where do they go? She is resolute against spending her advance, but she is moving toward the inevitable, toward the local hotel that charges salesman prices, covered by companies, not by ordinary people. She tries to look as forlorn as possible, but business is business. It does not matter that she is going to serve her country, or that her brother died defending it.

Something hardens deep within her.

She sits on the hotel bed and counts what money she

has left after paying for the cheapest room which shares a communal toilet down the hallway. She feels like crying.

I stayed in that same room. They kept records in a ledger and she was one of the last to register that night. There was a blot of water on the page, her signature shaky.

She hangs her new clothes at the end of the bed, lies down in a slip that stops at her knees. There are voices in the hallway. The stairs creak. Doors open and close. She waits until the sounds die, then puts on her coat and goes down the hallway to use the toilet.

The day slips past midnight. My mother is still awake, listening to the rattle of the window. She reads from the Gideon Bible, sets it aside, gets up and stares into the street. The snow has stopped.

There is something haunting about the slate blue moonlight.

The town looks two dimensional. She presses her face against the glass. She can see the Civil War memorial, the dark sentinel soldier glazed in ice. She turns away, but in doing so her eye catches the red pulse of something in the street.

Cupping her hand to the window, she peers out and sees a figure standing in a recessed doorway, shuffling from foot to foot. She sees the tattered leather case and realizes it is the kid from the diner.

He, too, had been waiting for a bus.

My mother puts her coat on over her slip, passes the amber glow of the lobby, and hesitates. A grandfather clock ticks away the seconds. She feels her heart beating as she opens the front door. She goes across the street to the kid. He is freezing cold; his face huddled into the collar of his flimsy coat.

She takes his hand in hers.

*

Three weeks later, on her way to her job at the munitions factory, she will feel a strange vertigo, her stomach queasy, not yet knowing the burden she carries, a child rooted to the lining of her uterus, pregnant by a kid who will be blown to pieces in the Pacific.

I learned this story from Louise, who cried because she was drunk and sad and so deeply affected by my mother's present condition. I didn't ask what had happened. My mother was pregnant, and then she was not pregnant. It was never mentioned again.

I went and viewed the attic conversion where my mother had stayed throughout the war, taking my book to gain me access to the boarding house. From the window, I stared at the remnants of the factory where my mother had worked, saw in that line of vision what she would have seen when she stooped and looked through that portal, the most improbable place you could imagine for making bombs. There were cows in the distance.

In the historical records of the town, her name was listed in a ledger of those who had served, all there in black and white.

I pictured my mother with those painted legs; I think the kid must have felt he had died and gone to heaven. Did he tell the story to other GIs hunkered down on the beach of some god-forsaken Japanese island?

Did that kid die in the Pacific? All the better if he died thinking of that night.

We need such saints at the door of heaven, the uncorrupted. What else is there, what is the alternative, the life of Lori's sweetheart, Donny, a guy holed up in a cinderblock house in a rundown part of Green Bay paying alimony?

On the other side of life there will, I hope, be a renewal of interests. I see a perpetual night in that room with the kid, or a replaying of that moment when my father stopped and took in the full extent of my mother's beauty. To see my mother in any other way would only diminish who she was. I think if there is a God, and a Heaven, these are the gifts that will be bestowed on us.

And so, in the silence of the apartment, I unplugged the answering machine and the phone, breaking the connection to her in this world.

Twenty-six

Aimlessy walking amidst a small enclave of boutique stores, I came upon Elena and Sergei eating ice cream at a vintage diner. Both had their backs to me, sitting on stools, facing an assortment of flavored syrups and gleaming metal mixers. I thought better than to approach them, especially given Sergei's temperament. He was absurdly dressed in a royal blue sailor suit and britches.

As I stood watching, Elena must have seen me in the reflective backing of a pie case. Dressed in a simple pinafore, like an Alice in Wonderland, she turned and winked at me in acknowledgement of our secret pact with the VCR recordings.

I smiled with a genuine kindness that maybe only a child could engender in another human being. She added a modicum of normalcy to life, our quiet alliance spanning a generational and cultural divide. I again saw in her a child-like Marina, inquisitive and impetuous, longing to be understood, to be taken seriously as an adult.

I moved on, trying to free my mind of everything, yet there was no escape. The independent bookstore featured, of all things, a display of Mitch Albom's book arranged in a pyramid, underscoring the reach of his words, tugging again at my own sense of failure.

I wanted to topple the pyramid.

I couldn't determine if my cynicism was just a self-defense mechanism against my personal sense of failure, my inability to seize and exploit any single event happening to me. I was still struggling with Fennimore's voice in my head, wanting to bring it forth, to attach a greater meaning to what we both had to offer. It was my last chance.

As I stood looking at the pyramid, I thought back to my initial instinct to try and capitalize on the infertility issue, how quickly it had gone nowhere with Schwartzy.

Understanding something was a particular madness, but capturing it was where genius lay.

Was there something wrong with me? It was hard deciding.

In retrospect, I understood my problem, or more exactly, I understood the cultural phenomenon of a Mitch Albom, of that sort of success, Albom's genius lying in the declarative title of his book, a masterful summary statement, a mini-narrative geared toward overworked publicists slogging through so many press release pitches seeking radio or TV interviews. The key was, you didn't have to read Mitch's book to know what it was about, the title itself descriptive and redemptive, posing and resolving a question, in Mitch's particular instance – The Meaning of Life.

It was so patently formulaic, working equally well for money management, dieting, relationships, drug addiction, teenage behavioral issues, anything in the sphere of personal responsibility and what could be overcome through willful self-determination or tough love. It was a format admirably suited to daytime TV, the introduction of a crisis along with an arbitrating life counselor in the first segment, while after the break, the quick wrap-up prescriptive resolution, the entire encounter reduced to what Warhol had so wryly defined as everybody's fifteen minutes of fame.

Again I came back to my own sense of failure. If it was that easy to deconstruct, then shouldn't it have been just as easy to reconstruct, to do as he had done? That was the charge Deb had leveled against me. 'Do something!'

Of course, I had done something, but that *something* just hadn't been what Schwartzy had wanted. I watched my reflection stare back at me in the storefront window. Why had I been unable to deliver on his directive for a declarative piece on the medical advances available to infertile couples? Why had I not at least established a relationship with him?

Of course, I knew the answer, for no matter what I could have given him, he was never going to understand its sociological import, this, a man whose sole contribution to modern culture centered on the illusive grail of a five minute workout for six-pack abs.

Just thinking back on the humiliating episode of his not returning my calls sickened me. I saw it as one of life's great injustices that an asshole like him didn't live anywhere but under a bridge, homeless, hungry and dying of syphilis, and not as he did, in some upscale East Side dwelling of cocktail parties, as a so-called socialite and barometer of New York couture and lifestyle.

Of course, all he did was sell magazines, that was his out, simply making a living, his gift most particularly hiding truth from people, deciding what not to publish, as much as deciding what to publish. He knew what people wanted, or didn't want. I thought back to what Fennimore had so vehemently argued on the phone, that in the so-called greatest democracy in the history of civilization, where you could say anything you wanted, there was in the end nobody really listening.

I understood now the absolute truth of that statement, thinking back to Lori's unsettling reaction to Glen Watson, understanding Glen made a better looking woman. It had prompted Lori's rambling confessional story of her life with Deb and their relationship with their father. She had been more comfortable revealing family secrets, talking about her abortion and the past than discussing what she was truly feeling. She had her answer for the Marinas of the world, the high school *sleaze* moniker, but how did one confront the courtship of this third sex, this enclave of alternative lifestyle, this co-opting of the feminine by males?

I guess the answer lay again in Deb's prophetic sperm bank quip, setting my intrinsic worth as troubled, discontented partner, against some anonymous donor sperm alternative – a subtle and ominous reality permeating, not just my life, but male life in general.

As I started walking again, I wondered how many of those here were truly gay.

Were we not, at some level, in the midst of a reactionary male protest or male fear?

I understood that though Glen represented a vanguard reactionary protest of an emerging preening maleness of hot waxing and silicone implants, it was ultimately a grand façade, whereas the brave new world of science was affording women real alternative choices. The option of the sperm bank had become one of those quantum power shifts between the sexes.

The reality was, a woman no longer had to be quintessentially feminine to attract a mate, and maybe this explained the emergent phenomenon of Hermaphrodite as abject metaphor of male obsolescence, a role reversal for males as the modern Madame Bovary of unrequited love.

I thought it a valid point, at least as relevant as anything Mitch Albom had to say. In my stay-at-home reality as solitary writer, I'd borne witness to the change, to the coven of daytime TV talk show hosts acculturating a generation of women to the idea of single parenting, the 'empowerment' card played to those trapped in loveless or broken marriages, boorish males dragged on stage, confronted by relationship counselors to 'shape up or ship out.' It was a revolutionary charge led by a new breed of self-directed females subtly, or not so subtly, eschewing heterosexual love for careers and independence.

So, why not this sperm bank alternative, this mantra of feminine empowerment against the shackles of marriage? Why not anonymous sperm bank insemination from a laundry list of checked genetic attributes, offspring spawned without the pain of courtship and heartbreak?

Against my better judgment, wanting to stay sober for the Cabrini Green vigil, I went into Ivan's triangle bar.

A chill had settled on my shoulders. My pores were still open from the steaming shower. I ordered a hot whiskey with a wedge of lemon.

For a time I tried to set my thoughts on something beyond the guilt of not heading to Wisconsin to be with my mother, casting my mind instead to the no-man's land near the Illinois/Wisconsin border, picturing Lori and Deb and a hapless Misty at the discount mall. I imagined them shedding the bittersweet memories of childhood and adolescence, reconciling the tumultuous affair family life most always was, but never bad enough to stop the majority from trying to do better. They'd had a pretty rough time by all accounts.

Maybe Misty could be saved from herself.

I looked up as a sudden eruption of noise broke my train of thought. Ivan and Vladimir had entered the bar, dressed in their Sunday best. Dasha followed behind.

I watched Ivan teeter and stare into the gloom of the bar, his hand on Vladimir's elbow for support. A half foot taller, in a simple white shirt, black slacks and with short cropped hair, Vladimir looked like a member of the Church of Mormon.

I shrank into my stool, moving my face out of the amber glow of an Old Milwaukee beer sign.

Dasha, holding a sack of quarters from the coin laundry, headed toward a poker machine along a narrow passage that led to the toilets. She saw me and said something to Ivan, who looked up.

Staring down the end of the bar, Ivan raised his voice. 'Ah ... Mr Karl! On a Sunday, where is this wife of yours, Mr Karl?'

'Working,' I said stiffly.

Ivan laughed. 'Working? This is something we must understand!'

He came toward me, with the over-intimacy of a drunk, taking my elbow. 'You are such a man who can make his wife work on a Sunday. We are looking for such a woman for Vladimir.'

He raised his hand, repeating what he had just said in Russian for Vladimir's benefit. Then, he put his index finger to his lips and, looking at Dasha, pressed my arm again with a conspiratorial air. 'Wait, we cannot have her hearing this secret.'

From across the bar Dasha scowled as Ivan stomped his foot in the most agrarian of ways, like he was dealing with a stubborn bovine.

Suddenly, Sergei entered the bar, and spotting Dasha, went toward her. He stomped his foot, demanding money. He was a miniature tyrant, underlining my decision to have him murdered in the early pages of the novel.

Elena appeared moments later in the doorway. She aligned

herself with Vladimir, getting on to a stool beside him, handing back change I supposed was from the ice cream parlor. I watched Vladimir put his hand on Elena's head in the most gentle of ways.

Ivan called towards Vladimir. He leaned into me, pulling at my arm. 'He is learning from the school books of Sergei.'

Smiling, I replied, 'The unambiguous sensibility of the second grade. Vladimir will speak like an innocent. Let me assure you, he will make the most eligible of husbands.'

Vladimir looked perplexed, his attention divided between Russian and English, awaiting the translation.

Elena took Vladimir's hand and said something in Russian. He simply nodded and turned toward me.

In that instant, he seemed suddenly diminished, his hand in hers, giving me a revelatory sense of solving what Fennimore had requested of me: I had found him a victim.

I would murder not Sergei, nor Vladimir, but sweet Elena. She looked at me with a quiet insistence, defending Vladimir; of all of them, she was the most cosmopolitan. I felt the sudden rapture of what it was to find a plausible thread of narrative. I would hitch the complicated dreams of Elena to my earlier observations of the family's collective existence, the entirety of her life and death suddenly coalescing in a series of director's takes, the lure of the VCR tapings a legitimate reason for Charles Morton having befriended her.

I found myself reconfiguring elements of the plot, settling on bringing a grievous existential pain to bear in this, the final book, the murder happening all because Morton had unwittingly left the snuff tape in the VCR instead of the blank cassette for taping *General Hospital*.

I imagined Elena caught in a wave of emotional uncertainty, having viewed the snuff tape, Charles Morton peering through the doorway, entering slowly, trying to placate the girl, to make her understand, catching hold of her to stop her leaving, trying simply to *explain*.

The tape could be destroyed if he could calm her down. I saw it as a spiraling sequence of circumstances, sweet Elena, someone Morton had grown to love with a paternal intensity. This was never meant to be! He would shout that inside his head, know this even as he suffocated her, trying to quiet her, her legs thrashing, her body going stiff, then limp; her murder ultimately involving her lack of faith, the same way my father's mistress had lost faith in him.

It was a revelatory breakthrough. I had a viable foil in Vladimir, this indentured servant manacled to the curious ways of the family. His alliance with Elena was well established.

Everybody knew it.

I even thought of allowing Elena a secret boyfriend for dramatic purposes.

Ivan's hand hit my back as I resurfaced. When he smiled his teeth showed black and crooked.

The bartender served up a tray of shots, the first of what proved to be a series of toasts.

I envisioned a dumbstruck Vladimir, under police suspicion by virtue of his sharing quarters with the family. I pictured him reduced to an agitated, monosyllabic defense, already condemned in the eyes of the law, turning violent, insistent on his innocence, the veins showing against the tautness of his neck.

In the days after his interrogation, I imagined Vladimir shivering, muttering to himself, struggling against the shadow of suspicion. I saw troll-like Dasha coming upon him, lifting her burden of laundry; the inchoate thoughts that might befall her, this boorish peasant with her withered apple face.

I felt the excruciating longing to get started.

I simply closed my eyes.

Then I decided it would be as I had first envisioned it, Morton, not Dasha, coming upon Vladimir in the basement. It seemed all so natural, the dragnet of accusation closing around a flagging Vladimir lost in this foreign country, Morton entering near the end of a tremulous bench press set, Vladimir struggling momentarily against Morton, before succumbing to the inevitability of death, the pressure of the bar slowly crushing his windpipe. This was Morton at his sinister best, a master orchestrator of converging events, playing them to his own advantage, throwing police off the trail.

It had the narrative hook of pulp fiction, a page-turner, serving both mine and Fennimore's interests, giving Fennimore's protagonist, Harry, a purpose, a single-minded obsession with what investigators were too quick to call a closed investigation, linking Vladimir circumstantially with Elena's murder.

Harry would prove them wrong.

I continued to let the drama unfold as another round of shots was set before us, all of which I obligingly paid for, since that was how it was done in Mother Russia.

I saw a blubbering Sergei, that pup, set before the cameras day in, day out in his little suit, speaking with a gathering earnestness of a child foisted with sudden responsibility, de facto spokesman for a family as the only one who could really speak English. This would be his coming of age in America, this incongruous, delectable little morsel set before a rapt audience of gays, his fifteen minutes of fame.

With the onset of a floating inebriation, I pictured a pitiful Ivan going down to the basement in the days following Vladimir's supposed suicide, turning his chess pieces in his pocket, pressing play on the cassette player and breaking down when he heard the plaintive homeland music.

*

Back at the apartment, I drunkenly worked up a brief outline of what I had envisioned in the space of a half hour and faxed the material off to Fennimore before belatedly heading out for *The Stranger*'s Reconciliation Vigil.

Twenty-seven

My vodka-induced boldness dissipated on the El ride downtown. Against the mottled sky, the ruinous grid of Cabrini Green's burnt-out project blocks looked post-apocalyptic, figures pushing loaded-down shopping carts as others gathered around oil drum fires amidst piles of rubble.

On the articulated arm of an industrial cherry picker, rising above a series of basketball courts, I saw Brandt in a director's heavy down jacket with a fur-lined hood shouting directions through a bullhorn to a cluster of people. There was a fire truck nearby and a pyrotechnical expert was busy rigging a car Brandt wanted driven onto the basketball court for a night-time re-enactment of Marina's murder.

Off to one side was a makeshift table under a tarp with a banner advertising *The Stranger*, the display featuring posters of the two suspects charged with Marina's murder, along with the magazine cover using the shot I had taken of her.

Except for a few Goths, the booth was relatively empty, social reconciliation and an easing of racial tensions clearly not of genuine interest to *The Stranger*'s readership. Their disaffection lay elsewhere, in a white suburban ennui best expressed in the primal lyrics of Nine Inch Nails' Trent Reznor songs I imagined being written in the fishbowl nightmare of a high school homeroom, or the back seat of a Dodge minivan.

As I approached the booth, a raccoon-eyed Goth earnestly

handed me a laminated sheet on one of the suspects charged with Hampton's murder.

I merely scanned it before handing it back to her. She had another sheet concerning the demographic breakdown of those on death row, highlighting a marked prejudice toward juicing young black men. The Goth asked me if I was against the Death Penalty.

Of course I was.

She had a petition she wanted me to sign.

As I passed it back, I said, 'I don't know why, but I have this vision of you baking tollhouse cookies in polyester pants at forty-five.'

She said, 'Fuck you!', rousing interest within the booth where I spotted the green fluorescent Mohawk of Chastity.

She glared directly at me. Nate was there too, looking every bit the double of Elvis Costello, in horn-rimmed glasses and a velour-tipped blazer, a stylized uniform more suited to London than Chicago. He was also wearing a silkscreen print featuring the younger suspect in Hampton's murder, DeShawn Tate.

Nate was in the midst of talking to a troupe outfitted as grubs and billy-club-wielding military police. They were rehearsing a scene. When he finished he came toward me, reaching into the inner pocket of his jacket and producing an envelope. It turned out to be my paycheck. He said with professional detachment, 'We didn't have your correct address. We thought you'd end up here.'

I didn't quite understand what that meant.

He didn't mention the messages I'd left on the answering machine, though of course it was glaringly obvious he had listened to them.

I said bluntly, 'I think I touched on some salient points about race, economics, feminism and nationalism in my article.'

'Editorially, we didn't know how to position the story. I hope it finds a good home.'

I felt my face flush. There was no appealing to him. Pointing at his shirt, I said loudly, trying to bait him, 'I think you should have gone with a parody of *Air* Jordan here, Nate, something like a *Scare* Jordan shirt – a silhouette of a black man flying through the air with a knife, you know, something more indicative of the true racial divide ...'

Nate made a move to turn away, but I grabbed at his arm.

He pulled away, shaking his head.

I could see Chastity talking with some of the Goths.

I said, 'Look at them, Nate. This is who you surround yourself with, these fuckups! I could have elevated what you put out, give it something of significance. You advertise cock rings in your magazine, and I'm the supposed sick fuck here, is that it? This was my story! You stole it from me! If you had any decency, you'd admit that!'

Chastity tried to intervene, but Nate said, 'I got this.'

He actually approached me again with a renewed boldness. 'I gave you a chance and all you did was incite. As a publisher, I have an obligation to heal. You had some vendetta against Jordan before this story. Well, here's the reality of the situation. Jordan is of his time. He sees himself as a basketball player, not a *black* basketball player. That will be his legacy, his essential colorblindness. Either he'll be a historical anomaly or he'll represent the future of our democracy, the ability to recreate a sense of self, to move on.'

I laughed. 'I love it, Nate! You're a fucking sociologist now? Go back to cock rings, Nate. You think Jordan can change the historical reality of slavery? What's an NBA salary, a surrogate payment for race reparations? As long as Jordan's happy, then everybody should be happy? That's what it amounts to!'

I heard a voice behind me and turned. It was Brandt. He said candidly, '"How come our sports heroes are more immune to criticism than our Presidents?" That's one of the better lines from your article, right?'

I was taken aback by Brandt's sudden intervention. A camera was trained on him as he changed the subject and said, for the benefit of the camera, 'This is the last person who saw Emily alive.'

I quickly corrected him. 'I was the last person to *speak* with her.'

Brandt nodded and pointed to a break between two low blocks, again, more for the camera than for me. 'Emily was initially raped in that alleyway.'

I was suddenly incorporated in what he was filming. He had me by the arm, leading me.

The camera lingered on the shot, the alleyway no longer cordoned off, a ribbon of torn yellow police tape flapping in the light breeze.

Brandt pointed to a hinterland of buildings beyond the ghetto, the neon light of a bar sign glowing in a strip of liquor stores and pawn shops. 'Her last call was from a bar two blocks away.'

He kept speaking to the camera in a narrative of events.

I removed his other hand from my arm and disengaged, taking a few steps back.

I didn't catch everything he was saying, lost in a silent contemplation of what had happened – a woman I had known so briefly, perhaps fallen in love with, had been raped and murdered right here.

I felt an overwhelming sense of sadness.

I flinched as Brandt raised his voice slightly. Seemingly, he had asked me something. 'What's interesting is this curious phenomenon police psychologists often describe regarding murderers who try to connect with their victim, showing up at the scene of the murder ...' He turned and looked directly at me. 'You ever hear of that phenomenon?'

'I came because Nate owed me money, Brandt.' I held up the envelope like it was evidence to the camera.

'... and your interest in Emily's site?'

I could tell this was an ambush. I turned to walk away, but the troupe converged. There was no obvious passage out. I regained a measure of composure. I looked at Brandt. 'Marina was *my* story originally.'

He said with a tone of outward provocation, 'Her murder?'

I looked directly at him. 'If you have a serious question, then ask it.'

'I find it interesting you're still calling her Marina. Let me ask you something, did she ever break out of character?'

'No.'

'And what do you make of that?'

'I think she believed in what she was trying to accomplish. I got a sense of a person trying to make a difference. We connected at a political level.'

'How did you feel when she called you at home?'

I said flatly, 'It felt like work.'

Brandt opened his eyes with an exaggerated incredulity. '"It felt like work"! Are you kidding me?' His voice got excited. 'A woman like that calls you, and "It felt like work"?' He looked at the camera and then at me again.

'How long did it take you to tell her it felt like work? Take a wild guess, go on. Or let me just tell you. I have it written down here. Fourteen minutes and seven seconds to be exact. I'm guessing it validated something deep inside you, to have her call you like that?'

I said, 'We connected politically. She wanted to be taken seriously.'

Brandt laughed. '"Connected politically!"' You're delusional. You know what she really thought of you? She thought you were a *joke* with your business card.'

I felt a flush of emotion. 'So why did she call me?' I kept staring at him. My voice got loud. 'You're a fraud, Brandt, and Marina knew it! Everybody knew it. There are testimonials plastered all over the site concerning her involvement with you. She called me from The United Center and said she was leaving you! You backed out on going through with the protest during the game! You were afraid of getting arrested and having a criminal record! She called you chicken shit to do anything real!'

Brandt looked toward Nate. 'Nate will back me up. You showed up at *The Stranger* with your face all scratched up after Emily's murder.'

Brandt turned and stared pointedly at me. 'Explain that! You met up with her. One of the suspects in custody stated Emily was already injured and disoriented by the time they found her. She left after talking with you. She went to meet you!'

I cut him off. 'Didn't you just say Marina thought I was a joke? Why would she go to see me if that was the case? You've got to get your story straight, Brandt. That's the first dictum of journalistic integrity. Get the facts straight.'

'How about the scratches on your face, explain them? I have two witnesses, Nate and Chastity.'

I felt a growing sense of ease that all this could be handled. Brandt had lost credibility in the swirl of accusation. It was obvious he was prejudiced against me. Even Nate was looking nervously at the camera. Did he want to be associated with Brandt's mockumentary after all?

'To set the record straight, Brandt, and this is purely out of personal consideration for Marina's family, not you, to help them put this all to rest and find closure, on the afternoon I interviewed you and your troupe, my wife *miscarried*. We'd been trying to get pregnant through IVF. Right before the interview she paged me. I didn't go home. I did the interview instead. I'd committed to doing it for Nate. Hours later I showed up, she wanted to know where I'd been, why I didn't call. We got into a fight . . .'

I stopped and started again. 'My wife's doctor's name is Dr Louis Goldfarb. It's all documented! You're responsible for Marina's death, nobody else. She stopped believing in you. That's the reality. You weren't what you pretended you were! She walked out of The United Center, and you let her!'

Walking across the vast expanse of tarmac, I saw a cluster of women holding up signs that all read – I Have Nothing To Sell You —

They looked like an etching, like a memory fading.

Back at the apartment, I set out a prepared meal of chicken with cornbread then lit a candle in the center of the table to mark the occasion of Lori's return.

She arrived home just after ten o'clock, weighed down with a cache of discount clothing.

She proceeded to parade around the apartment in an impromptu fashion show, twirling at the end of an imaginary runway with a goblet of Diet Coke in one hand.

She looked surprisingly good in high heels.

I toasted her. I was willing to cede to wherever things might take us. I smiled and didn't mention anything about Brandt and what went on at Cabrini Green. Nor did I mention my mother's condition, not on this night. Nor did Lori mention Deb or Misty.

The phone was still unplugged.

I felt we were immune from outside influences, from Cantwell, Brandt, Nate, and Hampton, too. It was the first time I saw her in my mind as someone other than Marina.

She was a Yale debutante. It would never have worked between us.

I clapped enthusiastically as Lori announced the steep discount on everything she'd bought, as in 'Compare at $—', walking back and forth with a series of labels marked with either a red, yellow, or blue circle, giving a running commentary: A 'sixty percent off 600 thread count Egyptian cotton sheet set with matching valence,' a 'one-hundred percent silk cocktail dress at eighty-five percent off, *thank you very much, DKNY!*' and a 'Ralph Lauren cashmere hoodie with matching gloves at sixty percent off suggested retail!'

She made the *ka-ching* sound of a cash register racking up each sale, pumping her arm like she was pulling the handle of an old-fashioned register.

I did likewise as a show of good faith: '*Ka-ching!*' This was my destiny. I smiled until it hurt. I never got the actual price of any item, but they were all, I was confidently assured, 'steals', and 'unbelievable deals.'

We were on the other side of whatever had troubled her. A decision to endure despite everything had been reached out in the burbs, where, once upon a time, we might have employed quiet contemplation and prayer, a beseeching intercession to a higher power and the fingering of rosary beads. Instead, her hands now ran through innumerable dresses, skirts and coats, a tactile shimmer of satins and silks, satiating longing and desire.

She produced my 'mid-calf Gold Toe socks at seventy-percent off' and I said, 'Ka-ching!' in unison with her. Ka-ching. Was there another word like it?

I felt the shrill ring of a cash register in my chest, at the center of my being, where the soul allegedly resides.

Twenty-eight

My mother passed five days later, peacefully, in her sleep. I took the call in the early morning, as Lori got ready for work. I never mentioned she had been moved to the hospital.

Lori had never met my mother, but she stopped in the bedroom when I told her and held me and cried until I could feel my own eyes water.

There was the meeting with Goldfarb to contend with the following Monday. Lori was also in the midst of a performance review at work. She had to get going.

She kissed the crown of my head, dressed and left the apartment with a discount tag hanging from her skirt.

Most of the arrangements for the funeral were made over the Internet, Lake-of-the-Woods Funeral Home surprisingly high tech with a website featuring coffins, urns and funeral wreaths.

I sent off an e-mail, angling toward the fact that I was the sole surviving relative. The director e-mailed me back minutes later, suggesting something discreet and dignified, a cremation ceremony at $3,800 with a floral arrangement and a Death Notice posted in three papers of my choice. It was a package listed under a pull down menu.

I hit the send button and got a receipt.

It was the first legitimate service I had paid for online – expedient, cold, and terrifyingly modern. At the beginning of my mother's life, could she, or any of us, have imagined such a reality?

I was back from the funeral by late Sunday afternoon in the last brushstrokes of failing light, and disconcertingly bumped into Glen Watson in the courtyard heading out.

He was dressed down, in flats and a sweatshirt, his hair pushed back off his face.

Evidently, even he seemed to celebrate the Sabbath.

I pretended to not recognize him. It was an awkward moment.

He was carrying a small perforated box that smelled like alfalfa.

Glen said, 'I keep looking for that book of yours that you used to quote from down at *The Portal*. I liked what you had to say.'

There was no comeback to a compliment, at least nothing worthy of what it can mean deep down to an artist.

I said, 'I'm still working on it.'

Lori called just after seven. She was running late. There was a last minute project she had to finish up given we were heading to Goldfarb's suburban clinic the next afternoon.

She didn't reference my mother's funeral, nor did I. It was an uneventful call.

I set the phone down. Across the way a light went on in Glen's apartment.

I stood up and hid behind my blinds.

He was standing in bra and panties by an open window, the intermittent glint of a cigarette burning against the gray dark.

I thought he saw me and moved away.

Retreating to my desk I logged onto his site.

His apartment came up in a slow sweep of jittery footage that switched between various feeds. There were camera icons you could select for various rooms.

I clicked through the various silent views for a time, seeing Glen on the screen and across the courtyard at the same time. It was a disconcerting feeling.

Minutes later Glen closed the window. He painted his toes sitting on a chair, raising his feet on the table.

I saw the perforated box beside him. When he was done with his toes, he picked it up and went into his bedroom, turning on a light over what turned out to be a large glass cage with a boa constrictor coiled under a heat lamp.

I clicked a camera icon, the feed materializing.

Rapping against the glass, I watched Glen's face level with the snake, rousing it. It uncoiled in slow motion.

The box contained two white mice.

He dangled the one and then the other by their tails.

It was over in a matter of moments, for the first mouse, the yawn of the constrictor opening to accommodate the passage of the creature through its body, the other left nosing the glass cage.

Fifteen minutes later I watched Glen pick up a bundle of mail in the narrow hallway and return to the kitchen. He started sorting through it, paying bills, balancing his checkbook, prompting me to get up and look across the courtyard, his frame illuminated by the jaundiced yellow of a low-wattage bulb.

It was like staring at a rip in time, inhabiting two dimensions simultaneously.

From my vantage point, an apartment above and across from his, I could see a TV on in the background, tuned to a televangelist program.

Picking up my remote, I scanned until I found the station. The sound added a sudden religious soundtrack, the minister's voice calling viewers to greater glory, reading off names of those who had pledged prayer vows, beseeching them to experience Christ's love by touching their TV screens.

A scrolling text along the bottom of the screen gave a toll-free number.

I dialed it.

Fifteen minutes later the minister called out my mother's name and the name Glen Watson.

I watched him look toward the TV as the minister expanded on the prayer pledge I had phoned in, calling on the Lord to help Glen figure out who he was.

I felt an invisible connection to the scene, a voyeuristic echo of how I had watched and called Frank Klein, and, further back, how I had dogged my father, trying to influence the destiny of others.

Moments later, Glen broke the fourth dimension. He opened his window and said across the courtyard, 'I'm sorry to hear about your mother.'

I felt my heart jump, but kept watching the screen. I didn't go to the window.

Glen turned away quietly. Maybe he thought he had been mistaken.

His circumstances were really no different from my own. His site was not so much about pornography, as a niche given to human understanding, seeking what may be our collective goal, to be observed, to know we are not invisible to those around us.

Before I logged off, the camera moved in a slow sweep, finding him alone in bed.

I watched him take his cock in his hand and begin masturbating, though in the streaming video it came across not as performance but as part of the shabby ordinariness of life.

Before ejaculating, he turned from the camera, cradling into the fetal position in what could only be described as an unadulterated aloneness, an isolation so many have run from, and the horror Lori intuitively feared.

Lori arrived home just after ten o'clock.

I pretended to be sleeping.

She came to the door, looked in on me like a mother, then went into the kitchen and filled out paperwork as I drifted toward sleep.

Twenty-nine

There was no mention of the funeral as we took a train out to Highland Park for our Friday afternoon meeting with Goldfarb at his suburban clinic. We got off by the manicured lawns of Ravinia Park in a barren woodland. Early in our marriage, we had made a summer ritual of riding the train out to hear the Ravinia Concert series, bringing a picnic basket, blanket and wine.

Lori took my hand, the same memory registering, though neither of us said anything as we stood facing the linked fencing of the desolate park.

I felt the pressure of her thumb against the palm of my hand. She said quietly, 'We'll be late.'

Goldfarb's office was as yet some three miles beyond the train station. We had gotten off early at the prompting of Goldfarb's secretary, suggesting the walk might give us time to clear our heads. A recreational trail, newly fitted with a series of Cardio Health & Lifestyle stations, straddled a woodland ravine.

Off to the sides were palatial lattice-windowed homes that could only be aspired to, although at one point in my life, I had entertained the possibility of actually owning one.

Trying to define myself against this wealth, this success, I looked askance at Lori. She seemed curiously unaffected. We lived such utterly different lives.

I was suddenly aware of the jingle of what sounded like a leper's bell, and looked up just in time to avoid being run over by a retired couple on a tandem bike. In their matching tracksuits, they looked like an advertisement for a geriatric daily vitamin.

As they passed, I spoke for the first time since we had gotten off the train, saying wryly, 'I bet he drank Bourbon and smoked right up to his quadruple bypass. Now his idea of a good time is a curative enema and prune juice.'

Lori smiled and squeezed my hand.

Through the leafless trees, I saw life pass by on a conveyor belt in the cruelest of game shows. A stylized rooster weather vane atop a multi-car garage fitted with a basketball hoop; a tennis court set near a kidney-shaped swimming pool covered over for the winter. Further on, resplendent crystal shimmered in what must have been a Tiffany chandelier, something I saw through the circular window of a marbled foyer. The quintessential image of a Jaguar parked in a crescent driveway.

All this had passed beyond me in the space of just a decade, as others had advanced up the corporate ladder that led to such places, if you were lucky.

What struck me, again, was the memory of my early success, that first book deal coming just after college, when others were starting out. It had been easy to view them as drones caught in the first stages of the corporate trap, in the seventy-hour-week hell of some management consultancy, in that beleaguering humiliation that supposedly built character, but most certainly built careers.

I understood in coming late to a relationship with Lori, in the wake of my failing career, in the affected swagger of bohemian independence and talk of artistic immortality, I had hidden, not just from her but also from myself, the true nature of what I *really* wanted – success and money.

Perhaps what had drawn me so intensely to Hampton's real story was her willful rejection of what I would have snobbishly clung to. I wanted to understand her sense of purpose, the artistic integrity of where true genius lay, in a sphere outside ordinary aspiration, in the solace of self.

Lori sensed the hesitation in my gait.

Despite my best intentions, I said, 'Do you envy them?'

She slowed momentarily, saying with level-headed banality, 'You can't change what is. All it will do is eat away at you.'

'You're right,' I said, my gaze lowered to the gravel fitness path, submitting to the crook of her finger like a hook.

Fifteen minutes later we were interrupted by the same couple on their tandem coming back along the trail. In a brief moment of eye contact, as the guy waved, I saw the real him, his grimacing struggle against mortality. It was one of those fleeting images that at one time I might have shaped into an exploration of our collective consciousness, tapping into the despair of my father, whereas now it was just a passing image, signifying no more and no less.

I sensed Fennimore lurking in the back of my thoughts, and knew deep down there was no novel in me, not anymore, at least not of the sort he wanted. We were pushing on with developing the murder of Elena. Though, in meeting her in the hallway, in the days she came and watched *General Hospital*, I found it hard to conjure the act of her dying. It seemed heedless in a world beset with so much pain. I wanted only good things for her.

There were harrowing days ahead. I was aware of that, of what I might I have to inflict upon her.

I felt the creative slippage in the way a football player might lose that extra yard. What I regretted was the indeterminacy of what constituted the end of something, short of that physical hit, something that maybe answered why so many before me in my craft had opted for a shot to the head.

*

In the sullen quiet of another mile we said little of significance to one another. Lori talked about Lyme disease and the profusion of the deer population in suburbia. We were, it seemed, a nation of *Bambi* lovers, or so she said with a not altogether sympathetic attitude toward the deer.

It struck me as strange coming from her, prompting me to ask, 'Have *you* ever hunted?' a meaningless question that hit into the heart of something I couldn't have anticipated.

The illustrious Donny had been a hunter.

I didn't catch Lori's exact words, but instinctively broke my stride, not at the mention of Don's name, but at the fact that she was still calling him Donny. He inhabited a time and place in her life that I would never occupy. He had been her first despite everything that eventually happened.

Tracking wild game was something Donny's family did each fall, a seasonal killing, gutting and skinning of some unfortunate Bambi. Lori went on to describe points on a buck with the authority of someone who knew what she was talking about.

It was the nearest I had got to the heart of the Donny story, aside from the abortion. Though in the end the story did lead back to the abortion, Lori answering in a roundabout way the question I had posed earlier, if she envied everything here.

Up in Milwaukee there was a rich suburb just like this along the lake shore. Every Sunday Donny and his parents used to drive there and play a game, Donny pointing to this and that house, asking his mother, 'How about this one, or that one?' then winking at his father, saying, 'How 'bout we pull over, and I make them an offer?' This always elicited the same response from Donny's mother, something Lori delivered with a foreign accent, 'I like what I got just *dandy* . . . I got me a chauffeur and the State Champion of the whole of Wisconsin.'

Donny's father and mother had been taking that drive for

an eternity of Sundays since they arrived in America, even before Donny was born, the suburban dreams always, seemingly, just within reach, but not quite.

I listened to Lori talk about Donny taking her on the same Sunday drive when she got pregnant, playing the same game, pointing at this and that house, all the while moving toward the subtle decision that would end in the taking of a life.

Again, the specifics were less important than her general tone, so I let her talk.

At the end of her story, she stopped and turned toward me. The angle of the light obscured her face. 'I don't think a life *here* was ever an option for me . . . It was always make-believe, just a game I played a long time ago.'

It was the closest I felt I would ever get to knowing who she really was, to understanding she had something to offer me.

I had mistaken her remark, 'You can't change what is. All it will do is eat away at you,' as level-headed banality, when it was, in fact, an instinct for survival.

Thirty

Goldfarb's office was located in a professional building from the Sixties, right down to its polka dot wallpaper, a place very much at odds with his office downtown, something I mentioned to Lori.

She said, 'It's the burbs, what do you expect?'

I had expected better.

Strangely, the listing under the address we had been given read *Gabriel's Promise*.

The office was on the second floor in a corner suite at the end of a long hallway that smelled of ammonia. Even the receptionist, a sixty-something woman wearing a turtle neck and shamrock brooch, seemed curiously in a time warp, her hair swept back in a bun.

She smiled as we entered the office. A nameplate on her desk read – Joyce Hartley.

After presenting our medical insurance card, I was given preliminary medical paperwork by Trina, a pregnant twenty-something medical assistant. She met my eyes with a warmth beyond professional courtesy. I was taken by her poise and apparent maternal glow.

Since the paperwork mostly concerned Lori, I let her fill it in.

It turned out *Gabriel's Promise* was *not* owned by Goldfarb, hence the obvious and vast difference between The Hancock Building and where we were. Lori had misunderstood, the agency being just one of many used by Goldfarb's practice.

I retrieved a glossy brochure detailing the agency's mission and services. It was essentially a catch-all for modern fertility counseling and placement services, the brochure's bulleted lists including open and closed adoption and fostering, gestational surrogacy matching, also a screening and matching service between infertile couples and potential candidates offering egg and sperm donation.

I looked up at Joyce and asked whether Goldfarb offered an in-house surrogacy service. The answer was No.

The suggestion that this was a step down from what we had expected hung in the air. In the uncomfortable silence, Joyce over-compensated and having read Lori's forms, said with a yelp of enthusiasm, 'How wonderful, you're a writer? I'm a big-time reader!', producing, as evidence, a worn paperback copy of Anne Rice's *Interview with a Vampire*.

I could have killed Lori for the wanton disclosure. We had previously agreed that on all questionnaires and applications, I was to be listed as a *Professor*.

I said, by way of imparting something meaningful on the subject of Rice, 'Did you know Anne got the idea of writing about vampires after visiting a relative dying of leukemia who had undergone a series of blood transfusions?'

That shut her up, affording me an air of professorial credibility.

I saw Trina look at me with a regard I only hoped to get from potential students, a look Lori had invested in me so many years ago.

In a private conference room, we were finally introduced to our alleged fertility expert, Mercedes Conrad, a thirty-year-old, who smelled like Puerto Rico and Spring Break.

Mercedes gave us an emotional account of her circuitous route to joining Nurse Joanne, relating how she had been a cocktail waitress at a hotel near Hilton Head, when she became an egg donor and eventual surrogate to her sister in Chicago.

There was no reference to any state accreditation or certification, just their self-professed abundance of nurturing, sensitivity, and love. She was still an egg donor with the agency, and was effusive in her praise of Nurse Joanne, reiterating the solidarity of those working at *Gabriel's Promise*. It seemed that the *lovely* admin assistant, Trina, was also not only an egg donor, but was currently wearing a state-of-the-art prosthetic pregnancy belly.

Trina was summoned over the intercom to the conference room, where she showed us *The Bump* – a realistic inflatable belly complete with the rolling, kneading motion of a bread maker. They had one they loaned out, and suddenly Lori was ushered from the room, leaving me with the literature and Mercedes.

In a valiant attempt at good humor, I glibly remarked that, at $799, the price induced a nausea not dissimilar to morning sickness.

Mercedes smiled with a condescension I wouldn't ordinarily have attributed to a Puerto Rican as she handed me a three-ring binder of what she called *Gabriel's Secret* – the agency's list of prospective donors and surrogates.

As Mercedes hovered near me, I felt obliged to peruse the intro. I stopped on the phrase 'Genetic Load Factor (GLF)', an in-house rating system for egg and sperm candidates, based on a laundry list of potential intellectual and physical attributes, including SAT scores, level of college attained, athletic abilities, and faith. The genetic load of what the agency dubbed Ivy League Donors (ILDs) was worth up to six times that of Traditional Donors (TDs), and eight times that of Anonymous Donors (ADs).

We fell under the domain of gestational surrogacy, Lori's eggs harvested and my sperm banked at an outsourced medical facility. All we needed from the agency was a gestational surrogate, an incubating womb. Our surrogate would be carrying *our* biological load.

As I waited for Lori's return, my mind turned again toward Fennimore.

Here was potential material for our novel, Charles Morton following Harry and his daughter to the place, stalking and then gaining the confidence of a Mercedes, fixing her punctured tire in the office parking lot, driving by in an unassuming manner, stopping to help her. They would strike up a conversation, Charles Morton intrigued, then wanting to sign up to donate his sperm.

I knew already in my gut Morton would kill Mercedes in order to gain access to the clinic, to the medical records.

In the latter part of the novel, I imagined Harry, caught up in a flurry of scenes that would see him delve into the vast complexity of the cryogenics industry. I saw him being lured out to a low rise medical facility amid some manicured industrial park for a final confrontation with Morton; passing through a luminescent deep freezer facility containing bodies in pods hooked up to frosted tubes and tanks of liquid gas, then on to a sperm bank of smoking cryogenic cylinders.

It was still a nascent idea, how it would all play out, but I had a chase scene in my head, something essential to any modern fiction that hoped to sell more than ten copies. It would be high tech, the gleaming chill of modernity. I thought of Charles Morton falling into a vat of liquid, eerily frozen in time.

You never wanted to kill off an antagonist, to really end a series. That was a dictum within the industry.

I felt a brave new world aura settling in the final pages of a series that began so long ago with the autobiographical scene of a kid in Vietnam.

Now, a quarter century on, I revisited an alternative ending I had fallen on back at the time when Schwartzy jettisoned me, an aged Harry staring at a ward of swaddled infants, facing the real possibility that his daughter, in the anonymity of a medically assisted pregnancy, might unwittingly have birthed the progeny of his mortal enemy.

There were some basic plot elements and issues of momentum to sort out, but Fennimore was a master of the genre. It was a subplot, but I saw it taking on a grander significance I felt might just eclipse Elena's involvement, saving her.

Mercedes made mention of the service's obligatory non-refundable $3,200 origination fee, bringing me back to reality. She felt the fee best paid without involving Lori, for obvious psychological reasons.

I stared at her painted press-on fingernails moving over the sheet listing the services covered – among other things, a pelvic exam, pap smear, urine pregnancy test, standard blood work, and setup charges associated with an Escrow surrogate account and coordination of the sharing of medical records with Gold-farb's office.

The fee was basically a figure pulled out of the air. There was, of course, no forthcoming disclosure as to the actual cost of the entire surrogacy process, an MBA double-speak reminiscent of PALS that immediately set me on edge, especially with the memory of my mother's funeral so recent.

As I handed over the check, I could hear voices in the hall.

Lori re-emerged into the conference room. She smiled in a self-conscious way, dressed in a maternity hoodie and magically pregnant, or looking so, with her inflatable belly.

The model was top of the line, featuring a realistic heartbeat and fetal kick, along with a pliable vinyl material that could be incrementally inflated and weighted to forty pounds, and an adjustable rib belt to induce lower back pain, bladder discomfort, shortness of breath, and fatigue.

Suddenly we were beyond the point of rational reflection, and I felt overcome with the unreality of reality as the transformation took place, Lori pregnant and not pregnant at the same time. At the back of things I was also mindful of an associated, but receding, memory of Marina as both Russian and American. Was Lori any different from Marina, or Glen Watson, who believed, despite a penis, that he was something other than a man?

Reality, in the end, was defined by our wants and desires, by how we saw ourselves within. I felt that truth sink in as Mercedes' voice faded.

I looked again at Lori, watched her come to believe she was truly pregnant, her hands instinctively reaching for her stomach in a pose of maternal contentment, her hips giving in, displacing the weight in the way only a mother could instinctively shift, while in perfect synchronicity, at that moment of true belief, Nurse Joanne entered the room and exclaimed in an exalted tone, 'Sister, pray not for a lighter burden. Pray for a stronger back.'

It broke the spell, Lori suddenly faltering, going down on her haunches, sobbing.

I watched her hold her midsection in a way I'd seen only once before, on the night she miscarried for what she felt had been her last attempt at pregnancy.

Thirty-one

On the silent train ride home, I sat facing backward watching everything pass in reverse. Lori sat across from me.

We were the only two in the compartment, given it was going in the opposite direction to the exodus of those heading for the suburbs.

I watched her leafing through the Potential Surrogacy Binder (PSB), complete with the social and personal history of each candidate. She was that old Lori who had intently scanned the parenting magazines months before. The binder came with a Score Card for personally rating the candidates. She didn't look at me. She had recovered from her breakdown at the clinic, The Bump set beside her in its own hard shell carrying case.

The day already seemed like the distant past somehow, the sky darkening as the glare of the train's interior became brighter. Beyond, I saw the trail running parallel with the tracks where we had seen the geriatric couple in their tracksuits hours earlier. I lowered my head.

There was no dignity to old age any more, no point of natural reflection left for any of us in the modern age. In former times, under the influence of religion and the promise of an afterlife, I felt a man would have been allowed, *no*, obligated, to stop and review his life, to make sense of things toward the end, to find solace and meaning in the companionship of a woman who had given of herself completely, borne him children, made a home for him.

It had not gone that way with my father. He lived in the most terrible of ages, at a time where there was no continuity between his life and mine, no trade he could pass on; no land for me to inherit. I was the most tiresome of burdens.

I saw that now.

He had turned away from my mother and me, not because he didn't love us, but simply to survive, looking toward the comfort of this other woman settled in the ease of her small ranch style house.

I could see my reflection in the double glaze of the glass. I breathed, and my breath fogged the window.

I looked again toward Lori.

I wanted us to be different, to acknowledge certain truths about life, to come clean about our fears and our wants. I wanted us to agree to take no self-improvement classes beyond a reasonable age, to succumb to the inevitability of decay with a reasonable sense that what we did on Earth mattered.

Maybe there was a reward in the great beyond. Why preclude such promises? It put me in mind of scripture, the prophetic vision of the ancients anticipating a Godless age, 'For what is a man profited, if he shall gain the whole world, and lose his own soul? Or what shall a man give in exchange for his soul?'

Eventually, I pulled myself away from such thoughts, shoring things up as best I could, asking, 'Are you hoping for a boy or a girl?'

For the remainder of the trip, we scoured the binder a second, then a third time, rejecting out of hand – or, more correctly, *Lori* rejecting out of hand – the unmarried and the young as high risk, given their economic standing and desperation in even venturing into such a proposition. There was something almost immoral, or at least disquieting, in our dismissal of so many lives, not to mention the fact that such a vast pool of surrogacy candidates existed, willing to sell their eggs or wombs on the open market.

In reading through the profiles, I imagined the counsel of the clinic's founder, Nurse Joanne, in some half-way house, courting runaways, taking what youth so often granted, fecundity, turning the former charity and her Christian vocation as a nun into a commercial venture. I imagined too an affable ex-priest, a sort of Father Flanagan look-alike, sending around a jar to his delinquent charges to fill up with anonymous genetic load factor (GLF).

The most viable surrogate on our first run through proved to be a blue chip medical student in her third year who was looking for room and board along with compensation – though, upon further consideration, Lori ruled her too risky, given her income potential. She could challenge us legally if she decided to keep custody of our child.

By far the most troubling profile was that of a Gulf War veteran's wife whose husband was suffering from a syndrome caused by neurotoxin exposure in Kuwait. The woman's bio described her as a non-smoker, non-drinker, listing her loves as family, the flag, and living her faith.

I would have opted for her on emotional and moral grounds, humbled by someone else's circumstance, at what had driven her to sell her womb on the open market, but Lori would have none of it. Her desperation did not lend itself to compassion.

As she kept reading, I put my face against the glass once more. We had already passed through the gilded land of SUVs and gated communities and entered Evanston and Loyola, a world of dropping property values just short of slum dwelling, an existence most people lived through in quiet desperation.

The train came to a shuddering halt in a barbed wire and

243

graffiti infested station swarming with a throng of gang-banger types in their oversized parkas and basketball high-tops.

Lori remained oblivious to it all, intent on the binder.

I felt a general sense of fear, aware of what money afforded, how it could remove you from such desperation, from such lives. As the train filled, I had a fleeting insight into the fanaticism that must have prompted the religiously extreme in the Dark Ages to recoil from earthly concerns, seeking through sexual abstinence to end a lineage going back to the Garden of Eden and the Fall of Man.

Against that sentiment, I felt Lori prod me, her index finger circling with quiet insistence the candidate she had decided upon.

I simply nodded.

In the purely utilitarian way livestock was bought and sold, I saw she had settled on a woman of meager means but moral standing, the wife of a mill worker caught in the economic miasma of rural life in Upper Wisconsin, a proven breeder with three kids of her own.

Thirty-two

In the expediency of how quickly someone can literally rob you blind, we were on our way North the next weekend to meet with our surrogate, Lorraine Ehrlichmann, passing through the no-man's land where I had first heard about The Ukrainian Prince and the abortion. It seemed such a small world, the intersecting moments of all our lives lived again and again.

Across the span of decades Lori was journeying to accomplish what had been so easy years before.

We were supposed to meet her parents at a diner just off the highway. Deb had informed them of our decision to seek a surrogate. It was her jab at Lori for getting back with me. I was anticipating the awkwardness of the encounter with her father. In a way, Deb had done us a favor. It took our minds off the Ehrlichmanns.

Lori talked in the incessant way she did when she was overly anxious, landing on some story about her mother and endometriosis, describing in detail how her mother, with a peculiar Catholic shame, had hidden her personal gynecological problems, making up an elaborate story of needing to help an ailing spinster aunt in Minneapolis, when in reality she had left for the city hospital to have her womb removed.

Complicit to the hoax all along had been Lori's father, who had made calls through the week, supposedly to Minneapolis, checking on the status of the sick aunt.

It was hard following her exactly, where any of it was really leading, yet I had given the conversation over to her entirely. It was easiest that way.

I picked up on the point of the story as she said, 'I was twelve when it happened ... I hadn't understood what was going on. Deb found Mom's estrogen pills when Mom got home from the hospital. She showed me the bottle ... When things deteriorated between her and Mom and Dad a few years later, she started referring to her cycles as "needing to take care of Aunt Flo," trying to eat away at Mom.'

I tuned in as Deb was confined to the attic, in what proved the last stand between father and daughter, Lori's voice tremulous with the memory of Deb being beaten with the buckle of a leather belt. According to Lori, Deb had been seventeen, with a D cup and a history of sexual exploits that made such a fight sexually indecent, if not bordering on a sex crime. It had taken place under the scrutiny of Lori's mother, arms folded, standing on the pullout stairs leading to the attic, demanding Deb pay for the hell she had inflicted on the family. A week later, Deb dropped out of high school, eloped, and married her first husband in a Justice of the Peace ceremony in Daytona Beach.

Lori looked out across the grey landscape, her voice distant, lost to the past. 'A month later I lost my virginity to a guy I didn't even like ...'

The story took us almost to our exit for the roadside diner, establishing a melancholy I didn't feel conducive to meeting her parents. We were minutes away from confronting the sad implosion of their life.

I knew too much about them to hold them in any great regard, and yet I wanted to feel sorry for the father at least.

I said, 'We can keep going if you want.'

Lori shook her head.

We were early by some twenty minutes. We ordered coffee and waited.

Twenty minutes later they showed. Lori's father didn't get out, instead handed an envelope to his wife. He kept pushing it toward her.

In the context of what I knew about his existence, I was glad he wasn't coming in. Even at this distance he looked as though he had aged. I had seen him just a solitary time over a dinner when I was introduced as a potential suitor, seated across from him in the awkwardness of having to face the father of the woman I was screwing. He had shown little interest in me, especially when he heard I was a writer, excusing himself to watch the Packers on a small TV in his basement.

He was now incontinent, diminished, and living in fear of wetting himself. There was talk of prostate cancer. This was the accumulation of facts revealed over the years, snippets of his life, this father-in-law.

I thought Deb a heartless bitch for having contacted them, for forcing the issue, setting them out here on a highway like this in their failing years.

I watched Lori's father stare at Lori, holding her gaze before looking away, his hands on the wheel of the car as it idled and he waited. This was a man responsible for seeding her existence, for shouldering the burden of her adolescent mistake. I saw in his obstinacy even now that same resolute look he must have possessed so long ago when he pronounced The Ukrainian Prince dead.

For all my misgivings regarding the encounter it passed in a matter of minutes in a tearful, albeit stiff embrace; her mother from a different age not given to public displays of emotion.

I remained in the offing on a torn vinyl seat and simply turned to face Lori's father.

He was staring across the lot at them.

It turned out the *something* he had handed over to his wife was the remittance of a Life Insurance Policy he had cashed in, wanting it put toward Lori's surrogacy.

Lori opened the letter after her mother got into the car, as both of them receded from our life, pulling back out onto the highway.

Lori held the check in its envelope on her lap for the entirety of the journey two hours further north. She cried and quieted and cried and quieted again.

It was the longest she had ever gone without talking.

She called home from a phone box as I stared at the depressed, rundown area of Oshkosh with its small circa early fifties era homes of a vintage and square footage no modern builders bothered to build anymore.

In the interim years of the Cold War figuratively and literally we had outstripped the dimension of what had once constituted realistic domestic living space. Here was the era of *one* bathroom homes, of a finite reckoning of the realistic prospects of returning GI soldiers, who, having survived the horror of war, had simply been willing to exchange it for the staid domesticity of a black-and-white TV and the so-called *privilege* of shackling themselves to a thirty-year mortgage and some dead-end job.

Ostentatious was not in their vocabulary.

I couldn't help but wonder when the modern American Dream had become so grossly abhorrent and self-centered.

Lori arrived back with a new determination fifteen minutes later. She set the remittance check in the glove box and began reviewing the binder we had on our surrogate, like she was cramming for a final.

I pretended to consult a map I'd brought along, awaiting her word.

She said a few minutes later, 'We'll be late,' not referencing the phone call.

I pulled away from the curb.

I drove slower than I ordinarily would have, given we were still early for the appointment, the area decidedly sad and yet ennobling, a place my father had aspired to, the attainable dream of union men set out there by the compassionate politics of FDR. And yet, even in those grand times, in the flush of our golden age, my father had failed to achieve even this level of mediocrity. He had reached too high, and fallen far short. Lives here, once upon a time, had been attained in the numbing conscription of factory work, in the willful knowledge you would go nowhere and still find satisfaction in life.

We arrived at a ranch house with those quintessential garage access back alleys, where kids had tree forts and sling shots, where worms were undoubtedly fried under magnifying glasses in summer while bees were held hostage in peanut butter jars – a childhood I'd never experienced.

I was at odds to what I really felt right then about everything, about the past and the present. What if I could exchange everything for this life? Of course, it was a moot point, this existence had bypassed, not just me, but the entire nation. Big industry had moved to China. This was the faded dream of a post-war age of American security, of blue-collar unions.

An assemblage of bikes and Big Wheels littered our prospective surrogate's yard as we surreptitiously drove by, three kids, all boys, out in the yard, anachronistically dressed in their Sunday best, even though this was a Saturday afternoon.

We saw, too, our surrogate, Lorraine Ehrlichmann, framed in the living room window, staring out, anxiously awaiting our arrival, but Lori said, 'No, keep going!' on the first of two such drive-bys of the block. On the second drive-by, our surrogate had already retreated to peeking out from behind a curtain. She saw us of course.

I felt slightly ashamed of us and embarrassed for her. She had, after all, submitted to a battery of tests, psychological and biological, along with a drug test the likes of which was usually reserved for elite athletes, all to prove her worth to us.

Disconcertingly, I didn't see the husband.

I stopped a block away by a convenience store that had seen better days, now a cigarette and booze outlet advertising cheap milk and Wonder Bread.

This was our last chance to change our minds.

Lori looked over the letter of introduction, going through the boys' names and ages again, along with their interests, repeating it half-aloud.

We had ostensibly picked the family for their Christian values and family cohesiveness, but in reality because they were no match against us – financially and socially – if push came to shove and things got ugly.

We had been informed through accompanying letters of reference that Gustav (Gus) Ehrlichmann, a veteran worker some twelve years older than his wife, a man unskilled and consigned to the vagaries of long-term unemployment, had been laid off from a grain mill two years earlier. He was forty-seven years old and vulnerable.

In the lot of the convenience store, we sat with the engine idling.

I said, 'This is the hell that is *Hamburger Helper*, life as it really is,' simply to see how far Lori's desperation went. We were out here in the middle of a dying city in the rust belt of America seeking a child, seeking life.

She faced me and said quietly, 'I'm scared!' She put my hand to her heart.

I knew this was the same sort of place where Donny lived,

further upstate in Green Bay, the same cold landscape of ruin, a nightmare Lori had been spared through her abortions; yet, here she was, at the cusp of menopause, seeking out the abject mediocrity of so-called normal life, roaming this landscape again.

In the end, I took our being there in a rundown lot in the dying Midwest as one of the great existential paradoxes of existence. I believed in that moment there was no such thing as God, not in the sentient sense of someone who cared or who could save any of us.

Lorraine was dressed in a gingham dress that hid her soft middle but showed a spread of hips, the dress falling to mid-calf, showing thick ankles in black shoes. As we'd been informed through her application, she had delivered her three boys all topping nine pounds, carried full term without complications, been in and out of the hospital in less than twenty-four hours each time.

All three stood like toy soldiers in a line, attesting to their mother's success as breeder and matriarch, all three on their best behavior, the younger two wholly ignorant and just curious. The eldest, Gus Junior, at thirteen, seemed to possess a modicum of pride and inherent knowledge that something catastrophic had taken place within the family. He was defiant and protective, looking between his mother, Lori and me.

I knew the look of unflinching pride that masked a deeper, menacing pain. Here was a boy growing up too quickly, facing down life. He reminded me of a younger, vulnerable me, put me in mind of my own childhood, of those nights in motels when my father was out drinking, when the weight of our future hung in the balance of his actions.

I wondered if Gus Junior knew what was really going on here.

I hoped our plight had been set forth as the abject story of a childless couple hoping to create a family of their own, a story spun in the fashion of my mother's caring regard, in the lies that keep us all going.

The tension was broken by the youngest kid who, in the megalomania of being six, said, 'You bring us any presents?' which of course we had at the strong suggestion of *Gabriel's Promise*.

It led to a natural separation between adults and children as we adjourned to the kitchen from where, for the first and *only* time, I saw out back Gus Senior sequestered in a small castaway tool shed.

I guess he saw us. A solitary glowing bulb was extinguished, auguring a lifelong abandonment and sense of mounting disaffection. He was the sort of lost figure the NRA would have us allow carry an AK-47.

Lorraine met my eyes when I turned from the tool shed.

She said, 'Please … sit …'

The kitchen was hot and redolent with the smell of a baking pie, the fridge, a shrine to child art with its requisite gold stars in the inflation of accomplishment that defined the unadulterated love bestowed on early childhood.

Lori was entranced by it. She turned and smiled and took my hand and sat down at the table.

Lorraine sat across from us with a frankness that suggested Gus Senior was not coming near the house, that this was as good as it got. I figured some uproarious fight had taken place earlier.

Lorraine had a habit of combing out the pleats in her skirt as she talked. She was still attractive. She said, 'I've been open and honest with *them*.' She averted her eyes toward the living room. 'I think that's the best policy.' It was something she said more for Gus Junior's benefit than ours, since he'd come to the edge of the kitchen doorway, along with his middle kid brother, Pete.

Pete said with some prompting, 'I'm hungry. I want cereal.'

I saw Gus Junior pushing Pete into the kitchen. Pete said in the oblivious way of a ten year-old, 'Where's Dad?' as he took out a box of cereal. He looked at me and Lori and then at Gus Junior, who had a defiant look about him.

Lorraine didn't answer Pete as he got up on a chair and took down a box of cereal. She said as a way of changing the subject, 'They grow so quickly.'

I smiled and said, 'You know, something like three percent of cereal is bug skeletons.'

Lori admonished me with a nervous laugh, 'He's just making that up. Tell him . . .'

I said, 'Honest Abe . . . I'm not lying. That's what gives it the crunch!'

Pete was pliable. He smiled at me, took a mouthful and said, 'Mmmm . . .'

He was ten years old, and I figured he hadn't a brain in his head. When it came to recounting childhood, his story would be at odds with Gus Junior's version.

Then Lori said something stupid. She looked directly at Pete. 'You know why we're here?'

Pete held his spoon over his bowl. He turned in a kid not-so-subtle way toward Gus Junior, who had his arms folded defiantly.

I said, 'Lori, leave the kid alone . . . He's eating,' but Pete piped up, 'You got a problem with your plumbing.'

The blood drained from Lorraine's face, Gus Junior smiling with a gloating sense of victory, standing right behind Pete who took another bite of cereal and said, 'I taste bugs. . . . mmm.'

He was on a roll.

Maybe it took a kid to set the natural order of things right.

The visit lasted another three quarters of an hour, Lorraine shoving a reluctant Gus Junior into the TV room along with a compliant Pete to whom I slipped a twenty.

We discussed meeting with local doctors and scheduling check-ups in anticipation of insemination in Chicago, because discussing the clinical aspects of the process allowed us to talk with greater authority and conviction, putting us back in control.

Lorraine had a younger sister outside of Wheeling whose husband was an architect. They were going to make a family reunion out of the trip down to Chicago for the procedure. She was going to bill us only for mileage. We were saving on having to spring for a hotel.

All in all, it seemed the best of all possible arrangements, though as we left, I saw in the living room window Gus Junior giving me the finger.

Thirty-three

We arrived home well after midnight. Lori had slept through most of the ride back. Things had settled with her. We were moving forward now. Suddenly it had all become real.

On the answering machine, there were two messages. The first was from Deb. Misty was on the run. I heard Deb crying down the phone.

I neglected to tell Lori immediately, wanting to give us time alone.

The other was from an investigator following up on Brandt's assertion I had met with Marina. The investigator wanted to arrange an interview with Lori and me, though there was no real conviction in the voice, or not that I could tell anyway.

Over a week had passed since Brandt had confronted me. It seemed all so remote, so distant like none of it had ever really happened.

I set down the phone. My heart was beating slightly faster.

It would take a strength of character to endure what was potentially on the immediate horizon, Lori drawn again into the details of what had happened the night Marina died.

Lori had not remembered scratching at my face. At the prompting of an investigator, would she admit this? Would she testify she had passed out cold during the hours when Marina died, negating my alibi that I was with her all night? If they probed deep enough, there was incontrovertible evidence I had left the apartment, closed circuit camera downstairs monitored all comings and goings. It would have undoubtedly picked me up on camera, but how long did they keep tapes like that?

I regretted taking the box cutter. I had instinctively carried it for protection. I knew what potentially lay down there in the ghetto at such an hour.

Of course, it didn't explain how I ended up cutting myself, and then I realized in the encapsulation of events nobody had made mention of a box cutter. This was about the scrapes on my face.

These were the sorts of slipups one could not afford, offering up too much explanation, too many details.

It was hard keeping it all straight in the minutes after listening to the call.

Then I thought it might actually be in my best interest to reference the box cutter in relation to opening a box in the kitchen, short circuiting Lori's version of things, aligning my story with what Lori would undoubtedly reveal.

Only time would tell.

I was getting ahead of things. Brandt had nothing on me. The police had the confession from Antonio Jones. Marina had died in the most brutal of ways at his and Tate's hands, raped and sodomized, her throat slit, her corpse set ablaze.

These were the facts.

I lowered my head, wondering how different things might have been if she had lived.

Would I be here?

In the background I heard Lori say my name. When I turned, she was standing between the bedroom and living room holding the remote control for our VCR. 'Since when did you start recording *General Hospital*?'

I felt the world implode around me.

She pointed to a can of Coke and a candy wrapper sitting in the middle of the floor.

'And when did you start eating Twizzlers?'

I could say nothing, and then her sternness suddenly gave way as she shook her head, 'Why are men so afraid to show their true feelings? You felt sorry for that poor girl, Elena, is that it ... so you recorded this for her?'

I answered in a quiet, but staid voice, 'She's a twelve-year-old, culturally adrift of everything we consider normal ... I thought ...'

Lori half smiled at me.

On the VCR, I saw a chisel-jawed doctor in the midst of an intense discussion, shaking a woman by the arms, a woman I assumed was his wife, because she wasn't beautiful in the way heroines were on the soaps. The truth was coming out between them in histrionics of fists and tears.

Pointing with the remote, Lori said in mock reproach, '*This* is her initiation to American life?'

I kept looking at the TV. 'Maybe ... How else do you come to understand America but through television? It's a perception that comes through the filter of the unattainable, or the magical, depending on how you see it.'

It was a statement that made no real sense, but had a transformative effect on Lori.

She looked at me. 'How come you can't ever give a straight answer?'

'Have you ever considered that maybe life *is* complicated?'

I could feel the intensity of her embrace as she drew herself to my chest.

She placed her fist to my heart and whispered, 'I don't care if I have to keep working. I know I can't just quit. It's not a realistic option. You can be the stay-at-home-parent. I'm OK with that ... I really am ...' then fragments of unadulterated praise, in which, according to her, I was 'the natural choice,' 'a man with the capacity to understand things at a deep level,' something she wanted 'bequeathed to *our* child.'

It was the first time she had expressed in any thoughtful way how she foresaw our life together. In her new version of reality, her life would go on as before, but mine wouldn't. It was a decision wholly hers, a gift bestowed on me, or so it appeared from the way she talked.

Ten minutes later, she emerged against the half-light of the bathroom, demurely naked save for her pregnancy belly, her hands finding that same maternal pose she had perfected at the clinic, in what proved our first trial run at make-believe.

In the silence of 3 a.m. and the wake of what Lori had outlined as my immediate future, I slipped silently from her side, making a desperate and valiant attempt to write with the lack of self-consciousness that had defined my early work.

Even at this dark hour, and with the portent of what lay ahead, I produced nothing.

Maybe tomorrow I would commit to the page what I had envisioned out at *Gabriel's Promise*, pushing forward, resurrecting Fennimore.

His voice had become so distant in these failing hours, all those calls on the phone to nobody, arguing with myself for days on end, willing something into being, going silently mad, feeding pages into a fax machine to his old fax number from the glory days of our first collaborative success, beseeching him to let me have a second chance.

He never did. I had alienated everybody in the rant over lunch in New York City, killed whatever there might have been.

I was a liability.

I felt myself trembling ever so slightly, the weight of the

years settling around me, the struggle to advance after the rejection of The Opus, wanting to will something into being, to be simply understood, to be taken seriously again.

It didn't matter anymore, or not on this night anyway.

A half-hour on, I got up from the computer, hearing the clank of the courtyard gate.

From my window perch, I watched Glen entering the building with another victim.

I lingered until a light went on in his apartment, feeling the slow churn of my scrotal sack, a tincture of passing interest.

I wanted to log on and watch, to observe the details of how others existed, to find that vicarious connection to a life other than my own, a voyeuristic instinct that went all the way back to my early teenage years, to those times when I had taken to following my father, trailing his headlights in the vast openness of farmland.

In retrospect, my desire to please him seemed such a pitiful and embarrassing sentiment, his influence on my work lamentably Freudian. I had tied such significance to his disaffection and loss, his wry lament, 'We start out with such high expectations,' a refrain I thought transcended the ill-fated saga of one family.

For a time I did nothing but sit alone, drinking the dregs of the previous evening's black coffee.

I listened again to Deb's message. I whispered, 'Run Misty, run!'

Through the window, I watched the cold eye of the moon moving amidst a parting of clouds. In my lifetime, we, as a species, had been there and back, and in so doing unlocked its mysteries to a point at which we had lost interest.

I thought, maybe that was how life, even whole epochs,

went; the desperate search for understanding, then the anti-climactic end. It had gone that way with the legacy of putting us on the moon – we came back to more earthly concerns, the horrific nightly images of Vietnam, through Nixon's impeachment and our withdrawal from the South East Theater of War, so by the seventies, all our collective consciousness could settle on as horror was the cinematic inanity of *Jaws*, a marauding great white shark with the potential to ruin, God forbid, a Fourth of July weekend at the beach.

As I continued to wait for the coming dawn, I set my head into the cradle of my folded arms. Everything around me felt dark, indistinct, and numbing.

I was aware there had been a time before, a time when I had been able to sustain an intellectual rigor and commitment to the audacious notion that the art of fiction could yield some greater sense of meaning than ordinary life. It was a belief that had supported me, body and soul, enabling me to lock myself away against an external reality I considered inferior, degenerative, and meaningless.

Through my early writing, I had remained immune to the horror of the world's tragedies on the nightly news, the killing fields of Cambodia, Bangladesh, Ethiopian famine. I had lived solely within my head, turning with a cold indifference from so many late night appeals begging for my intercession, the perennial *Save the Children* appeal of a bearded saint-like Samaritan walking eternally through an unnamed cholera-infested South American slum, the most photogenic of doe-eyed children set amidst cesspools of shit in order to wrest from me what the Samaritan tabulated was a pittance of my Western wealth, the mere 'price of a cup of coffee a day' to alleviate such misery.

In all those years, I had never once called the number on the screen. So, how was it now that the simple awareness of other lives going on in parallel to my own within an apartment complex was enough to distract me?

I knew the answer: the intellectual awareness of these lives as *real*.

The acknowledgement of their existence diminished what I had to say, relegated the primacy and importance of what had been my own story to a solitary voice, a tale told by an idiot full of sound and fury, signifying nothing, a chilling Shakespearean lament.

Something had died within me, some synaptic loss at a molecular level. I would go on as before, outwardly remaining the same. It would be a wholly personal death of uncertain significance, this night ostensibly a requiem to my life as an artist.

Maybe Fennimore and I would prevail. He was out there, just beyond my conscious grasp. He might call again, seeking understanding, but for now, none of it mattered. I hadn't the will to resurrect him.

In the immediate future, there was the investigation into Marina's death to get through. I had not killed her. That was the essential truth. Any revelation about leaving the apartment would have no bearing on the murder case. It would simply compromise my relationship with Lori.

She would stand by me. We would endure. I knew that in my heart of hearts. She was practical that way. She saw only what she wanted to see.

We all do.

And so, turning from the outside world, I slipped quietly back into bed, spooning her, feeling the mechanical motion of the bump's fetal kick. It was a surreal and yet comforting experience, a heel-like pressure of a supposed human foot against my hand.

It put me in mind of an experiment I had read about in a

psychology textbook concerning the nature of love and need, the article featuring an image of the experiment's abject control subject, a wide-eyed baby monkey, separated from its natural mother.

Clinging to a surrogate terrycloth effigy, the experiment underscored that all things are possible, that one can learn to love almost anything given time.